Dear Reader,

To my mind, a week in the wilderness of New Hampshire was a triple-task assignment: complete a magazine shoot, brush up on survival techniques and steal a little well-earned R and R.

Well, that was before Jessie Meyer and her triple-threat teenagers. They're as uncontrollable as a new load of recruits. But I'm going to teach those three adolescent girls to live in the wild—without a curling iron and a telephone.

And I'm going to teach their *mother* a thing or two about survival. Seduction. The birds and the bees. And making babies.

Mark Elliot
Colonel, USAF (Retired)

— New Hampshire

1. ALABAMA
Full House • Jackie Weger
2. ALASKA
Borrowed Dreams • Debbie Macomber
3. ARIZONA
Call It Destiny • Jayne Ann Krentz
4. ARKANSAS
Another Kind of Love • Mary Lynn Baxter
5. CALIFORNIA
Deceptions • Annette Broadrick
6. COLORADO
Stormwalker • Dallas Schulze
7. CONNECTICUT
Straight from the Heart • Barbara Delinsky
8. DELAWARE
Author's Choice • Elizabeth August
9. FLORIDA
Dream Come True • Ann Major
10. GEORGIA
Way of the Willow • Linda Shaw
11. HAWAII
Tangled Lies • Anne Stuart
12. IDAHO
Rogue's Valley • Kathleen Creighton
13. ILLINOIS
Love by Proxy • Diana Palmer
14. INDIANA
Possibles • Lass Small
15. IOWA
Kiss Yesterday Goodbye • Leigh Michaels
16. KANSAS
A Time To Keep • Curtiss Ann Matlock
17. KENTUCKY
One Pale, Fawn Glove • Linda Shaw
18. LOUISIANA
Bayou Midnight • Emilie Richards
19. MAINE
Rocky Road • Anne Stuart
20. MARYLAND
The Love Thing • Dixie Browning
21. MASSACHUSETTS
Pros and Cons • Bethany Campbell
22. MICHIGAN
To Tame a Wolf • Anne McAllister
23. MINNESOTA
Winter Lady • Janet Joyce
24. MISSISSIPPI
After the Storm • Rebecca Flanders
25. MISSOURI
Choices • Annette Broadrick

26. MONTANA
Part of the Bargain • Linda Lael Miller
27. NEBRASKA
Secrets of Tyrone • Regan Forest
28. NEVADA
Nobody's Baby • Barbara Bretton
29. NEW HAMPSHIRE
Natural Attraction • Marisa Carroll
30. NEW JERSEY
Moments Harsh, Moments Gentle • Joan Hohl
31. NEW MEXICO
Within Reach • Marilyn Pappano
32. NEW YORK
In Good Faith • Judith McWilliams
33. NORTH CAROLINA
The Security Man • Dixie Browning
34. NORTH DAKOTA
A Class Act • Kathleen Eagle
35. OHIO
Too Near the Fire • Lindsay McKenna
36. OKLAHOMA
A Time and a Season • Curtiss Ann Matlock
37. OREGON
Uneasy Alliance • Jayne Ann Krentz
38. PENNSYLVANIA
The Wrong Man • Ann Major
39. RHODE ISLAND
The Bargain • Patricia Coughlin
40. SOUTH CAROLINA
The Last Frontier • Rebecca Flanders
41. SOUTH DAKOTA
For Old Times' Sake • Kathleen Eagle
42. TENNESSEE
To Love a Dreamer • Ruth Langan
43. TEXAS
For the Love of Mike • Candace Schuler
44. UTAH
To Tame the Hunter • Stephanie James
45. VERMONT
Finders Keepers • Carla Neggers
46. VIRGINIA
The Devlin Dare • Cathy Gillen Thacker
47. WASHINGTON
The Waiting Game • Jayne Ann Krentz
48. WEST VIRGINIA
All in the Family • Heather Graham Pozzessere
49. WISCONSIN
Starstruck • Anne McAllister
50. WYOMING
Special Touches • Sharon Brondos

MARISA CARROLL
Natural Attraction

New Hampshire

Harlequin Books

TORONTO • NEW YORK • LONDON
AMSTERDAM • PARIS • SYDNEY • HAMBURG
STOCKHOLM • ATHENS • TOKYO • MILAN
MADRID • WARSAW • BUDAPEST • AUCKLAND

HARLEQUIN ENTERPRISES LTD.
225 Duncan Mill Road, Don Mills,
Ontario, Canada M3B 3K9

NATURAL ATTRACTION

ISBN: 0-373-45179-2

Published Harlequin Enterprises, Ltd. 1985, 1993

Printed in the U.S.A.

Chapter One

"Mr. Elliot, there's no way on earth I can pack up three teenagers, enough food and blue jeans to keep them from turning mutinous and meet you in Hampton Beach in six hours. It just isn't possible." Jessie Meyer flicked a straying wisp of auburn-streaked brown hair off her hot forehead and frowned at the thermometer outside the kitchen window. Eighty-three degrees in the shade. The grimace marring her smooth, high brow was a look the aforementioned three teens would have avoided like the plague. Unfortunately, the man on the other end of the phone line couldn't see the warning signals.

"I know you're on vacation this week, Jessie." The voice went on as though scanning her mind while she scurried mentally through a list of excuses. "You told me that when you dropped off the proofs from your last assignment, remember? And I'm not asking you to go to the ends of the earth." The masculine tones overrode the beginnings of her polite but firm refusal. "Just to the ends of the continent, actually." He chuckled, a low, vibrant sound that sent tiny flickers of energy twisting along Jessie's nerve ends. Mark Elliot's voice was the most attractive thing about her client and sometime boss.

Sometime boss.

The phrase struck her forcefully—right in the center of her common sense. One did not willfully antagonize the man who paid at least part of the bills, however indirectly. "It doesn't make any difference," Jessie broke in, in an even, friendly style, trying hard to keep her temper under wraps. He'd never been witness to one of her rare but legendary lapses in that respect. To top it all off, she didn't dare forget he was a valued client of the firm of Abrahms and Mahoney, CPAs, of which Jessie was the most junior associate.

She liked moonlighting as a photographer for Mark Elliot's regional publication *Meanderings*. So there wasn't a lot of future in giving in to her impulse to simply hang up on him. She scowled down at the phone and held her peace. Raising and educating three children alone wasn't easy, she reminded herself unnecessarily. The free-lance photos she took for *Meanderings* made making ends meet a lot easier. It varied her daily routine and was more interesting by far than the usual run-of-the-mill tax problems and accounting snafus she dealt with in her alter ego as a CPA.

To be totally honest, the well-sublimated poet and artist in Jessie's soul thoroughly enjoyed the assignments to photograph the rugged beauty of New Hampshire: the grandeur of the snowy peaks of the White Mountains, in the north; the hustle and bustle of rejuvenating industrial towns; the softer, rolling strip of lowlands along the Atlantic Coast. Her practical side quickly reasserted control. She wouldn't jeopardize that. She could feel herself capitulating.

"Jessie, are you still there?"

"Yes, Mr. Elliot." She hated the infinitesimal bit of meekness that crept into her voice. At times like this Jessie always found herself wanting to say Colonel Elliot.

"I need your typical family unit. Now."

Jessie gave in to temptation at the staccato command. "Yes, sir!" She snapped to attention, rolling her brown eyes heavenward at her mother's frankly curious expression. Marta Young had been sitting with Jessie at the kitchen table cleaning the first raspberries of the season and bemoaning the unusually long August heat wave. Now she gave up all pretense of attention to the bowl of fruit and stared at her daughter.

"What exactly are you asking, Colonel?" Jessie inquired, playing for time as her mind continued to sift through various overused excuses. He already knew she was free of obligations to Abrahms and Mahoney for another week, so that was out. She raised her brows at her mother's continued scrutiny. It was best she let the man know she would not be intimidated. But her stomach was distinctly uneasy. Her stomach always reacted first when things were going wrong. And Jessie knew very well what he was about to say.

"My nieces backed out of this trip," Mark reported with a hint of cajolery singing along the wires that Jessie couldn't resist. It was his way of acknowledging she'd scored a hit with her reminder that he no longer commanded a unit of military engineers. "They were going to be my 'voluntary castaways.' You know how important this layout is to me."

Of course she did. Everyone who was connected to the magazine at all knew about the wilderness experiment he'd planned.

"It's the highlight of my first spring issue. And *National Geographic* is interested in the idea. I canceled their photographer when the girls deserted me, but I think I can still get them to take the article with your pictures. The assignment is yours, if you agree to come along."

"*National Geographic*!" The name danced in front of Jessie's eyes like a golden mirage. It was a twenty-four-karat carrot he was dangling on his stick. It was the one bribe—besides a substantial bonus—he could offer guaranteed to hit home.

"An eight-page color spread—" Mark added silkily, sweetening the pot "—complete with byline. All I need is you, your camera and your charming daughters. . .for the next six days."

Six days. Sanity returned with a rush to stiffen her sagging backbone.

"Mr. Elliot." Jessie reverted to his civilian title to underscore the seriousness of her next words. "You don't understand." He'd never met her children. He'd only taken over publication of *Meanderings* a year ago. He had no idea what he was asking, or what he was letting himself in for, Jessie thought spitefully. "My children have never been camping in their lives." That was the understatement of the twentieth century. Ann and Lyn, the twins, were sixteen and tied to electrical umbilical cords of various lengths: curling irons, blow dryers, makeup mirrors, tape players, you name it. It was a major operation just getting them onto the school bus every morning without overloading the circuit breakers.

And Nell, thirteen just last week, was still a gawky, awkward tomboy who couldn't spend fifteen minutes with her older sisters before a riot ensued.

"And my car's in the shop," Jessie revealed triumphantly in a last-ditch attempt to weasel out of the tight corner. The aging Chevy station wagon *was* on its last legs. That only left the VW and that was a penance she wouldn't submit to for anyone.

"I see." There was a moment's hesitation as he digested the information. Jessie could hear the background noises of a busy highway. Where was he? His neices had, indeed, waited until the last moment to back out. She hardened her heart to his plight. "The company car's at the plant." The infuriatingly assured male voice came back at her with all the decisiveness Jessie was sure he'd applied in combat situations overseas. "Take that."

"But I've explained why it's impossible," Jessie sputtered in her haste. Her hand waved in unseen argument. Her mother put her elbows on the Formica table and clucked a warning at the rising pitch of Jessie's tone.

"All right, Jess. You drive a hard bargain," Mark replied. There was a note that might have been amusement in his raspy voice. "I know I'm asking a lot and I'm running out of time. Here's my final offer. I'll give you one hundred dollars a day as a bonus for every day you stick it out. Is it a deal?"

Jessie's mouth popped open as the last of her scruples crumbled like so much dust before the wind. Six hundred dollars. That would get the Chevy out of hock and put the search for a more reliable means of transportation, derailed by the breakdown, back on track.

"You have a deal, Mr. Elliot," she said tightly with just a sliver of grimness in her soft voice. Jessie ignored her mother's silent facial gyrations. She prided herself on being a woman of character, but sometimes principles had to take second place to practicality. "When do you want us at the dock?"

"Good show," Mark said approvingly. "I'll expect you in five hours and fifty-seven minutes." His words were brisk, as though he were indeed staging a military campaign. "It'll give you plenty of time to pack and leave Manchester before rush hour. And, Jessie—"

"Yes, sir?"

"I think it's about time you started calling me Mark. Mr. Elliot is so formal for two people who are going to spend the next week together on a deserted Atlantic island." He hung up before Jessie could form a suitable retort.

She replaced the receiver thoughtfully, wondering what had come over her to cause this sudden loss of common sense. Was it the heat, unusual for New Hampshire? Or the restlessness of having spent half a summer with three bored and bickering teens? Or just that she was only thirty-five and already becoming senile?

That was probably it, she decided with a self-conscious little laugh as she turned to face her mother. "The girls are going to have me committed," she stated with conviction.

"What's this all about?" her mother exploded, sugaring the raspberries with a heavy hand. Marta had fallen for Mark Elliot like a ton of bricks when she met him at the magazine's Christmas party.

"The girls and I are going camping." Jessie sounded as if she didn't quite believe it herself—which was the truth. "They're going to have a fit," she prophesied with more conviction.

"Camping?" Marta stared at her only daughter as if she'd taken leave of her senses. And she probably had,

Jessie admitted with private candor. "With those three? The man's deranged."

"You can't say I didn't warn him," Jessie said, grinning with some satisfaction. "Repeatedly. But he offered me a hundred-dollar-a-day bonus and a chance to have my work in *National Geographic*. A little judicious bribery worked on me," she confessed with a pang for her bent ethics. "It'll work on the girls. No more arguing. We have to get packed. And so do you."

"Me?" Sugar and berries ricocheted out of the crockery bowl onto the tabletop and floor.

"Yes, you," Jessie affirmed, laughing at Marta's plump, careworn face. "You're going to your class reunion. Call Aunt Lettie and have her get your room ready." Her mother had been a rock, a safe harbor, in a world suddenly gone mad seven years ago when Jessie's husband was killed in a senseless and tragic sawmill accident. She'd left her own home in Pennsylvania and come to Manchester. She'd stayed on, making Jessie's bewildering transition from wife and homemaker to widow and sole breadwinner as easy as she could. Marta had given up a lot for the four of them in those years. Now Jessie was determined to give her something back.

"Go back to Red Lion? I can't. Driving that VW would be like putting a loaded gun in my hands. I hate stick shifts."

"You don't have to drive the bug," Jessie soothed. She doubted if the little import could make the trip anyway. She only drove it around town herself.

"I get sick on the bus," Marta pointed out inarguably.

"You're not taking the bus. Let's call the airlines. I'm sure a no-frills-flight can't be that much more expensive. It'll be my treat. Please, Mom. Somebody should benefit from this fiasco. It might as well be you.'' Jessie jumped up to swipe at the melting white granules of sugar with a damp dish towel.

"I don't know..."

"No more buts, Mom," Jessie ordered, her voice muffled as she bent to clean the spilled sugar off the floor before a horde of ants found the sweet offering. "You're going and that's it." She straightened with a little grunt, wishing she'd taken the time to work off the extra ten pounds that gave her figure its lush, full curves. Maybe she'd find the time to diet when the girls got back to school. "It's not every year you have a forty-fifth high-school class reunion."

"Don't remind me," Marta replied tartly, double chin quivering. Jessie got her figure from her mother. Marta was what Jessie's father had always termed a "fine figure of a woman." Her blue eyes danced with excitement. "I really would like to go."

"Of course. And you will. We don't have time to go through it again. Help me round up the girls, and I'll tell you all the details while we pack."

But Jessie did end up explaining it—more than once. In fact, it was the main topic of conversation for the next five hours and fifty minutes.

Marta led off, insisting she could pack herself in a twinkling when they were safe on their way to the small private coastal island somewhere just south of the New Hampshire-Massachusetts state line.

"My daughter's work in *National Geographic*." Marta intoned the publication's name with blatantly mock reverence but there was a sparkle of pride in her eyes as she stuffed a bright red turtleneck sweater into

Nell's tote with little regard for what it would look like coming out.

"Nothing's definite," Jessie reminded, not wanting to let anyone know how exciting the possibility really was for her.

"Nonsense. Have faith in your own abilities," Marta lectured in precisely the same tone of voice she'd used since Jessie was twelve. Nell's swimsuit followed the sweater. Jessie nodded automatically, her thoughts already skipping ahead to the twins sulking in their room.

"I wonder what Ann and Lyn are packing? I think I'll throw in all our heavy jackets just to be on the safe side. It's bound to be cool on the water."

"Good idea. How much do they pay? *National Geographic*, I mean?" Marta interrupted Jessie unceremoniously.

"Is that all you can think of? Money? Mom, I just agreed to spend a week on a deserted island with a virtual stranger. Doesn't it bother you that your only daughter and your grandchildren might be going off with a Granite State Jack the Ripper?"

"Don't be silly, Jess. Mark Elliot is no such thing. He's a Rotarian and a veteran." That was enough for Marta. "Look on this as an advernture, an opportunity to explore *strange new worlds*." The italics in Marta's words were almost visible. She and Nell were hopeless "Star Trek" fans. They watched the ancient reruns six days a week.

"Well, Mark Elliot, Lt. Col., USA, Ret., is 'bravely going where no man has gone before,' that's for sure," Jessie agreed spitefully. "Especially if the twins decide to be really difficult. Have you considered what that will be like?" Marta didn't have a retort for that remark. If Ann and Lyn were miserable they were perfectly capable, in their adolescent selfishness, of making life a penance for everyone else.

"Do you think he can handle it? Is he used to children being around?" Marta plopped down on Nell's unmade bed, her round face serious, as she considered the matter at hand.

"I haven't the slightest idea. I barely know the man. He's never been married. His nieces backed out on him at the last minute.... Neither of those circumstances lead me to believe this expedition has a snowball's chance." Catching her mother's eye Jessie shrugged. "I wouldn't be surprised if we're all back here by tomorrow evening," she concluded fatalistically. She'd learned the hard way that three children could send even strong men running for cover.

"It's entirely possible, of course," Marta agreed. "But you'll think of something to keep them in line for the whole week. You always do." Marta changed the subject after that vote of maternal confidence, sending Nell off to find a temporary home for the hamsters while Jessie forced the twins out of their self-imposed exile.

Lyn marched off grudgingly to the Petersens' next door with the raspberries and a request to feed the cats. Ann was prodded to the phone to notify the paperboy and the post office to hold the mail. Marta arranged a ride to the airport with one of her friends from the senior center at the Congregational church before setting off with Jessie to pick up Mark Elliot's car.

"AND THAT'S ABSOLUTELY the last grousing I'll listen to on the subject." Jessie directed the ultimatum mechanically to the pouting twins in the back seat of the late-model sedan as she searched for a place to park along the busy streets of the happy little resort town of Hampton Beach. She checked her watch. Seven minutes ahead of schedule. Jessie hated being late for any reason.

Ominous silence greeted her words. "You made a deal," she reminded. "Six days of living off the land in return for the use of the VW when you get your driver's licences. No reneging."

"Yes, ma'am" came the reluctant response.

Jessie had made her offer flat out. There hadn't been time to do otherwise. She'd have the VW overhauled and pay the insurance until the twins graduated. No bargaining. There wasn't time. The girls had put up a brief but spirited debate, more for show than anything. But they, too, had finally succumbed, their adamant refusal to leave the civilized world as they knew it bowing to the lure of their own "set of wheels."

"I didn't ask for anything special, did I, Mom?" Nell chirped righteously from the passenger seat where she had her nose buried in a dog-eared survival primer she'd borrowed from Mrs. Petersen, the retired librarian next door. She gave Jessie a broad, innocent, silver-capped grin. Jessie cast her mind back hurriedly to the Savings and Loan calendar on the refrigerator. Had she neglected to cancel an orthodontist's appointment during their mad rush to meet Mr. Elliot's arbitrary deadline?

Giving her youngest daughter a severe look, Jessie wheeled the car into a lot near the docks where they were to meet Mark Elliot. She was exhausted from the midsummer heat wave, the long drive in bumper-to-bumper "summer complaint" traffic and the entire lunacy of the present situation. Maybe she ought to save the girls the bother and commit herself.

"This is gross, Mom," Ann wailed as Jessie heartlessly yanked a cosmetic mirror and blow dryer from an
overstuffed tote in the trunk. "How can we dry our
hair?" She looked as if her mother had drowned a favorite kitten before her eyes.

"It will dry nicely in the sun." Mark Elliot materialized beside his car before Jess could reply with what was
obviously a more short-tempered suggestion.

Jessie Meyer's daughters were going to be beauties
someday, too, Mark decided, letting his regard linger on
each girl for a few appraising seconds. Perhaps it
wouldn't be the racy-sleek, haute couture model type
that was in fashion now, but womanly beauty—the kind
their mother possessed so abundantly. Jessie's lush,
rounded curves were already becoming apparent in the
twins' slender forms. Then there was the youngest.
What was her name?

Nell. He pulled the fact from the recesses of his brain.
Her bone structure was as intriguing as her mother's,
and her smile was enchanting, despite all the expensive
hardware affixed to her teeth. It had been Jessie's smile
that first attracted Mark in the stuffy mahogany-pan-
neled offices of Abrahms and Mahoney last fall.

First her smile: friendly, open, just a tad shy; then her
face: strong, oval-shaped, with high-angled cheekbones and a willful, determined chin; lastly there had
been the photographs she had taken. Several of them
hung on the walls of the reception area and in her own
small cubbyhole office. They were beautifully composed, sensitively rendered studies of plants, barns,
rocks, trees, sea and sky. She captured ordinary, everyday scenes with a skill and compassion that gave them
great depth and feeling.

On a whim totally foreign to his cautious nature and lifelong habits, Mark had asked her to free-lance for *Meanderings*.

Just like that.

And to his surprise she'd accepted.

Just like that.

It was that willingness to explore new avenues, to experiment with new opportunities; her zest and spirit of adventure that came through in her photos and was so at odds with the businesslike facade she tried to project at Abrahms and Mahoney that had given him the courage to broach this latest venture.

Jessie hadn't disappointed him today, either, although she drove a hard bargain. He recalled ruefully his promise of the bonus money. There was no doubt whatsoever in his mind that she'd stick it out to the end—and her daughters with her.

"There's no way we can get a ten-mile extension cord, dummy," Nell's shrill voice intruded into his thoughts. "Don't you know there won't be any electricity where we're going?" she summed up piously for her sisters.

"That's enough, Nell," Jessie cautioned automatically, turning to confront the expedition's leader. Her face brightened involuntarily from a combination of chagrin and afternoon heat.

Mark Elliot looked every bit as imposing in jeans and a Black Watch plaid shirt with open collar and sleeves rolled to just below the elbow as he did in his conservative three-piece business suits. He had the chameleonlike quality of adapting himself to the environment around him. It fascinated Jessie, being a trait she both admired and envied.

It seemed at times, lately, that without her camera and array of lenses she wasn't really a person. She was only somebody's mother, who used to be somebody's loving wife and friend, but who was now too often a woman alone. It worried her a little—when she had time to consider the situation.

"Hello," Nell piped up. "All they think about is their hair ...and boys." Her smile was genuinely friendly as she pronounced judgment on her sisters. Jessie refrained from commenting on her rudeness, preferring to let it sink into oblivion. Nell held out a tanned, grubby hand. "I'm Nell Elizabeth Meyer. Are we really going to live on a deserted island and eat weeds and raw fish for a week because your nieces are a couple of spoiled brats?"

"Nell!" Jessie couldn't let that one pass. She was horrified at her progeny's lack of manners. Unfortunately, she also recognized her own unguarded words to her mother in the speech. Mark's nieces might have left him high and dry, but with her luck they had probably managed the feat with impeccable manners.

"I certainly hope not." Mark chuckled low and deep, accepting Nell's hand with dignity. His carriage was tall and straight, without any of the stiffness you'd expect from preconceptions of a retired military officer.

Nell's coltish face fell, mirroring her disappointment. "I mean," Mark hurried to explain, "I hope we don't have to eat anything raw that wasn't meant to be ingested in that form."

"Gross" came the inelegant reply from both the twins.

"Not if I can help it. You must be Annette and Lynette," Mark continued without skipping a beat as he turned his riveting, gold-flecked blue gaze on the twins. Jessie wondered fleetingly where he'd learned the girls' names. His charming, boyish grin seemed to be holding them in thrall. She felt a spurt of momentary annoyance at his easy camaraderie with the three teens.

In all truthfulness, she was genuinely surprised at the twins' docility, until Nell bounced to her side and said in a stage whisper that carried to the far corners of the parking lot: "They never believed it when I told them you said he looked like Tom Selleck."

Jessie groaned in silent mortification, catching Mark's quirking grin of amusement. Perversely, his even temper made her angrier still. He was laughing at them! She slammed the trunk lid closed, missing her finger by a hair breadth. Drat the outspoken child and her devastating candor.

Unfortunately, her observation was true. Mark Elliot was a shade over six feet tall, broad-shouldered, narrow-hipped, with not even a hint of a paunch—although Jessie knew for a fact that he's just passed his forty-sixth birthday. She stole a furtive glance at Mark as she pretended to count duffels on the ground beside the car. He was a great deal sexier, in her opinion, than the hearthrob TV sleuth. There were lines fanned out around his eyes that told of years spent out in the wind and weather. His hair was cut a little shorter than Jessie liked, but she guessed it was an attempt to control—without a great deal of success—a decided tendency to curl above his ears and at the nape of his neck. There was only a tiny, attractive hint of gray sprinkled in the sable pelt. He was intelligent, interesting...the kind of man that had always appealed to Jessie.

"Tom Selleck is four inches taller and he has green eyes, I'm sure," Jessie hissed sotto voce. "I never said that," she lied, bold-faced and unrepentant. Nell seemed ready to dispute her mother's word, thought better of it and was distracted from further altercation as the twins broke into speech.

"We're fraternal twins," Ann, the eldest by several minutes, said, preening under the masculine attention.

"That's why I have brown eyes and Mom's reddish hair," Lyn offered with a comical moue. She wanted nothing more this summer than to be tall and leggy and blond. At five-seven, she was well on her way to the tall and leggy, already matching Jessie's height, but blond was out of the question—not while she lived under Jessie's roof.

"I look like our dad," Ann supplied. She was an inch or so shorter than her twin and five pounds heavier. Her hair was dark, almost black, as her father's had been. All three of the girls had inherited Carl Meyer's straight nose and tip-tilted eyes. Lyn had his even temper, Ann his quick laugh and Nell his love of books as further legacy.

"You all look like your father," Jessie chimed in, amazed at the ease with which she spoke. Was it true that time did heal all wounds, as corny as the phrase sounded? Carl had been gone seven years. Her life was speeding by so quickly that some moments she wanted to reach out and stop the world as it spun along. It was sad and wonderful all at the same time.

"If you're ready, ladies." Mark included them all in his engaging, crooked grin. Did he practice it in front of a mirror, Jessie wondered, annoyed. "There's our transportation to the staging sight." He gestured with a wonderful economy of motion toward a lobster boat moored at the end of the concrete pier. "We'd better hurry. It's a two-hour trip. We don't want to pitch camp after nightfall."

Jessie felt her frazzled temper shorten like a snapped rubber band. To her it seemed as if his teasing tone was directed patronizingly at her own lack of organization. Of course they were late getting started. It had been *his* nieces who had chickened out.

Her own girls stared in patent disbelief at the mode of travel before them. Three mouths opened in collective protest. Not even Nell was taking this development in stride. The trawler did appear to have seen better days, but it looked somewhat sturdy and the brasswork gleamed in the fitful afternoon sun.

Jessie frowned her daughters down, making a gesture of shifting gears with her free hand as she grabbed the nearest tote. She shoved it into Nell's hand. It was all the hint required. Each taking a duffel, the twins marched to the end of the pier as though the tumbril waited at the far end.

"They'll do fine. Don't worry," Mark assured, bending to pick up a duffel in each strong, tanned hand.

It was the last straw. He didn't know how her children would react. "I'm not so sure." Jessie's tone was sharp, admonitory. She wasn't certain herself how the girls would behave when push came to shove. She resented—now that there was no turning back—what she perceived as Mark's unfair means of getting her to agree to this foolhardy adventure. Jessie felt as though she'd been tricked, that he'd appealed to her baser instincts and won. It suddenly occurred to her that she was no longer in complete control of her life, or those of her daughters. The knowledge gave her a jerky little moment of panic.

They'd been on their own for seven years. She was too long out of practice in a partnership of any kind to immediately recognize Mark's willingness to work together in the venture. Jessie was aware only that she couldn't give up command to a man she barely knew.

"Call them back if you want," Mark directed stiffly, watching the conflicting thoughts flicker across Jessie's expressive features. Would she? Had he been wrong in thinking Jessie would meet his challenge? He hoped not. Mark held his breath, feet planted firmly on the gravelly sand beach. She wasn't like the typical, stoic New Hampshirite he'd come to recognize in the two years he'd spent in the state. She was warm, smiling, easy to talk to and to laugh with—until now, when he'd ruffled her maternal feathers.

"I said we'd go and I meant it. But remember this," Jessie cautioned, a long, clear-tipped finger shaking under his Roman nose, "you asked for it, Mark Elliot. Every minute of the next six days."

"And you don't think I'm man enough to handle all of you, is that it?" Jessie blinked. So he'd hit a nerve. A slanting black brow raised toward his hairline. Male arrogance seeped into the statement, try as hard as he would to keep it out. Gut-level instinct told him that wasn't the best way to deal with Jessie. She wouldn't be bullied. But it was too late for a retraction. He'd have to be very careful from now on when he confronted this exasperating, intriguing woman.

"I'm not sure you are," Jessie stated bluntly, meeting his regard with a steady, assessing evaluation of her own. "What do you know about living with children, teenagers yet? They're a totally different breed. A career officer..." She trailed off, obviously embarrassed at the personal line of attack she'd been about to pursue.

Mark hid a smile. She was no quitter, that was for sure.

"I don't even know what equipment you've packed." Jessie opened up a new field of fire. "You shanghaied us into this deal so darn fast I didn't have time to ask how you intend to house us all." Telltale temper lines appeared between her brows, heightening the resemblance between mother and aggrieved daughters. "Do you have a first-aid kit...a radio for emergency messages?" Jessie sputtered to a halt.

"You'll just have to take my word for it, won't you?" Mark summed up gruffly. He seemed to address her resentment without alluding directly to it. Jessie was ashamed she'd stooped to such petty arguments. Mark would certainly have everything they needed. His next words confirmed her thoughts.

"Trust me to know what's best for all of us. My hide's on the line in this deal, too. Can you do that, Jess?" He waited patiently, his stance relaxed, his shoulders braced easily against the weight of heavy canvas packs. "We can't do this experiment by committee vote. If you can't accept my authority, say so now."

Was it only her imagination that read a measure of tension in that proud tilt of his head? Trust him. She'd have to. She'd given her word.

"After you, Colonel Elliot," Jessie snapped, good intentions giving way to purely human pique. "But don't say later I didn't warn you." Lord, what a scathingly brilliant retort. She could have bitten off her tongue once the words were out of her mouth. She was as bad as Nell when it came to having the last word— and not half as witty.

Chapter Two

In the end the embarkation went surprisingly well. They landed on the tiny wave-lapped dot fifteen miles off the northern coast of Massachusetts late in the afternoon. Overhead the halfhearted sun had given up its protest against the thick gray clouds and disappeared altogether. Maybe that accounted for the gloomy atmosphere that seemed to hang over the islet like an invisible fog. A few seabirds called forlornly as they soared above the tidal flats in search of a meal. It felt like rain. Jessie shivered in sympathy with a screeching gull. Rain—just what they needed.

She surveyed the granite and pine-studded landfall glumly, estimating its size to be no more than a square city block or so. It rose to a ragged crest roughly a hundred feet above the sea. Ahead of them a granite ledge jutted out into the water, creating a fairly level plateau. Their campsite? How did Mark expect five people to live off the dubious bounty of such a rockbound speck for a week? It couldn't be done. She wished she could hop back on the boat and escape, and if the horrified looks on the twins' faces were any indication, they shared her sentiments.

"Rocks and trees and noisy, dirty birds," Lyn mourned, leaning over the side of the fishing boat at a precarious angle.

"The birds can't smell any worse than this tub," Ann seconded with a fastidious crinkling of her nose.

"It's not so bad," Nell defended. She seemed to be reserving judgment, on her best behavior after her one monumental gaffe at the dock only minutes before they sailed.

"We'll starve to death," Lyn continued her lament. "Nell probably knocked most of the supplies overboard back on shore."

"I did not," Nell maintained. "Mark said it wasn't anything we had to have to survive, didn't he, Mom? It was an accident."

"We know that, honey. But I think you should apologize for your..." Jessie searched for an appropriate word as she watched a tanker, the only visible sign of human life, slide over the edge of the horizon far out to sea. It was a lonely sight. A sigh eased past her lips.

She still didn't know how the incident in question had occurred. It never did take much to set off an eruption of knobby knees and gangling elbows where Nell was concerned. Before anybody could move quickly enough to save it, one of the heavy canvas duffels had been jostled away from its fellows and lost forever in the murky waters off the pier.

"I'm a klutz," Nell wailed in a fit of self-pity, infected no doubt by her sisters' sullen attitudes.

"You're not a klutz, just overeager," Jessie soothed. She'd made a supreme effort not to yell at the youngster back on the dock; something she might not have done if they'd been alone. The twins had looked suitably smug, making Jessie's palm itch to slap them. Nell had promptly burst into tears.

Mark Elliot, to give him credit, had taken it like a man. He bit off a sharp exclamation that Jessie was positive would have added unsuitably to the girls' vocabulary and interestingly to her own. A hurried inventory didn't pinpoint the missing objects but ascertained that the lost equipment wasn't absolutely essential to survival. He'd slanted a quick, icy-blue glance in Jessie's direction. "What do you think, Jess? Should we call it off?"

Had he been giving her a way out, Jessie considered in retrospect? Perhaps he had, but she'd refused to be drawn, ashamed at her own irritation with the girls and chagrined that he'd been witness to it. She was determined to uphold her end of the deal. "You're the boss" was all she'd said and stepped onto the boat. With a jaunty salute Mark had followed her.

Jessie hated to admit it, but Mark Elliot was a born leader. From the moment they landed on the rocky spit, the girls seemed to shake off their gloomy lethargy and jumped to obey his slightest wish. He assumed the role of con artist cum Prince Charming as though born to it. Jessie found herself more than a little jealous at the ease with which he handled her brood.

The tents, three two-man nylon affairs with bright yellow-and-blue rain flies, went up like magic. Maybe their vivid color was what tempted the sun to peek out from behind the tattered clouds. Maybe it was Nell's delighted giggles floating on thermals over the island that piqued its curiosity. Jessie wasn't sure, but in any case the whole island took on a different cast in the mellow golden light. Dull gray boulders acquired subtle shading of umber and copper glints; pine trees showed variations in texture and hue that had been hidden in the mist. The sky was so blue in spots it hurt to look at it. Jessie's innate sense of optimism began to take control of her thoughts. Maybe it wouldn't be so bad after all.

Nell was drafted to make a circle of stones to house the campfire while Ann and Lyn foraged for driftwood. Jessie was secretly relieved to learn that the actual cooking would be done on a propane camp stove; there was no way on earth her culinary skills would match up to an open fire.

"Quit looking as if it's the end of the world, Jess," Mark teased, squatting on his haunches as they unpacked the cooking utensils under a plastic lean-to he'd erected on what Jessie could have sworn was solid rock. "We're not here to put Outward Bound out of business. Think of it as a week-long clambake." Jessie made a face to show what she thought of that suggestion. "We're only trying to show that man can live off the land and eat well if he has to. Nothing more."

"In this instance I believe it's more accurate to use the feminine case: 'to show that woman can live off the land.' We outnumber you four to one." How could he be so damned casual about the whole thing? Didn't he know they were sitting on an adolescent time bomb? The twins could go off at a moment's notice, taking Nell with them. Yet he sat there, perfectly at ease, as if he had nothing more serious on his mind than continuing his bantering conversation with the mother of three walking booby traps. "You don't seem to comprehend what you've gotten yourself into."

"I think I have a good idea." He grinned as though he didn't have a care in the world, swiveling on the balls of his feet to watch the twins carry in a load of driftwood for the fire. "We'll get along just fine," he reiterated with such complacency Jessie longed to shake him. Rising, he smiled down at her from what seemed a great height as she crouched squawlike over the box of kitchen supplies. Without another word he turned and headed for the driftwood crew with an effortless, fluid grace.

Jessie was still considering the witty, scathing remarks she should have made when Nell's voice broke into her thoughts. "Mark, it says here in my book that you shouldn't use stones that have been in the water to make a bonfire. They could explode." Nell's tone dropped a reverential note. "Could we experiment to see if it's true?"

Jessie hid a smile at the child's enthusiasm but not at her suggestion. Mark's answer was lost as the breeze died as suddenly as it had sprung up. Jessie was sure his pronouncement would be as informative, as diplomatic, as it was firmly negative.

She would probably have said, "No!" flatly and emphatically. "You can afford to be so patient with them, Mark Elliot," Jessie muttered under her breath, opening the lid on the propane cooking stove to survey its unfamiliar controls. "You don't have to see them turn into competent, happy, successful adults. I do. It's a big job, mister. But, of course, the perfect 'uncle' type can afford to humor them, to be so damned obliging, so much fun to be with."

Mark appeared to be able to handle her daughters every bit as well as their father would have. Jessie nearly stabbed herself in the foot with a fork at the thought. He did handle them well—and seemed to enjoy it. There weren't many of those old-fashioned, family-oriented guys around anymore. She knew that all too well. And he was fun to be with. They'd never had time in their brief working sessions at *Meanderings* to have learned much about each other's personalities, but now Jessie decided she'd like to know much more about Mark Elliot.

Before her musings could gain complete control of her, Jessie called to Nell across the small clearing. "Honey, come here. Do you suppose there are critters already in residence on this island? Can raccoons swim? Ask Mark if we should put any of these things up off the ground?" That should do it. Tending to business was the best antidote for daydreaming that Jessie'd ever found

The awful reality of latrine facilities—or lack of them—set the tone for the rest of the evening as far as the twins were concerned. The second depressing piece of information—that fresh water, brought along in two large plastic drums, could only be used for drinking and cooking, not bathing—pushed even the horrifying specter of a shovel and those rolls of odd-looking toilet paper out of their heads. The strictures on water use brought immediate and vocal protests from all the Meyer women.

"We can't wash our hair in salt water," Lyn said gently, trying out the dynamite smile that had stopped more than one senior boy dead in his tracks. Mark returned the smile but looked in no danger of expiring from joy.

"And I'm not bathing in a tidal pool," Ann added for emphasis, in case he'd misunderstood her sibling.

"I wouldn't want you to," Mark said with utter conviction. "Those tidal pools are ecologically delicate. Not to mention the fact that they'll be providing much of our food supply over the next six or seven days.

We're here to coexist with nature, not to alter it with protein-enhanced shampoos, herbal body scrubs and artifically perfumed soaps.''

Jessie brushed at a curling wisp of shoulder-length, nut-brown hair and wondered fleetingly where he'd learned about herbal body scrubs. From the absent nieces?

"I don't care," Ann went on with adolescent omnipotence. "I won't get in the ocean. It's too cold." Jessie cringed inwardly at Ann's condescending tone, but it was a telling argument. It was far cooler out on the water than it had been when they left Manchester sweltering in the August afternoon. Jessie didn't intend to get in the chilly gray Atlantic, either, if she could possibly avoid it.

Experience told her to side with Mark. Two adults divided over the first test of authority weren't even fair game for three teens bent on opposition. She'd learned that lesson the hard way after several painful bouts with the twins. But her own dismay at the primitive conditions was stronger yet. She moved closer to the twins, subliminally closing ranks against the intruding male in their midst. Jessie avoided looking directly into his eyes, wondering why all of a sudden she was reluctant to do so.

"I agree with you about the tidal pools, naturally, Mark. But, on the other hand, I'm not much of a swimmer. Surely there's some way we can work around this problem?''

Jessie looked inordinately proud of her logic and her tact, Mark concluded. And it wasn't hard to see how difficult it was for her to take a secondary role in ordering her life. He found himself admiring her spunk.

"That does pose a problem." He lifted a hand to his chin, seeming to consider the problem as he tapped his cheek with an index finger. "I could probably rig up one of those plastic groundsheets we brought along to catch the dew and any rainfall."

"God forbid," Jessie interrupted from her heart.

"Yes, God forbid it should rain." Mark didn't try to hide his smile this time. She was being a trooper about the whole thing. "That is unless the groundsheets went over in the duffel."

Nell looked down at the scruffy toes of her pink tennies peeking from beneath the cuff on her jeans. Jessie gave her youngest a timely nudge. "I'm sorry that happened, Mark, truly I am," came the muffled reply. "I'd like to help you to make up for it."

"You don't have to make up for anything. It was an accident." The quick, bright glance from Jessie told him he'd said the right thing. "I'd appreciate your assistance on the project, though."

"Really?" Nell's eyes shone brightly.

"Really. Let's get going." Mark glanced out over the sullen gray Atlantic where the sun shone red below a cloud bank. "There's only an hour until nightfall. Shall we get to it, ladies? Ann and Lyn, down to the clam beds I showed you. We'll need about three dozen for dinner. You can pick up some *Mytilus edulis* at the waterline before the tide starts to come back in."

"*Mytilus*...what?" The twins exchanged a private, wary glance.

"*Mytilus edulis* are ordinary blue mussels. They're delicious. You'll have to learn some Latin if you're going to really get into this nature business."

"I don't think I want to get any further into this 'nature business,'" Ann said, skirting the edge of insolence.

"Then you'll go hungry," Mark answered reasonably, but there was an edge to his words as a quarter century of wielding authority underscored the statement. "If we don't cooperate we'll all go hungry, and that's hardly fair to your mother or Nell." Had he handled that correctly? He waited for their answer.

"It *isn't* fair to spoil it for Mom and Nell." Lyn had hesitated a moment before making the observation.

"No, I suppose you're right. *Mytilus edulis*, huh? Down there?" Ann pointed down the boulder-strewn slope to the waterline. "Can we wear gloves? Mom brought a pair of those rubber ones."

"Good idea." Mark nodded, relieved the first test of his leadership had resulted in an equitable settlement. Handling teenage girls wasn't all that different from dealing with a unit of new recruits if you made considerations for gender and the situation at hand. The duo marched off, a little dazed, down the rocky slope to the shore where the outgoing tide had nearly doubled the size of the island, exposing acres of tidal flats alive with seabirds feeding off unlucky crustaceans unable to scurry to safety.

"You handled that very well," Jessie said when the twins were out of earshot. She wanted to make herself as scarce as her daughters but didn't know how. What was the matter with her? Was she so out of practice that she couldn't carry on a conversation with a man if one of her children wasn't present? In her heart she felt she owed Mark a warning. He looked so pleased at his performance, yet he was a novice at this game.

"You keep winning skirmishes and pretty soon you've won the war," he explained with a shrug of his shoulder.

"Applying military tactics to getting along with my daughters won't work," Jessie said bluntly. "You'll probably have a real battle with them in the morning. They won't wash their hair in salt water." Why in heaven's name did she have to sound so defensive? She didn't want to wash her hair in salt water, either. The whole situation was ridiculous. Jessie planted her feet firmly on the granite and stuck her hands in the pockets of her fisherman's knit sweater.

Mark laughed. "Is that what has you so stirred up, Jess? You sound as if it's the end of the world. Lighten up. I'm prepared to negotiate. You never throw all your artillery behind the first assault. I think if I allow fresh water for rinsing their hair and whatever—" he gestured up and down the length of Jessie's curves "—we'll get along just fine."

"Don't be too sure of that. I've heard that old chestnut dozens of times. Usually from unsuspecting new babysitters or inexperienced camp counselors."

"Doesn't it sound like a workable solution to you?" Mark ignored the unflattering comparison. One black brow raised inquisitively. "After all, you are their mother. What's your expert opinion?"

Jessie thought it over. "It does sound satisfactory," she replied grudgingly. He'd touched on a sore spot. Jessie often didn't know what was the right path to take with her girls. Some days she felt this mothering situation getting totally out of hand. She worked hard at it, but it never seemed to get easier for her. Mark's solution was so simple. Why hadn't she thought of it herself? The man was a natural.

"Did you expect me to order you all into the sea?" Mark continued in the same lazy, teasing tone that appealed to Jessie more than she liked to admit.

"The thought had crossed my mind, Colonel Elliot." She couldn't control a tiny twisting smile, but it disappeared as quickly as it came. The awful realization that she'd surrendered, to some extent, her authority over her daughters to this man bounced unbidden into Jessie's head. She couldn't turn her responsibilities over to him, to anyone, even for a short time. They'd been on their own for seven years. The girls were her responsibility—no one else's.

"And risk a full-scale mutiny my first night out?" Mark came back, diffusing her anger before it could boil over. He laughed, and Jessie was suddenly hard-pressed not to laugh with him. "To tell the truth, I'm not all that keen on salt water myself. This was a perfect excuse to try jerry-building a passive collector." He continued to watch her, aware of the fluctuations in her color, entranced by the clear smoothness of her skin, the curve of her cheekbone. "Satisfactory?"

"Satisfactory." Jessie's smile was brilliant.

"Good. Now, I'm putting you in charge of foraging for the salad course, I think sea-salted glasswort." He pointed informatively to a spiky, yellow-green plant nearby. "The stem tips are best, by the way, and orache will compliment the clams nicely."

"Ugh," Jessie echoed her offspring, making a face as Mark propelled her toward the natural garden among the rocks. His hand was warm and strong on her back. Jessie moved forward with a jerky little hop. It was the first time he'd ever touched her. She hurried into speech to gloss over her momentary confusion. "Whatever you say, boss," she quipped, chagrined at the tiny quiver in her tone. "But don't forget my warning. Teenagers can be lethal to your sanity. Especially if you aren't exposed to them daily."

"I'll remember," Mark said seriously. He was suddenly all business. "Orache's that low, crisp-leaved plant near the waterline. Do you see it?"

"It looks a little like spinach," she admitted after a dubious inspection of the stubby plant he'd pointed out. Jessie was grateful for Mark's casual return to the subject of dinner.

"Actually, it's a relative of both spinach and chard," Mark lectured. "Doesn't even need salt. A bucketful will do nicely." He'd embarrassed her again. He'd have to watch it, go slowly. It had been a long time since he'd tried to establish a relationship with a woman. He wasn't sure he even remembered how. *Don't push it,* he warned himself. He wanted Jessie to consider him her friend. *Take it slow, keep to the script.* "Jess."

"Yes, Mark?" Jessie looked up from where she'd kneeled to inspect the plants.

"I'll keep your advice in mind. I'm not trying to undermine your authority with your daughters, you know that, don't you?"

"Yes." Did he really understand her unease? Could any man who had no children of his own?

"This expedition will turn out fine if we work together as a team."

"I understand." Jessie frowned again. Teams. Partners. Two by two. Parenting was something that should be done in teams, but it wasn't always possible. She couldn't explain to Mark how hard it would be for her to go back. Learning to share all your responsibilities with a man, then having his support taken away, hurt far too much to try again—even on a temporary basis.

MARK WASN'T LUCKY ENOUGH to have everything continue to go his way. He looked totally frustrated, a little angry but endearingly human when they gathered around the campfire in the cool evening darkness. The crisp, cool air smelled of wood smoke and seawater and countless unfamiliar exotic odors that went straight to Jessie's head like a rush of adrenaline.

If only the twins hadn't refused, adamantly, to eat "seaweed and fish eggs," as they termed the salad Jessie had dressed with oil from their stores and the pale orange sea-urchin roe served along with clams and mussels steamed on a bed of rockweed, she might have enjoyed the natural banquet more herself.

"Try them at least," Jessie urged as the juice from a steamer dribbled inelegantly down her chin.

"We did," Ann retorted, sniffing. She turned up her snub nose at her mother's lack of finesse in handling the tasty shellfish. She grabbed one of the two rather soggy ham sandwiches left from lunch and confiscated an apple from the cool rock shelf that served as the larder. "Can we finish these in our tent?"

"*May* we finish these," Jessie corrected automatically. "Yes, you might as well." It was the path of least resistance when they were in this kind of mood. Mark remained silent, not questioning her reasoning of her authority, and she was grateful to him for that.

In a matter of seconds taped rock music, so soothing to jangled teenage nerves, poured from the tent at a volume that would have split Jessie's skull in similar crowded surroundings.

"Do you think they'll stay there as long as they did when you said they couldn't get their ears pierced again?" Nell asked with a hopeful gleam in her eye.

"No, they will not," Jessie said forcefully. She wasn't about to repeat that sustained battle of wills.

"Do you mean they wanted their ears pierced more than once?" Mark asked in an interested tone. He was peeling an apple in one long strand. Nell watched the procedure with great interest until he handed her the skinless fruit. "I had braces once, too. They're a hell of an inconvenience when you're eating apples."

"They sure are. Thanks."

Mark looked at Jessie again, waiting patiently for an answer to his question. "It's the latest thing in their school," she said finally. "Some of the girls have their ears pierced three or four times. I don't think it's necessary." Jessie shrugged, obviously wanting to change the subject.

"You have your ears pierced," Mark observed, reaching out a long arm across the small space that separated them. He brushed back Jessie's fine silky hair to reveal a small golden stud. Her skin was cool and soft beneath his fingers. He let his touch linger a fraction of a second longer than necessary before moving his hand away.

"It's a fad. Someday they'll be sorry they did it." Was Jessie's melodious soprano just the slightest bit breathless? "One artificial hole in each ear is mutilation enough for any man or woman." Her hand rubbed the spot where his fingers had rested. This was the second time he'd touched her in as many hours. What had gotten into him?

"Mom's just sore because she has to wear real expensive earrings and the rest of us don't," Nell supplied. "She can't even wear a watch. They die on her."

"Her watch died?" Curiosity got the better of Mark. He slipped almost without thinking into the exaggerated Viennese accent that had always sent his younger sister, Ellen, into gales of laughter at Nell's age. He continued to scrape metal plates into a plastic garbage sack as he talked. "How iss dis, Frau Meyer, that you keeled a vatch?" He rolled his eyes at Nell, twirling the end of an imaginary mustache. Nell giggled merrily, just as Ellen always had.

"I'm allergic to base metals," Jessie answered tightly. "These earrings are all gold. That's why I only have one pair."

"She loses them all the time," Nell interrupted to clarify the matter with devastating candor. "We aren't that poor."

"And the doctor says you could all become sensitive to metal in the same way at any time. The matter was settled weeks ago, Nell." It didn't take a great deal of intelligence to see she was embarrassed by Nell's forthright speech. Jessie wiggled her finger at her daughter's grinning face. "Nell Elizabeth, change the subject."

"I hope they starve to death." Nell obeyed her mother's wish to change the subject as Mark cleared his throat to hide a wayward chuckle. The child was a treasure. He picked up one of the twins' barely touched plates of food. Nell watched its disposal with ghoulish relish. Mark handed her the sack, pointing in the direction of the trash container. He couldn't help but enjoy her enthusiasm for life and living. It was addictive. It made him feel like a kid again, too.

"Your sisters will eat when they're hungry," Mark assured her. Nell began to pitch empty clam and mussel shells back into the sea.

"They're always eating even when they're on a diet. Say, this is a neat way to get rid of garbage, isn't it?"

"I have no doubt they'll eat," Jessie informed Mark dryly, unsettled by her own wandering thoughts and Mark's perversely even temper. Her skin still burned where he had touched her. She resisted the urge to rub her fingers across the spot. His hands had smelled of apples, and the scent still lingered on her skin. "One thing you can count on with teenagers is that they will eat. But whether or not they'll be satisfied with what they wolf down is something else altogether."

"It sure is dark out here." A small flashlight appeared in Nell's hand. "I'm going exploring along the shore. Isn't this great, Mom! I never knew there were so many stars in the sky." Jessie was proud of her youngest daughter. She'd tried every item on their forager's menu gamely, and although she'd had trouble with the mussels, the clams were a hit and the sea-urchin roe hadn't caused open rebellion as it did with the twins.

"The sky is always more beautiful away from city lights," Jessie agreed wistfully. "I can see the North Star and the Big Dipper. And there's Venus, the Evening Star. Make a wish, Nell."

"I did ages ago, Mom." She scurried off, her flashlight beam a small, bouncing beacon in the darkness.

"She's a trooper," Mark said. He was alone with Jessie for the first time since they'd set foot on the island. He tried to recall his earlier mental strictures on how to deal with her. Friendships required time to grow. Slow but sure.

"Did you enjoy your meal?" he asked politely, gathering up utensils to drop in a plastic pail.

"As a matter of fact I did." There was a faint tinge of surprise in Jessie's tone, as though she couldn't quite believe it herself.

"Well, then, our first day hasn't been a complete failure." Jessie hesitated a moment before accepting a refill of her plastic coffee mug from the pot he held out to her.

"All things considered," Jessie tried again, hoping to find the right light note, "I really am sorry about the twins' behavior. I'm afraid it has a lot to do with their age." How much did he know about the fragile equilibrium, the monumental eggshell-thin egos of sixteen-year-olds? He'd never been married and had spent most of his adult life in the military, cut off from the ordinary lives most people led. All at once it seemed a sad and lonely way to live as far as Jessie was concerned.

"It'll catch up to Nell in the next few months," she added with a sigh, leaning back against the sun-warmed boulder that had served as both dining table and chair. Nell's flashlight beam winked along the shoreline about a hundred feet away. Jessie began to relax a little. "Only I think I'll be able to recognize the symptoms more easily with her, avoid some of the pitfalls I've encountered with her sisters. At least I hope so."

"Experience is the best teacher, they say." Mark watched the play of firelight over her strong, fine-boned features.

"They just can't seem to look past the moment at this age. It'll pass, my mother tells me, but now things like having their ears pierced again or bathing twice a day assume monumental importance—not to mention washing their hair. Be prepared for another crisis tomorrow if there's no water available." She took an experimental sip of the hot drink.

"We'll think of something before then. I remember how it was with my sister, Ellen. It might have been a generation ago, but I don't think girls have changed all that much over the years." He smiled, sloshing hot water over the plates and silverware. It was the first mention he'd made of his family to anyone in a long time.

"Where is your sister now?" Jessie found herself watching his reaction closely. "Is she living in Manchester?"

"Portsmouth. My brother-in-law is a retired naval officer. That's where I called you from this morning. I went up there last night to load them up for the trip. This morning she and my nieces backed out."

"No other brothers or sisters?"

"One brother. He lives in Idaho. He runs my aunt and uncle's sheep ranch."

"Is that where you grew up?" Jessie leaned forward, cradling her mug, eager to hear him talk about himself. "Do your parents live there?"

"My parents died when I was sixteen. My aunt and uncle took in Ellen and Keith. They were hardly more than babies, six and eight. I couldn't cut it," he said tersely, the words coming hard, as though he hadn't told the story to anyone for many years.

"Did you run away?"

"Yes. I paid a guy fifty dollars to say he was my dad and sign the papers. The army gave me an education, a career, and I gave them twenty-four years of my life."

"But you were just talking about Ellen as a teenager. Did you go back to Idaho while they were growing up?" Jessie hoped so; the army was no substitute for a family.

"I was stationed in Washington State for two years after I got back from Nam. I got to see them pretty often, and got to understand my aunt and uncle a little better, too. It must have been hard for them at their age, saddled with a whole family all of a sudden like that.

They weren't ready for an insolent, grieving adolescent as well as two small children. We're all good friends now. So you see I'm not such a greenhorn when it comes to teenagers after all."

Jessie could feel her color heighten; she was thankful for the darkness. "I'm sorry it had to happen that way." All around them the sea murmured sleepily. The wind had died away, taking with it some of the restless energy of the ocean. The tide had turned; the seabirds were gone. It was still and quiet for a few precious moments. They might have been alone in the world.

"Don't be sorry, Jess. It was a long time ago. The army was the best thing that ever happened to me."

"I'm glad."

"Your turn," Mark insisted, refusing politely to allow the conversation to focus on him any longer. He sloshed hot water over the dishes. "Have you always lived in Manchester?"

"No, I was born and bred in Pennsylvania, in a little town not far from Harrisburg. Red Lion, have you ever heard of it?"

"No."

"That's not surprising. It's in Amish country—fertile, prosperous."

"So you're a New Hampshirite through the back door. By marriage, right?"

"That's about it. I fell in love with Carl, my husband, then I fell in love with New Hampshire—the mountains, the scenery and the sea. I love New England."

"Me, too," Mark admitted. "Especially the sea."

"Then you should have settled down in Maine, not New Hampshire. Unless you're a ski nut."

"I do like to ski, but it's not a passion. I guess I didn't check to find New Hampshire only has about fifteen miles of seacoast before I took over *Meanderings* from old Mr. Peavy."

"Are you sorry you didn't? Move to Maine, I mean?" Jessie hesitated a second before taking the warm hand he held out to help her up from her place by the fire.

"Good Lord, no, Jess. I was joking. Lighten up."

"I was joking, too," Jessie replied. "I think I'm out of practice though." She laughed lightly.

Mark likened the sound to chiming golden bells, high-pitched and melodic. No woman for a long time had affected him quite like this one. He didn't know why or how it had happened, but Jessie Meyer fascinated him. He felt comfortable with her, at ease. He wanted to learn to know her, to be able to reach out and smooth away that worried frown that so often settled between her bottomless honey-gold eyes. He wanted to tell her she didn't have to keep apologizing for her daughters' behavior.

"In any case I'm glad you didn't choose New Hampshire strictly for the skiing. I'll make a confession if you swear never to reveal it to another living soul." She gave his hand a squeeze.

Mark looked down at her hand nestled comfortingly in his. It felt good, natural, as though it belonged there cradled within the strength of his palm. "What's that?"

"I can't ski. I don't want to learn to ski—ever. I can't imagine why an otherwise sane human being would strap those tiny strips of wood to his feet and go barreling down the side of a nearly perpendicular mountain. There, are you shocked?"

"When you put it like that I have to agree with you, but a lot of other New Englanders would argue the point. It's great fun."

"That's what my brother, Tim, tells me. He's the only one I have, by the way, so I think he's kind of special, but every winter he comes up here to ski. I can't understand it. He was always the brighter one of the two of us." Jessie chuckled again at her own facetiousness. She couldn't remember when she'd had so much fun talking to someone. The giggle ended in a sigh. She looked down at their joined hands as if seeing them for the first time. She gave a little tug but Mark only tightened his hold on her fingers.

Jessie halted the attempt to free herself and looked up questioningly into his darkly shadowed face. "I think we should call it a night."

"I've missed out on a lot of things in my life," Mark stated wonderingly. His breath brushed her skin, his after-shave mingled with the rich, deep smells at the edge of the sea. "But I just want to thank you for keeping this dream alive, for coming out here with me, Jess. The spring issue could spell the difference for *Meanderings*."

Jessie didn't move. "I know how much the magazine's success means to you, Mark. I just hope this week turns out the way you want it to, that we don't disappoint you." Her breathing was ragged. Whatever was the matter with her? Had it been something she ate? Or was it some unknown element in the sea air? "Good night."

"Not yet, Jessie." Mark's voice was low and rough. "Stay just a little while longer. He could see the rush of blood through the vein in her throat. Her body was inches from his. He could feel her warm breath on his cheek.

"It's getting late, Mark." The sound of his name on her lips was sweet in his ears, and Mark was sure the taste of her mouth on his would be equally as sweet. He bent his head a fraction of an inch; Jessie remained motionless.

The taped rock music issuing from the twins' tent died. "Mother!" Jessie jerked back. Mark dropped her hand. The spell was broken. Jessie blinked in surprise. A moment ago she could have sworn the stars had left the sky to glitter and dance on the broken surface of the tidal pool. The moon had certainly been more than a wispy sliver of cold light far up in the inky velvet blanket of the sky. It had been right here, inches above the treetops right over her head. "Mother!"

"What is it, Ann?" she called.

"There's nothing to put under our sleeping bags. It's going to be awful sleeping on moss and rocks. It's all Nell's fault for knocking the duffel overboard, losing the air mattresses and the first-aid kit. Now she has to go to the john and we're already undressed. Will you take her?"

"They're such sissies." Nell's brown head popped out of the tent.

Jessie thought she heard Mark utter a curse under his breath, but she couldn't be sure it was because the girls had interrupted their tête-à-tête. "I'm coming, Nell. Get your flashlight. Good night again, Mark." She wanted to be alone to have the luxury of savoring the precious minutes of companionship they'd shared. Had he truly wanted to kiss her a few moments ago or had the stardust in the sky played tricks on her reason?

"Jess—"

"Ready, Mom." Nell's piping voice overrode Mark's words.

"We'll get to work on something to double as mattresses first thing in the morning." He hoped she hadn't realized he'd been about to kiss her before the girls' timely interruption. She'd probably figure he'd lost his mind, or worse. Yet the thought of her soft lips under his refused to be banished from his mind.

"I know just how to do it," Nell broke in, tugging at Jessie's hand as she explained the finer points of wilderness camping she'd picked up from her paperback guide. "They're called browse beds. And, Mom, it says here you can even drink fish blood if you have to, to stay alive! After Mark rigs those two a shower we'll probably have to do that when the water runs out."

"That's enough, Nell." Jessie laughed, following the bobbing flashlight beam into the darkness. "Hurry along. I'm so tired I don't even think sleeping on solid rock is going to keep me awake tonight." But the pleasant memory of her time with Mark certainly might.

Chapter Three

Jessie slept late, awakening to the sound of Nell's trilling laugh, the twins' whispered giggles and Mark's deep, authoritative voice issuing instructions and suggestions as he passed by. Evidently she was the only slugabed.

Rummaging through her tote for toothbrush and undergarments, Jessie made a discovery as she hurried to join the busy crew outside. In the rush to pack and make Mark's deadline, she'd left her underwear behind. That posed a problem. She'd never been sorry for the full, sweet curves of her breasts, but neither had she felt comfortable going without a bra. She was the mother of three, a member of the chamber of commerce, PTA vice-president. She was beyond such behavior, wasn't she? Now it appeared she had no choice.

Why not? She didn't look too bad in the old white T-shirt she'd slept in, Jessie decided. She tucked in her chin, scrutinizing her figure beneath the thin cotton. Not bad at all, if she did say so herself. Grabbing another shirt, equally old but red in color, she dragged it over her head, pulled on her jeans, and bent to tie her shoes. At the last moment she added a sweatshirt because the weather was cool, not because of her braless state; she ran a brush through her hair, pinning it into a soft swirl on top of her head with ease, and crawled—as gracefully as she could manage—out into the beautiful sun-washed morning.

"Mom! Come look at our shower," Ann called, dancing toward her from a small stand of spruce trees directly behind and above their tent. "Mark rigged it up this morning, just like he promised. Didn't you hear him pounding on that rusty old bucket Nell scrounged up off the beach?"

Jessie admitted she'd slept through the operation.

Ann sniffed at Nell's pack-rat proclivities and continued. "He's got it working great. He scoured it with rough moss and hung it on a tree branch. Come look." She laughed self-consciously at her own enthusiasm. "The branches come down around like a screen. There's even a rock to stand on and pour more water into the bucket."

As if on cue, Lyn appeared in the clearing, her cinnamon-colored hair gleaming in the bright, clear light. "Hurry up, Ann," she directed. "The water's finally hot. Mark must have started the fire hours ago. "'Morning, Mom."

"'Morning, honey," Jessie replied faintly. This was the last thing she'd expected. She'd been bracing herself for another long sulk by both of them. But here were her temperamental twins, bright-eyed, bushy-tailed and smiling!

"What's for breakfast? I'm starved," Nell called, emerging from the trees as if she'd been produced by a magician with a hat. The magician himself followed close on her heels. Mark hadn't shaved yet that morning and the stubble of dark beard on his sharply angled face gave him a rakish, piratical air. In his black-and-red plaid wool shirt and soft faded jeans he looked totally at home in the rustic setting.

"Good morning, Jess. Breakfast's just about ready. We have bayberry tea, powdered juice for the girls, coffee if you need it," he added with a smile for Jessie. "Fresh raspberries, scrambled sea-urchin roe, which I promise you won't be able to tell from scrambled eggs, and toast. That's the last of the store-bought bread, by the way. Today we bake our own."

"How?" Jessie queried. She knew the propane stove wasn't anything like the oven she was used to back home.

"You create your own Dutch oven by placing a pan on top of the one you're baking the bread in," Mark explained. "That keeps in the heat and bakes the bread all around." After all his years of camping, this method had become second nature to him, and he was quite adept at creating some unusual tasty treats. "Got it?" he asked the group surrounding him.

"Understood," Jessie answered for her brood.

While they ate, Mark passed out assignments that set the pattern for that long busy day and the next. After breakfast, with the camp shipshape, the twins would disappear with towels, shampoo and buckets of water that they collected from the surprisingly efficient setup Mark rigged.

Later they all worked at gathering beach peas, small wild cousins of the domestic variety in Jessie's garden. The shelling was tedious, but time was plentiful.

Mark added snow-white cattail hearts to the menu when he found them growing in a deserted nineteenth-century quarry. Together with bay leaf and clam juice they made an excellent stew, as he promised. For lunch they snacked their way around the island: goose berries, tart and juicy; more raspberries, full and ripe; and rose hips, large as plums.

"Want to come with us, Jess?" Mark asked on the middle of their second full day on the island. "I'm going to show Nell how to fish in the deep water off that spit of rock. I think fresh fish would taste good tonight."

"I'd love to. Wait until I get my gear." There wasn't anything she'd rather do than spend the day with Mark and her girls. She snapped happily away, more relaxed, more rested than she could remember being for a long time. She'd never had the luxury to spend so much time at her photography. Busy with the camera angles and shutter speeds from dawn to dusk, Jessie knew she was doing some of her best work ever. It gave her a special glow of pride and accomplishment.

It was easy when you had good subjects. The girls always made interesting studies, and Mark's rugged good looks gave added depth and substance to the shape and textures of gray sea and rocks. Nell, small, quick and bright, her slight, red-jacketed form framed by dark pine trees and blue sky above, was echoed tirelessly by the restless movement of the choppy surf.

When the sun climbed high and the fresh breeze off the water died away, Jessie would pull off her sweatshirt and open her arms to the sun like a greedy flower. She never gave the fact she was braless a second thought until she looked up to catch Mark's intense blue gaze touch for a second on the opulent curve of her breast. Her nipples tightened automatically and pleasurably. Jessie turned her shoulder, amazed at the response of her body, but managed to meet Mark's eyes head on when they lifted to hers.

At that moment, fortunately, Nell hooked a silvery, toothsome mackerel. Mark leapt up to help her land the large fish, and the awkwardness evaporated as Jessie hurried to join in the fun.

The twins kept busy, too, although they were generally off on their own pursuits. They kept the camp policed: they gathered soft new balsam boughs to pile on sapling frames Mark cut according to the directions in Nell's beloved wilderness primer. The gesture pleased Nell no end. And the result was remarkably comfortable as well as the most delicious-smelling bed Jessie had ever slept on.

Mackerel steaks, beach-pea-and-bay-leaf stew, boiled cattail hearts and rose-hip tea left them all replete the third evening of their wilderness sojourn. Mark promised clam fritters and cranberry muffins for breakfast. Ann, Lyn and Nell each gave him a brilliant variation of Jessie's smile before retiring politely and in the best of spirits to their tent to play a game of Trivial Pursuit.

"Sleep tight, girls," Jessie called after them, leaning back against the sun-warmed rock she'd designated as her own. The granite was only beginning to lose its heat although the stars had come to life in the high, black arch of the sky.

"'Night, Mom. 'Night, Mark," Nell called over her shoulder. The twins waved.

"Good night." Mark returned the gesture amicably.

"How do you do it?" Jessie quizzed, genuinely impressed with the way he handled her girls.

"Nothing to it. I'm a natural," Mark said, shrugging off the implied praise. "You just have to put yourself in their shoes. You told me what's most important to them. I try to supply it. Easy."

"Oh, no, it isn't." A painful dart of maternal jealousy skidded across Jessie's heart. He made it sound easy, but it wasn't. Not for her, not easy at all. "I think I'll make use of the girls' shower," she said as much to change the subject as anything else. "There's plenty of hot water left." The sun and salt spray had left her skin feeling sticky and dry. "I should have asked them to pour my water before they started the game."

"At your service, madam," Mark's voice came out of the darkness at her side.

"Oh, no. I mean it's not necessary...." Jessie stumbled over her words as she watched him secure the trash bag for the night. His suggestion sent little sparks of warning dancing over her skin.

"Come on, Jess, you're a big girl now. I'll keep my eyes closed. I promise."

"I know I'm a big girl now," Jessie retorted, finding her equilibrium once again. "That's precisely why I don't want you acting like a Roman slave," she quipped with a laugh she hoped was worldly but suspected merely sounded nervous.

"Whoa! Wait a minute. Back up! Weren't those poor devils usually eunuchs?" Mark yelped. For a moment there he'd been afraid she'd revert to her usual overserious mood, but she'd risen to his challenge. "No way. I was only volunteering in the name of cooperation and friendship." He laughed, watching her tense silhouette relax as she curled her hands around her knees and stared into the dying fire. "Come on, Jess. There's plenty of warm water, as you said. Don't forgo the pleasure because you're a prude."

"I'm not a prude," Jessie shot back, sitting up straight to fix him with an admonitory glare. "I'm very open-minded."

"Then what are we waiting for? Grab a towel and your soap. I'll meet you in the clearing."

"What if the girls need me? How will I explain showering with a man?" Jessie could feel her face burn. She was glad for the shadows of twilight. "I mean, having you there while I shower...oh, dear."

"Jessie, lighten up. Your worry lines are showing again. Give those three credit," Mark urged. "Give yourself credit for raising intelligent, caring children. They'd think you were taking a shower. Nothing more. Besides, this way you'll owe me."

"Owe you?" Jessie retracted the hand she'd extended to him. Mark reached down, pulling her to her feet despite her protests. "Owe you what?"

"Owe me a favor in return. I certainly don't want your daughters improving on their biology lectures by pouring water over my back. I intend to make use of the contraption tonight, too. Later, of course." His laugh was full and rich.

"Sounds like you're the prude, Colonel Elliot." Jessie echoed his mirth. It's what he wanted to hear. It felt so good to make her laugh. How empty his life had been, and he hadn't even known it until Jessie and her effervescent brood had invaded his staid and quiet existence. Is this how full and satisfying Ellen's and Keith's lives were? He'd never considered how lacking his own was until these past few days.

"On the contrary. I'm very open-minded."

Now Jessie wished there was more light when moments ago she'd blessed the darkness. Was that a dark stain of color creeping up his high cheekbones? Mark Elliot blushing? Impossible. She laughed again, but her merriment carried a new current of excitement that coursed between them. "If you bring the water I can fill the reservoir myself," Jessie said, moving back a prudent few steps.

"I'll meet you in five minutes." Mark turned away to kick at the burning embers of the fire with his shoe. A vast shower of glittery sparks danced and leaped skyward. His expression carried little of the amusement that had edged it moments earlier. Had Jessie felt that shimmer of excitement, too, he wondered.

Jessie arrived in the clearing ten minutes later. The only illumination came from the waxing moon. Two buckets of steaming water stood beside the low-hanging branches of the old pine. Mark was nowhere in sight, yet stepping naked into the mossy circle under the tree was one of the hardest things Jessie had ever done.

She lifted the bucket high, filling the salvaged reservoir, wondering how what was so obviously a milk bucket had found its way to the island's shore. Warm, sweet water flowed over her in a comforting rush. It felt marvelous. She soaped and lathered, intent on the silky glide of flesh on flesh. She could have stayed there for hours.

The water stopped. Before Jessie could react she heard a rustle of movement and smelled the distinctive spicy odor of his skin. The bucket was refilled. "Mark?" Her voice was thready with nerves and something else, brighter, hotter, that she preferred not to name. "Go away. What are you doing out here?"

The moon shone, benignly lessening the deep shadows around the pine but little more. "Don't worry, Jess. I can't see a thing. I brought more water. Do you want to wash your hair tonight?" His words were soft, almost lost in the night. *Slowly, slowly, don't frighten her off.*

"No..." She stumbled over the lone syllable, swallowed, tried again. She wanted to attribute the hesitation to pique but it was closer to panic. "No, thank you, not tonight. I..." How could she tell him she lacked the poise to carry on a conversation in this vulnerable state? "It takes so long to dry...."

"Yes, I imagine hair as thick as yours does take a long time to dry." He should have thought of that before he returned to the clearing. Still, the offer was only an excuse to be with her. He cleared his throat to erase the husky note of strain he'd detected lurking there. "I should have thought of that. Perhaps in the morning."

"Yes, in the morning. I'll have the girls help me," Jessie said, pleased she'd reasserted some control over her wayward senses. "If you leave I'll be getting dried off now."

"No more water?"

"No," she retorted. "No, thank you," she continued more softly now, muffled as she toweled her face and neck. "I'll see you in the morning."

"I was hoping to be able to say good-night with a kiss." He moved to intercept her as she stepped from the screening boughs clad only in a towel that was damp and clinging. Mark wished all at once that she was wearing the ratty old bathrobe with its wide, full sleeves and concealing folds he'd seen her in yesterday morning.

"I thought you'd gone." Her tone implied criticism at his ungentlemanly behavior. Mark ignored the stricture.

"Shh." His hand reached out to circle the back of her head. He wanted so badly to touch her. "You've got more material in that towel than in most bathing suits you see these days." He wished he could convince his clamoring senses of that fact. "I admit I'm not shining to my best advantage at the moment, but I didn't mean to embarrass or frighten you in any way, Jess."

There was genuine regret in his voice but something deeper and darker, too, that called to Jessie's femininity, keeping her from answering as pertly as she wished.

"I'm not frightened, just uncomfortable. I don't usually carry on conversations with male friends in the nude...or as close to nude as I am." Jessie wished she could have found something more sophisticated to say than that. She wished it wasn't Jessie Meyer, CPA, mother, practical businesswoman standing there half-naked under the trees.

It should be Jessie, worldly, provocative, self-assured as she'd like to be for just fifteen minutes or so. "But I would like a kiss," she heard herself say, amazed at her temerity. "I've wanted you to kiss me for quite some time, actually. I mean, if you want to, of course." *So much for women's lib,* Jessie thought disgustedly; she'd certainly muffed this chance to be assertive.

"I don't want to rush you, Jess. I'm not about to take advantage of the fact that you're more or less at my mercy on this blasted island."

"Is that what's bothering you, Colonel Elliot?" Jessie gurgled, relieved she hadn't scared him off with her unaccustomed boldness. She was deeply touched by the evidence of his thoughtfulness. "I suggest if you do want to kiss me we'd better get at it or my built-in trio of chaperones will pop up on their way to the latrine or something and show you just how little at your mercy I really am." Jessie surprised herself again with the directness of her suggestion.

"Yes, ma'am," he mimicked her occasional teasing use of his military title. "Is that an order?"

"Merely a request, Colonel. Despite your background, you don't seem the type to be good at taking orders."

"You're sure right, there." He pulled her closer, all the time his fingers working tactile magic on the back of her neck, soothing the tightness, melting her inhibitions.

Mark began to wish Jessie hadn't knotted the towel so tightly that there was no danger of it slipping an inch. He had no intention of pushing this fragile new intimacy further than she wished it to go, but he would have liked to learn the feel of his mouth against her breasts as well as her lips. Jessie's eyes were closed; there was a faint frown outlined between her brows. She looked as if she were bracing herself to be inundated by his kiss.

Mark's kiss, when it came, wasn't at all what she expected, but it was what she wanted. It was light, tentative, restrained, making no demand for something she wasn't ready to give. He pulled her deeper into the shadows of a twisted pine, cradling her soft, damp shoulders in his hands. The sensation of being held in a man's arms was wondrously familiar, yet somehow new. She leaned closer, trying to bring their bodies into more intimate contact while Mark tried to maintain a small distance between them.

Jessie lifted her face, letting the tip of her tongue explore the full curve of his lower lip. "Kiss me, Mark. I'm a woman. You don't have to treat me as if I'm made of spun glass. I won't break. I'm a big girl now, remember."

Mark groaned, taking her face between his rough, strong palms. "I think I've wanted to kiss you since the first night we got here." He nibbled lightly at the soft parted moistness offered to him.

"Why didn't you?" Jessie whispered without a hint of provocativeness. He moved his feather-light caress to her hairline just above her ear.

"Because in my day a guy didn't kiss a girl he was trying to impress on the first date," Mark replied, but his voice was husky and his lips lowered to tantalize the curve of Jessie's ear, nipping at the earring nestled there.

"An officer and a gentleman." Jessie sighed in defeat. "You're not going to step one inch out of line, are you?" She was dizzy with wanting, her voice a mere whisper in the louder whispers of pine boughs and night breeze. She'd never felt quite like this before, not even with Carl, not even in the white-hot blaze of first love all those years ago. "Something's happening to us. But I'm not sure what it is. It's just that I've never considered you...I mean, I didn't intend anything like this... Oh, dear." Jessie faltered. "Perhaps you should go now. I'll stay here and dress."

"I've got a better idea. I'll stay here and try out the shower. All by myself," he added meaningfully. "It is too soon for us, Jess. There's something beginning; you feel it, too." Jessie nodded, dazed. "I'm not used to this kind of thing hitting me like a bolt out of the blue. I don't think you are, either?" He made it a question.

"I'm not used to this kind of thing at all," Jessie confessed with a last quick, light joining of lips. Her hands had lifted to circle his neck of their own will. Now she let them slide down the column of his throat, trace the hard firm planes of his collarbone to rest lightly on his shoulders, then the smooth muscles of his chest beneath the soft flannel shirt. "You're right. It is too soon." Jessie couldn't stop the sigh that followed her words as Mark lifted his head slowly and reluctantly. "We both need time to sort it all out."

"Time together." Mark liked the sound of the words. "I'd like to take you foraging tomorrow—without the girls."

"We'll see," Jessie hedged. She hadn't meant to become attracted to this man. Perhaps it was just the moonlight, the starlight dancing on the ocean and its constant throaty murmur in the background that made her feel so unlike herself. She needed time alone to consider, yet she wanted very much to be with Mark, learn all about him, try to judge the strength of her growing pleasure in his company.

"The girls will be fine without you for a few hours. Trust me." Mark's finger touched her slightly parted lips, then dipped to follow the line of terry cloth across the rise of her breasts. "We deserve some time alone together, time to get to know each other, to comprehend what's happening between us. Say you'll come with me." He could feel her start to relax as she reacted subconsciously to the uncoiling tautness in his own body. Would she agree to come with him? Or would she retreat yet again behind the shield of responsibility to her children?

"I'd like that very much. I'll be ready whenever you are."

"No!" THE NEGATIVE WAS EMPHATIC. "I do not believe you got a Purple Heart by being thrown through a bar window in Da Nang because you'd taken on one marine more than you could handle." Jessie laughed delightedly, screening her eyes from the bright sun with the brim of her disreputable old straw hat. "And I do not want to see your scars!'' She held up a purple-stained restraining hand as Mark's fingers went to the zipper of his faded brown cords. ''I take it all back. If you say so, it must be true. I believe you, every word.'' Jessie fell silent a moment, sorting out leaves and stems from the small wild blueberries in her hand. ''Do you want to tell me what did happen?'' Her eyes cloaked him in warmth and concern.

''No.'' Mark shook his head to soften the harsh syllable. How had they even gotten on the subject? He couldn't recall. It was extraordinary how easy it was to talk to this woman. He didn't have to tell her the shrapnel scars on his left hip came from what was left of his sergeant's helmet, the helmet his friend had been wearing moments before he stepped on the booby-trapped mine. She understood so quickly and didn't press when he wanted to gloss over the details of those three long, dangerous tours of duty—six years of his life, a quarter of his military career.

''Vietnam left most of our generation with scars of one kind or another.'' Jessie didn't elaborate on the observation.

Mark added another handful of berries to Jessie's bucket. He picked berries as he did most things: with purpose, efficiency and great economy of movement. The sun was high, but clouds loomed not far away, fat and gray. They were in for rain. ''Was your husband in Nam?''

''No. Carl was an only child. His parents were adamantly opposed to the war. But I don't think he ever gave it that much thought. He would have gone if he'd been drafted, but he wasn't.''

She flashed a private little smile that twisted something deep in Mark's gut. He didn't like to admit he could be jealous of a dead man, so he ignored the ache.

"They sent him to college to keep him out of the service. I met him there at the University of Pennsylvania. We fell in love and got married. Carl dropped out after his sophomore year. By then we had the twins." A dull red stain colored her cheekbones. Had Jessie been a proverbial pregnant bride, Mark wondered absently. He'd have liked to see Jessie round and smug with child. "All Carl really wanted to do was work in the woods, among the big trees. He died there in a logging accident seven years ago."

"I'm sorry." The words sounded inadequate, as they always did when one sincerely meant them.

"So am I. He was a good husband and a good father."

And lover? That was another tangent he didn't intend to follow.

"Enough of the past." Mark wasn't aware his words were a growl as he dragged Jessie up from her knees, out of the prickly, low-growing blueberry bushes. He wasn't jealous because Carl had known Jessie first, he assured himself, or loved Jessie first. "No more talk of the past. Look at that view, those clouds, that ocean. Where's your camera?"

"In the boat. I'm out of film at the moment. I'm going to have a lot of trouble picking proofs for this one." Mark had included an inflatable, two-man rubber raft complete with small outboard motor among their equipment. They'd used it to putter across a choppy mile or so of open water to this larger sister island. It was just the two of them, alone together. "I think it's going to rain."

"Don't be such a pessimist, Jess."

"I'm not, only practical. I didn't bring an umbrella on this outing."

"It's not going to rain," Mark pontificated.

"So now you're a weather sage on top of all your other abilities." Jessie made her tone as sarcastic as she could manage.

"I'm a natural wonder," Mark admitted with great modesty and a theatrical flourish of his hand. He loved to make Jessie laugh. It had been another good day. They'd talked about everything under the sun. They discussed politics, on which they disagreed. Jessie was decidedly more conservative in her outlook than he. It would make for interesting conversations come the next presidential primary.

Over lunch they'd discussed the playoff chances of the New England Patriots in the upcoming season. Mark was surprised to find Jessie liked football and was knowledgeable about the game. Jessie was surprised he'd let his chauvinistic leanings show by even mentioning the fact and told him so. And with Hershey bars smuggled over by Nell and bargained for by her mother as their dessert, they'd come to the satisfying conclusion that either of them could do a better job with the economy and the budget deficit than anyone in Washington, if only they had the chance.

Yet they'd been equally happy to be silent, listening to the wind and the sound of the sea, the calls of high-flying gulls riding thermal currents till they were specks in the far blue of the sky, drinking in the stark beauty of granite shores and the untamable sweep of the cold, gray Atlantic.

They were becoming friends, Mark discovered happily. How good the words sounded echoing in his thoughts. He'd been alone so long he hadn't even realized he was lonely—until Jessie and her girls set his well-ordered world on its ear. They were becoming friends. And friendship could lead anywhere.

"Why do you do this, Mark?" Two fishing boats passed across her vision far out on the horizon. Closer in, a yacht under sail slipped gracefully along the swells making for Portsmouth or some other safe, snug port. Jesse sat down, reluctant to leave the island. "Do what, Jessie?" Mark prevaricated, dropping down beside her on the fern and grass-covered lip of rock. The crash of breakers on the far side of the small headland made Jessie strain to hear his quiet words.

"This business of living off the land." Jessie made a gesture that included the sea, the berries and shafts of wild strand wheat they'd gathered, and the island off in the distance where the girls were spending the day on their own.

"To sell magazines, of course." He grinned, stretching out on the sun-warmed ledge. "Lighten up." It had become a joke between them, that phrase. This time Jessie didn't respond. "You're much too serious about this adventure, lady. I want you to enjoy yourself. I've told you that."

"I am enjoying myself." That much was true. At least it was only a white lie. She did enjoy every minute she wasn't worrying about how to deal with him. "I didn't mean to be so serious. Bringing up three children alone tends to make you that way, I suppose," she said candidly, then wished she had not. It came too close to voicing more of her private philosophies. She was liberated by necessity, not choice. He was so damned quick to take up on her moods he'd probably already divined that fact. "I'll try to do better, sir. It's a big responsibility." The quip fluttered to the ground and fell flat on its face.

"I'm aware of your responsibility and how you've handled it. I admire you for it. But it's a fact you seldom let me forget. Don't be so damned defensive about your girls."

"I'm not defensive. Am I? It's just that...well, some days I get so angry at Carl for leaving me alone. As if he had any say in it." She gave a rueful little shake of her head that was filled with the pain of loss.

"It's hard to understand and cope with," Mark said gently. "Now you've given up on finding anything like you had with Carl. You must have loved him very much."

"I did love him. It's sad to think there may not be any more men with his qualities left in the world, at least not for me. Now you know almost everything there is to know about me. Turnabout. Answer my question. You owe me." Jessie hoped the painful residue of old grief wasn't coming through in her voice. She thought she'd handled it all very well. It hadn't been as difficult as she feared, telling him her very private hurts.

Mark wasn't about to let her know the agony showed quite plainly in her expressive eyes. "I've forgotten exactly what you asked me," he sidestepped.

No censure for her confession of maternal doubts was in his tone. There was no pity in his brilliant blue gaze, Jessie noted from beneath lowered lashes. Yet something flickered in the gold-shot depths of his eyes, something darker and far more meaningful.

"I asked you why you brought us out here. To serve what purpose?" she reminded him.

"To sell magazines, naturally." He laughed at the awful pun as Jessie winced. He ran his hand over his jutting chin, contemplating his answer. His beard was thicker today. He really ought to shave.

"You said that already." Jessie looked mulish.

"I did?"

"Yes, besides, I don't believe you do it just to sell magazines."

"You've never contradicted me so adamantly before, Jessie Meyer. I like it. No tiptoeing around my ego this time. I wondered when you'd show a taste of that skillfully concealed temper of yours."

Good grief! He knew she had a temper. Jessie stared down at her jeans-covered legs in confusion. She'd been so careful to keep it hidden. She'd been a model parent all week, and barely even raised her voice to the girls. How could he know?

Mark laughed again, loud and heartily. "I listen to office gossip when it suits my purpose. Does that surprise you, Jessie? No doubt being the boss I don't hear as much as you do." Jessie didn't remind him she spent very little time at *Meanderings*. She didn't feel comfortable learning she was the occasional topic of conversation. His conversation. "You'd rather I didn't know that about you, wouldn't you, Jess?"

"Yes," she replied with candor. "And that was still one more nonanswer to my question. Why are we here?"

Mark shrugged. Iron-hard muscles rippled under the soft, dense weave of his chambray shirt, distracting Jessie as effectively as his conversational red herrings. She pulled arched brows together as much to banish the image as to spur his confession. "I do it for the pure enjoyment of nature."

She looked stern, waiting. But she felt far more at ease now that the focus of attention was no longer herself.

"More detail?" Mark looked up from his equally intense study of blades of grass. She nodded. "I want to prove man can live in harmony, nondestructively, with nature. I spent a lot of years building things to destroy or be destroyed. But while I was at it I also learned a lot about nature and what she provides us with. I want to make up a little for what I destroyed. I'd like to pass that knowledge on to others."

It evidently wasn't all that easy for him to share his deeper feelings, either. Jessie liked that. She felt he had repaid her confidences with something of his own. "Go on," she urged. "Why *Meanderings*—a regional magazine on its last legs? That's about as far from the Army Corps of Engineers as you can get."

"You're right, there." Mark had suddenly become very interested in the fronds of a fern growing near his left elbow. "And New Hampshire is as far from the jungles of Southeast Asia and South America as you can get, too. I've spent most of the last twenty-five years of my life in that kind of climate, in the corps and later as a consultant for a Portuguese engineering firm. I wanted some place where the air is crisp and cool, where there are rocks and open sky and lots of clear running water."

"How did you meet old Mr. Peavy?" Jessie found herself being caught up in the unfolding story. It seemed so right, so natural to be sitting here listening to Mark, talking to Mark as if they'd known each other for years and years.

"Hiking on the Appalachian Trail. He's a remarkable old coot. We got caught out together during a thunderstorm two years ago, sheltered in a dilapidated old sugarhouse. My sister had just moved to Portsmouth. I was visiting her and needed to get out on my own for a while. One thing led to another. He's a persuasive old bastard, and before I knew it I'd agreed to buy *Meanderings* as an investment. Six months later he had me talked into running it myself and trying to make a success of it.'' Mark shook his head as if he still couldn't believe the selling job the crafty octogenarian had done on him. "It was the best move I ever made in my life.''

"Even if it goes under and you lose your life savings?'' Jessie couldn't imagine herself taking such a gamble. But for Mark it was the kind of calculated risk he'd lived with all his life.

"It won't go under.'' There was steel in his voice. No, it wouldn't, Jessie realized. He wouldn't let it happen. Warning signals screeched like air-raid sirens in her brain. How could she know that about him? For a woman as private as Jessie, it was a frightening prospect to be attuned to another human being so suddenly—frightening but exhilarating.

Jessie abandoned the line of thought with a jerk that pulled her gaze level with Mark's once again. He still watched her tenderly, absorbingly. Jessie jumped up, grabbing her berry bucket. She was disturbed by the strange yet familiar gleam in his eyes. Was it desire? Mark plucked at her pant leg, still stretched out in his prone position.

As she hesitated her shadow disappeared from the ground beside him. Jessie stared at the spot as if she'd never witnessed the phenomenon before. She looked up to find the sun obscured by the bank of fast-moving rain clouds. Low on the horizon, fog followed in their wake.

"We'd better go. You were wrong about the weather. I told you it's going to rain."

"But I'm not wrong about us. Don't be in such a hurry, Jess. There's time." She sank back to her knees, her aluminum pail rattling on the rocks.

"The berries...I promised the girls a pie for supper. I don't think there are enough...." She stuttered to a halt. Jessie knew she sounded as witless as a babbling brook.

"I'll help you with the pie. I want to be able to help you with everything." Mark reached out slowly, hesitantly, imprisoning her face in his large capable hands. Her hat fell off, freeing the shoulder-length waves of her auburn hair. It spilled over his wrists. He buried his fingers in its softness. "I'd like very much to be there for you, Jessie."

His kiss was as gentle and restrained as before. Until she opened her mouth boldly to his probing tongue, inviting him within the secret places, pulling him out of control. "God, Jessie, don't do this," Mark groaned against her lips. "You're ruining my battle plan. I don't want to go too fast, scare you away. I knew this would happen if I took you in my arms again." He pulled her down beside him on the hard, stony earth. Pebbles pushed into her hip; ferns tickled the back of her neck. Jessie didn't mind the discomfort. She was too taken up with her own delighted response to his kiss.

It was all that she wanted it to be—a kiss between a man and a woman. Jessie felt as if she'd grown a hundred feet tall, flown a million miles away, become a child at Christmas, a woman desired above all others. All were sensations she'd thought never to experience again in this life. She returned Mark's kiss as tears prickled behind thick, spiky lashes. If he had asked, she couldn't even have told him why she felt like crying.

"I didn't mean for this to happen," he mumbled low in his throat. "I meant to go slowly, work my way into your confidence, your affection, not play the caveman on some desert island. I want us to be friends before we become lovers."

Friends before we become lovers. He sounded so positive of the fact. His hands had tangled themselves in her hair. Jessie luxuriated in the power of his strong fingers, the tangy smell of salt and sun on his skin, the brush of his beard along her jawline when he dipped his head to nuzzle at the golden stud earring.

She let her fingers stroke over the soft curling hair at the nape of his neck. It was thick and fine as she'd known it would be. Jessie lost herself in the tactile exploration while Mark's caressing fingers moved over her shoulders to the fullness of her breasts.

"Jessie." Her name was a hoarse groan of pleasure. "Such a contradiction, velvet on the outside, steel beneath. Demure and aloof for the world to see, smoldering and passionate here, with me alone."

"Shh, you talk too much," Jessie whispered. His words were evocative and erotic. They undermined her equilibrium. She was determined to remain untouched emotionally despite the singing of her senses. This was nothing more than a lovely interlude between two mature, consenting adults. It wasn't a prelude to a commitment. She couldn't expect that; indeed, she didn't even want to consider it. But it was so good, so right. She longed to be joined to Mark completely, to experience all the joys of her femininity with such a man.

He had called her a contradiction but so was he. Outwardly decisive, dynamic, aggressive, yet beneath he was sensitive, caring and passionate in his own right. All the qualities Carl had possessed. All the qualities she admired and wanted in a man.

Her breasts responded to the touch of Mark's hands. The sun returned to feast on the glory of Jessie's awakening passion as eagerly as his hands molded the soft curves. "You haven't worn a bra since we got here, Jess. Are you doing it to drive me wild?" Two buttons parted, exposing the beginning rise of creamy skin.

"No." She meant to be emphatic, but the word sifted past her lips in a breathy sigh. "I'm not a tease. It's your fault as much as mine." She challenged him with eyes as dark as winter earth. "You made us leave Manchester in such a rush I forgot to pack my undergarments."

Bright flames kindled the gold flecks in his eyes. His laughter was a short, triumphant bark of amusement. "Hoist by my own petard. I was so set on talking you into this expedition that my impatience is my own undoing. Now I suppose you'll tell me you aren't even wearing a lacy little wisp of panties under your jeans?" One brow climbed toward his hairline.

Jessie could barely string two words together coherently as his hands continued to mold to her form. His palms circled the straining globes with exciting roughness. She could feel her nipples harden in response to the stimulation of his caress.

"I'm not wearing anything...." This wasn't the staid everyday Jessie talking, that was for sure. Where had she gone? Where was she hiding?

"Always truthful," Mark mumbled, brushing her breasts with the rough stubble of beard on his chin. Desire roared through Jessie like a steam engine.

"I think I'm beginning to enjoy it." The woman who stretched among the ferns and brake of a deserted Atlantic island, the woman who moved with such ageless feminine grace in Mark's arms, wasn't the same hardworking CPA who'd left a drawerful of sensible cotton underwear back in Manchester four days ago. That Jessie would never have allowed herself to be seduced by her own passion. That Jessie would have retreated in confusion from such erotic give and take. "I may burn all my bras and panties when we get back."

"That's guerrilla warfare, Jess. I never thought you'd stoop to such tactics. I planned this assault so carefully." Mark looked down at her fumbling fingers as she parted the buttons of his shirt. Jessie concentrated fiercely on her task to keep the blood from rushing indiscriminately to her cheeks. She didn't want him to guess how very new this role of aggressor really was for her. "I've made so many plans alone in my tent these past nights. Now you've blown it all sky-high. Ambushed me."

His mouth covered her mouth, and his body covered her body as he rolled his lean, strong length atop her.

The brush of his hard-muscled chest against her soft, conforming curves drove all rational thought from Jessie's brain. She'd been alone so long, been lonely so long. She needed someone to be with. A friend...and a lover. Her heart sang.

She let her fingers trail across the rough, curly hair on his chest. Her palms fitted to the tapering V of his ribs and sidled lower to the stiff, unnatural barrier of his belt. Reality collided with desire as their eyes met. Mark's were as dark and liquid with passion as her own. "I want to touch you, Mark," she whispered.

"Do you, Jessie?" His voice sounded as hushed as hers even though they were cut off from other human beings. A fine tremor communicated itself from Jessie's fingertips along his hand.

"I think I do. I'm not sure. I haven't done this for so long. It shouldn't be so difficult. It isn't any different...." But it was different, very different from being with Carl, her husband, the only man she'd ever loved.

"God, Jessie, you're so sweet and innocent." Jessie sniffed scornfully but the continued stroking of his fingers along her nipples precluded speech. He switched the attention of his lips from her neck to her breasts. He sucked gently, the scratch of his beard on her skin threatening to send her plunging into a great glittering void of sensation.

"Mark." His name was a shadow on the wind. She wanted to tell him she was frightened of rediscovering the wonder of a man's body. His passion was blatant, an exultation of her femininity. He was hard and smooth, tempered like fine steel, and she reveled in his nearness. But the fine trembling in her arms and legs wouldn't stop.

"I won't rush you, Jessie." The pale shadow of indecision, that tiny hint of fear, was back in her candid gaze. Her eyes were truly the mirror of her soul, the crystal ball that forecast her every emotion if one only made the effort to look into the reflecting depths.

"I'm confused," Jessie said. "It's all happening so fast. I'm not very good at relationships anymore."

"Neither am I," Mark admitted. "It's just that you make me feel like a kid...a teenager with his best girl in the back of his old man's Chevy. Remember?"

"Yes, it was awful. *Should I let him kiss me or will he think I'm fast? Better not, I might get lipstick on his shirt. Would his mother call mine if she found it?* I don't ever want to go back.'' Jessie sighed, and the brief moment of amused remembrance broke the tension hovering between them like the rain clouds moving up quickly over the horizon.

"That bad, Jess?"

"Yes, it was awful. I'm sorry, Mark. It's just happening so fast between us. You seem to know so much about me without even asking. It's not fair. I feel so confused. It's upsetting." Jessie watched Mark refasten the buttons of her shirt. She didn't trust her shaking fingers to reciprocate the same simple task.

"That's one good thing about not being so young anymore. We don't have to go rushing off to meet tomorrow head-on. We have all the time in the world to learn about each other."

"We do?"

"I intend to monopolize a great deal of your time from now on—up to and including having my taxes audited to provide an excuse."

"My Lord, you are serious." Jessie pushed herself up off the hard ground. Now that the sensual attraction between them had retreated to a simmering awareness lingering beneath the surface of their casual banter, Jessie found the rocky soil uncomfortable. Was she crazy for coming out with it point-blank like that?

"You better believe it. I'm very persistent in pursuing my objectives." Jessie should have been warned by the climbing black brow, the hint of a smile in the mobile curve of his lips.

Mark draped her arms around his neck. He dropped a quick light kiss on the tip of her nose. The tension of the last few minutes was all gone now, sublimated into a warm, anticipating glow. She would be his someday, he was sure of it now. But he had to go slowly, one step at a time. He'd almost frightened her away with his need to make himself a part of her. He'd have to be very careful not to make the same mistake again. "This fog won't last, but the girls will think it's what's delaying us." He made his tone meaningless and teasing. "I have a suggestion...."

"Which is, Colonel Elliot?" Jessie retorted, picking up his mood.

"Let's neck."

Chapter Four

The rain came quietly behind the fog, no more than a heavy mist at first, but by late afternoon, when Mark and Jessie returned to the camp, it was coming down in a steady concentration. For a time the girls were too busy breaking out rain gear, securing firewood stacks and watching Mark skillfully bank the fire to pay much attention to Jessie's dreamy smile and inattention to detail. For that small blessing she was mighty grateful.

The evening meal, cooked over the propane stove and eaten in the shelter of the kitchen lean-to, was calculated to keep the girls happy. Deep-fried clam strips, chowder made with powdered milk and fresh bay leaves, the blueberry pie Jessie had promised and managed quite well, despite having to improvise a rolling pin with an appropriately shaped, well-scrubbed sea stone provided by Nell, scavenger extraordinaire.

They separated early, Mark and Jessie exchanging a visual caress that still managed to make her breath catch on the pulse beating hard in her throat. Nell had replenished the balsam boughs of their mattresses that morning, and the damp, heavy air filled the little tent with woodsy fragrance. Mother and daughter settled down by the light of one of the remarkably compact candle lanterns, Jessie to daydream, Nell to plan for the unlikely but secretly longed-for prospect of being stranded on the island indefinitely with only the guidance of her dog-eared wilderness primer.

Jessie hummed an old Beach Boys tune under her breath, brushing the tangles from her hair with sybaritic pleasure. Here it seemed they were always busy; yet there was also time to do what you wanted to do. Wasn't that what life should be like, Jessie mused in a lazy, half-philosophical kind of mood. When was the last time she'd been able to sit down with her mother and really talk, just the two of them, of things close to their hearts, on matters not essential to the smooth running of a totally female household? It was something she'd like to change when she got back home.

And right now she could luxuriate within herself. She could lose track of man-made time in the tug and glide of the brush through her hair and think about what had passed between her and Mark earlier in the day. She could contemplate the future.

She needed a man in her life. Equality of the sexes, women's liberation, her own independent nature notwithstanding, it was good to be involved in a partnership again. The girls needed a male figure in their lives, too. Allowing Mark to be in control of their immediate destiny these past few days had brought back all the good memories of being married for Jessie.

She smiled at her shadow on the tent wall as it mimicked her movements in larger-than-life-size pantomime. A few short days ago she'd been irrationally angry at Mark's assumption of that authority. Now she could see more clearly, recall the joy of sharing the decisions, the everyday problems of life, the good times and the bad. He was a great help with the girls. She appreciated that; she hoped she could accept his contribution with more grace in the days to come.

Being independent, a businesswoman and, with heaven's help, a successful single parent had its advantages, to be sure. But it was a lonely job. Jessie didn't want to spend the rest of her life alone. For her, that was a basic and fundamental truth. She wanted to spend her future with a man, a partner and a lover. A man like Mark.

And oddly, thankfully those thoughts, Mark's presence, his appeal and easy rapport with her daughters didn't stir the embers of past sorrows. But it did give Jessie pause. She'd put her mourning for a lost love behind her. But was she ready for a new involvement? Her body had understood that before her brain; hence the conflicting signals between heart and head that afternoon. Again Mark had read the signs, reacted with tact and sensitivity, giving her options, not ultimatums, forging new links in the chain of friendship that was beginning to bind them.

"Mom!" It was Ann at the tent flap with Lyn behind her, their faces lost in the shadows of hooded rainproof ponchos, that pulled her from her reverie. "We are starved."

"Already?" Jessie was becoming resigned to two-hour feedings. It was almost like having infants in the house again, except they required far larger portions of a more varied menu than they had sixteen years ago. "We barely finished KP an hour and a half ago." It was pitch-dark and the sound of rain was loud on the tent roof.

Nell strained to be heard above the drumming downpour. "Me, too. I ate all the stuff I brought along for snacks. You took the last of my Hershey bars this afternoon, remember?'' A not too subtle hint.

"Our stuff's all gone, too,'' Lyn lamented. "I didn't think I'd be so hungry out here. I wish this place had a McDonald's.'' That it didn't have any fast-food restaurants was one of its chief selling points in Jessie's eyes, but she didn't voice the thought aloud.

"Will popcorn be an adequate substitute?'' Mark's words startled Jessie into dropping her hairbrush. She'd never get used to how quietly he moved.

"Popcorn?''

"I've been saving it for an emergency. I guess this qualifies, since both your mother and I contributed to the junk-food crisis.''

"I love popcorn,'' Nell gushed, gesturing with her book, index finger marking her place. "We don't have any butter, though. I like mine with lots of butter.'' An edge of disappointment peeked out of the statement.

"I brought some butter-flavored salt. It's not bad. Will that do?'' Mark cajoled with a grin that sent Jessie's pulses careening—if not her daughter's.

"Sure.'' Nell gave him a thousand-volt, silver-plated smile in return. "We have to make do out here. Besides, it beats eating grubs and grasshoppers. That's the chapter I'm on now: 'How to Stay Alive Anywhere, Anytime.'''

"Mom, shut her up,'' Ann begged.

"I'd rather starve, 'anywhere, anytime,''' Lyn added emphatically.

"I wouldn't,'' Nell stated with scientific disregard of her sisters' disdain. "Did you ever have to eat those kinds of things in the jungle, Mark?'' Nell's steamroller approach had apparently gathered as many details of Mark's past as Jessie's gentle probing.

"No, thank God. But C rations aren't all that fantastic." Nell looked disappointed. "I did have roasted snake meat in Brazil once," he added to soften the blow. Nell looked impressed and opened her mouth to request further details.

"Enough," Jessie intervened. "You'll spoil my appetite. Snake indeed."

"It's true," Mark insisted. "It was a bushmaster, very poisonous. We killed it when it crawled into camp."

"No more." Jessie shivered. He was in all likelihood telling the truth. What a varied, interesting and dangerous life he'd led. It made hers seem so stodgy in comparison.

"We have a couple of cans of Coke we saved," Ann admitted in a rush of magnanimity. "We'll get them." The two camouflaged ponchos evaporated into the dripping gloom, leaving only Mark's face peering in at the tent flap.

"Enterprising trio. Have they been supplying you with contraband all week?"

"To keep me quiet about their cache. That's how the black market works. We've had munchies and soda every night." Jessie was secretly proud of her daughters' initiative. "I thought you might not approve, given the reason for our being here." Jessie's stubborn chin was high. She'd given him her explanation, not an apology.

"Not approve? That chocolate bar this afternoon saved my life," Mark said, grinning. The smile included his entire face, ending with sparks of light in his dancing eyes. "I was beginning to have withdrawal symptoms. Hadn't you guessed my dark, shameful secret? I'm a chocoholic." The theatrically whispered confession sent Nell into paroxysms of shrill giggles. "The popcorn will be ready in a few minutes. Perhaps you'd better put on a sweater or something, Jess. It's chilly." Mark's tone was rough around the edges. He spoke over the top of Nell's bright, inquisitive head as the generous child searched through her tote for an overlooked chocolate bar that might have escaped her eagle eye.

Jessie was flustered by the abrupt change in tone, the strain she heard so clearly, until she realized he was looking directly at her breasts. She'd already changed into the white T-shirt she wore to sleep in. Her curves were outlined now in the rush of cool, wet air from the open tent flap.

"Thanks, I'll do that." She didn't blush, but it took a direct effort of will.

They ate apples and popcorn in the kitchen lean-to while Mark told stories of the early days in New England that the girls had never heard before. He confessed a little reluctantly that he'd gleaned them from old Mr. Peavy when he was taking over *Meanderings* from the former owner. At that point Nell embarked on a ghost story that Ann and Lyn were bound by sibling honor to top. Jessie hid her surprise at their not retiring immediately to the privacy of their tent and dredged up an old scenario from her Girl Scout days that involved a one-armed mass murderer, terrifying massacres in out-of-the-way places, and ended up having the narrator grab the nearest person as she hissed the frightening punch line in the unsuspecting ear.

Nell screamed right on cue. Even the twins caught their breath before giggling derisively at their less-so-phisticated sister. But Mark's offering was best of all: involving pirate curses, phantom clipper ships, ghostly revenge and pieces of eight. It sent the Meyer women off to bed in a mood of scary, shivering delight that made sleep a long time coming.

Unfortunately, by the time the rain dwindled to a spotty drizzle and was finally chased away by a fresh breeze the next afternoon, the mood was long gone. The girls were bored and restless. Nell was whiny, the twins glum and testy by turns. As soon as the sun popped from behind ragged, gray-edged clouds, Mark assumed the role of taskmaster and sent them off on various errands guaranteed to work off some of their frustrated energy and bad temper.

"Thanks for taking them off my hands," Jessie confessed. "I can take only so much of them, all at once, in confined spaces, when they're in that mood."

"No problem. I spent a lot of time with my brother and sister before our parents died. I enjoy doing things with your daughters. I like kids; I always have. Especially girls." He was wearing army fatigues, cut off and neatly hemmed just below the pockets. Jessie was careful to avoid staring at the long, corded length of his thighs. Often now he'd dropped details of his boyhood into the conversation. Jessie was pleased he felt comfortable enough in her company to do so. "They just need a firm hold on the reins."

Mark waited, expecting Jessie to bristle at what she must construe as a slur on her parenting, not a compliment to her handling of a rough situation. A few days ago she would have done that, but today she only looked thoughtful and nodded. Maybe he was making progress, getting past some of the prickles, getting her to look at things more lightly. He found he wanted to take her strain away so she could enjoy her daughters as she should. He wanted to be there with her to share that enjoyment and far more.

"I'm going to take that statement at face value." She cocked her head to the left and surveyed him seriously. "I don't think you said that just because you need us all in a good mood."

Mark leaned on the handle of the short camp ax he'd been using to split driftwood into smaller, more manageable pieces for the fire. "I'm glad. I meant it as a compliment. Not that I wouldn't be above a little judicious flattery if I thought it would keep things going more smoothly."

"Scowling, teenage faces on the cover won't sell magazines." Jessie met him one on one, not backing off in confusion and a welter of hurt feelings.

"Exactly, Jess. For *Meanderings* I can be very charming."

"For any reason," she replied boldly and turned back to her camera with a smile. He laughed at her final sally and returned to his wood chopping. He was right about needing them in a good mood, of course, Jessie admitted to herself later. But he seemed to be enjoying the lazy stress-free days as much as she was.

It was very nice to think no further than your next meal, to wander over the hilly, rocky islet in search of beach peas and bay leaves for stew. When all that was required of you was that you admire Nell's harvest of sea-urchin roe, which provided fat "that might otherwise be lacking in a forager's diet," as Mark had sanctimoniously lectured before popping a large bite into his mouth. Then he nearly choked on his laughter when Ann pointed out that it would be a forager who'd run out of Hershey bars who suffered such a fate.

For a moment, during that interchange at lunch, Jessie couldn't help falling into a pattern of self-doubt, feeling left out of the camaraderie, thinking Mark might be chiding her for the ten extra pounds. Then she saw the rakish teasing light in his eyes and laughed as loudly as the rest at Ann's sally. It was that memory that had helped her through their latest exchange.

Still, the thought remained. She would go on a diet when they got back, she promised herself as she checked the focus on her telephoto lens. If she didn't hurry, the light would change and she wouldn't be able to capture some of the texture of sun and shadow presented by the ever-changing patterns of clouds in the sky. She did want to look her best, she realized. For herself and for Mark.

Somehow that self-admission, small in itself but indicative of larger things, made everything brighter. Jessie looked up, smiling serenely. The wind caught at her hair and whipped it into her eyes. She brushed it away, narrowing her gaze against the sudden sparkle of sun on the sea. It wasn't just that the sun had come out from behind the clouds. It wasn't just the brisk sea air, the insistent soothing beat of the surf or the sighing of the wind in the spruces. It was Mark's presence that made Jessie feel young and desirable and so very much alive.

"Mama! Mama, come quick. It's Nell!"

Apprehension blossomed in Jessie like a thorned vine, twining around her heart, squeezing her throat and shutting off her breath. Ann never called her Mama anymore. And her voice was high and strained, her face tight and pinched with fear. "Ann, slow down. What's happened? Where are Lyn and Nell?"

"At that old quarry. We told her not to do it. Oh, hurry and come. Maybe you can talk her down."

"Talk her down? Told her not to do what?" Instinctively Jessie turned to Mark. He'd stopped his work at the sound of Ann's voice. Now he grabbed his shirt as he looked up to see the stricken faces regarding him. The ax bit into solid wood, its handle quivering in the sun. *Funny, how such small things linger in your brain when you're scared,* Jessie found herself thinking. That's what she'd remember about this moment forever, the quivering ax handle. She dragged her attention back to Mark as he grabbed her shoulders.

"Jessie, what's wrong?"

"It's Nell. I don't know the details." She drew courage from his calm, no-nonsense attitude, managing to keep her voice steady.

Ann, too, became less agitated, more coherent. "Nell is stuck on a ledge at that old quarry. We were getting more cattail hearts for a salad. She saw some of that stuff...sheep sorel?" Mark nodded, urging her on as they walked swiftly in the direction of the abandoned granite quarry. "That's the stuff you said made such good soup, isn't it?" Jessie wanted to scream for Ann to get to the point but she didn't. "We told her not to do it, Mom, honest, but you know she doesn't listen to us."

"It's not your fault, honey. But couldn't you have been a little more emphatic about it?"

"Mom!" Frustration poured out of Ann's voice. Jessie didn't add to it. What good would it do? It wasn't Ann's fault, anyway. It was hers, for letting them go off unescorted.

"Where is she exactly?" Mark's voice was authoritative. Ann responded to it and so did Jessie, breaking off her self-castigation.

"On the far side. On a little ledge. I don't know how she even got up there. Lyn stayed with her. Down below, I mean." She looked frightened, white and shaking, near to tears once again. "Mom, it's almost straight down from where she's standing."

Jessie wanted to run to her child, but Mark touched her arm, halting the first step of her headlong flight. "You can't do Nell any good with a broken ankle. Slow down." His face was concerned but composed.

"I never should have allowed her to go off like that." Jessie bit her lip so hard she tasted blood. It was her fault, too, that she'd let Carl go off to work that day and die.

"How could you have stopped her from being the bright, inquisitive kid she is, Jess? Don't blame yourself." Was he getting through to her? He could read her like a book. She'd blame herself today if anything happened to Nell just as she'd probably blamed herself all these years for not being there for Carl.

"You're right. I'll be careful." She couldn't have changed anything today. She couldn't have changed anything seven years ago.

"All set?" Mark saw her catch hold of her fear and subdue it with an effort that was almost physical. "Ann, lead the way."

It wasn't far. Nell was huddled on a small ledge ten feet below the edge, twenty-five or thirty feet above the overgrown floor of the old quarry.

"How did she get up there?" Mark asked. There wasn't any discernible path; the ledge sloped up wider at the far edge but was still dangerously narrow all along its length.

"Who knows," Ann wailed, goaded by fear. "She thinks she's Spider-Man or the Human Fly or something. How can we get her down?" She wasn't speaking to her, Jessie realized, but to Mark. The leader. The one Ann sensed most able to deal with the situation.

"Nell, baby." The words, torn from her mother's heart were only a whisper as Mark's grip tightened warningly on her wrist.

"Don't let her see you yet, Jess. She'll only be more frightened, more anxious to get down. Lyn looks like she's doing a good job of keeping her occupied. Let's work our way over there, get a look at the situation up close."

"Ann—" He pointed with a long, tapered finger, another gesture without a wasted motion caught forever in the meshes of Jessie's memory. The beauty of the moment stretched out, enveloping the stark glory of the landscape, the scurry of cloud shadows, the wind slipping through the high grass. "Go down to Lyn. Tell her we're coming."

Mark took Jessie's hand, starting off around the edge of the quarry at a pace that was swift but sure, leaving Jessie with no excess breath to speak. She had no idea what to do at the moment. No solution presented itself in the swirling mass of confusion and fear in her mind.

"It's funny," she managed to whisper in a breathy sigh that was half a sob. "Whenever one of them is hurt, I freeze up inside. I get this sharp, wrenching pain, right here, low in my middle. Just like labor pains, you know? No, that's silly, of course you don't know about labor pains." Her brave attempt at a smile fell short of its goal.

"I can guess. Don't worry, Jess." His voice carried all the confidence in the world, but he failed to meet her anxious gaze. "She'll be fine. There's got to be a safe way down. I just wish we had a rope."

"Did that go over with the ill-fated duffel, too?" Jessie wanted to sound as serene and confident as he did. She intended to convey her trust in his handling of the situation, but her voice cracked and broke. She gave up any further attempts at conversation when he shook his head vehemently.

"Damn it, no. I didn't think there'd be any need to bring one. I should have been prepared."

Jessie stopped short, pulling back on his arm, spinning him halfway around to face her. She wasn't going to let him shoulder the blame. Now she had all the confidence in the world. "Don't say that. You couldn't have known this would happen. Don't mention it again." Her eyes flashed with conviction; her chin took on the obstinate tilt Mark was coming to recognize.

"You're my responsibility." Agitation showed in his sharp words if not in his quiet hands and strong body.

"Nell is my responsibility, no one else's. I made the decision to come out here. Don't mention it again."

"Yes ma'am." A ghost of a smile curled at the corner of Mark's lips. "I'll get her back for you. I promise that."

"I know you will. But we'll do it together."

"Together." Mark walked swiftly to the edge of the quarry, dropped to his knees and leaned over. "Nell." His voice was even, low, completely assured and reassuring. A tear-streaked gamine face looked up at him, fear and hope competing for dominance in brown eyes so like Jessie's.

"Where's my mom?"

"I'm right here, honey. How did you get in such a pickle?" Jessie was proud of the matter-of-fact tone she managed but her nails almost drew blood, she curled them so tightly into her palms. Nell was so far away, so obviously beyond her reach. Irrationally, Jessie longed to be able to swoop down over the ledge, pull her child close and return to safety all in one swift leap.

"I don't know how I got out here. I was climbing. It was easy coming up. And I found this weed growing in the cracks. I mean this plant Mark said made such good soup...." She reached for a small sack propped beside her on the narrow ledge. A crumbling piece of moss and lichen-covered stone dropped over the edge with a hollow thud. Nell flattened herself against the face of the quarry, a great heaving sob escaping her trembling lips. "That happens whenever I move. I can't figure out how to get back down."

"Don't cry, honey," Jessie said with loving sternness. "It won't help. I'm right here. Can't you try going back very slowly?"

"No! I told you. It creaks and pieces fall off."

"Okay, we'll think of something else." Without hesitation Jessie turned to Mark. He was frowning, concentrating on the problem, working through various solutions in his mind. Why couldn't she make her brain slow down from its whirling, useless befuddlement and help him? She took several deep breaths and willed herself to a semblance of calm.

"Could you climb up this last little bit of rock? I'll lean down and help you." Jessie lay on her stomach and stretched her hand down. Last little bit of rock—ten or twelve feet of pockmarked granite. Nell was still much too far beyond her grasp.

"I don't think I can," Nell replied, sobbing. "Mom, I'm scared. I want to get down from here."

"Hold on, Nell. Your mother's got the right idea. I think I see a way down." Mark's voice was quiet and convincing.

"Mark? What are you talking about? Can she make it by herself?" Jessie couldn't see any way at all of accomplishing the feat.

"Not alone. I'll help her. See that fissure in the stone? It goes all the way to the bottom. It's not too wide. I can get from there to the ledge. I'll steady her until she gets far enough up the rock to reach you safely. She'll never go back the way she came. And I seriously doubt it will hold my weight, too."

"I can't let you do that, Mark. I'll go. I'm smaller." Jessie eyed the split in the quarry face dubiously. It was two or three feet wide, jagged and ugly. A great chunk had broken off, making a small depression that did, indeed, open out onto the ledge where Nell was stranded. It would be possible to climb down, but very, very dangerous.

"You don't have any choice in the matter, Jess. I'm still the leader of this expedition, remember? I know what I'm doing. I've climbed a little before when I've had to. No more argument." The last words were an obvious challenge. He tucked in the tails of his denim work shirt as he spoke, buttoning the cuffs over strong, sinewy forearms. "Agreed?"

It wasn't the time for arguing, or hysterics or tears, although Jessie felt prone to all three. She wouldn't argue with him. She wouldn't break down and cry. She had to be brave for the girls—and for herself. "All right. You're the boss. But for God's sake, be careful. I can't have you on my conscience, too."

"Don't worry about me. I'm tough." Their eyes met and held, underscoring the hidden meaning in their exchange. "Trust me, Jessie." His hands were on her shoulders, strong and sure. She didn't have to search to interpret his meaning this time. Reasssurance was there for her to see. Jessie drew strength from his touch without embarrassment, using it to restore her dwindling reserve of courage.

"I do trust you." She reached up on tiptoe and kissed him quick and hard. "Hurry. I'll lean as far over as I can to take her hand. She'll make it then."

"Of course she will. She's your daughter, isn't she?"

On those words he was gone. Jessie went to the edge, flopped down on her stomach again, explaining calmly to Nell what was happening and continued to talk to the frightened child. Afterward she could never remember what she'd said. They were silly inconsequential things that required answers and diverted Nell's attention from her dilemma and Mark's climb.

Nell couldn't see his descent or the rapt, attentive faces of her sisters. Jessie wished she couldn't see them, either. Their excitement and fear for Mark and Nell were mirrored too clearly in expressive faces so like her own. Endless moments later, Mark dropped down in a welter of dislodged stones that bounded off the ledge onto the quarry floor.

"I can't go back up there like you came down, Mark," Nell admitted tearfully. "I tried. It's too wide. I'll fall just like those stones." She swiveled her head downward to mark their course when the stones came to rest at the foot of the sandy knoll where the twins waited.

"I know, baby. You're going up," Mark soothed.

"Up?" Nell turned her attention to the rock wall above her, then focused her tear-bright gaze on Jessie's face.

"Will you help me, Mom?"

"That's what I'm here for," Jessie assured, forcing a smile to her lips that made her face ache with the effort it took to produce.

"Okay, then, I'll do it. What about my sack?"

"I'll take care of it; don't worry." Mark wished he could take his own advice. Nell was right. There was no way, without the proper equipment, to get her back up the split in the quarry face. He wasn't too sure he could get back up that way himself. His climbing skills were rusty. He was ten years older than he'd been the last time the need arose. But he'd find a way to get Nell to safety. He had to. They were counting on him, all the Meyer women.

"Put your hands in the cracks, then your sneakers, Nell," he instructed with all the certainty twenty-five years of military service could muster in his voice. "Your mom will help you up the last few feet and I'll steady you from down here."

"I can't!"

"Yes, you can, Nell Elizabeth, or you're going to be there a long, long time. There's no other way." Jessie's tone was as everyday as she could make it, as though she were scolding for nothing more serious than a spilled glass of milk on a newly mopped kitchen floor. It worked.

"Okay. Here's my sack." Nell handed Mark the bag filled with pungent, lemony sheep sorrel. "This soup had better be good."

Mark laughed, tossing the sack to the waiting twins. Lyn caught it deftly, holding it over her head in momentary salute. Mark waved back. Jessie's spirit showed brightly in all the girls, but Nell was most like her. In her it burned highest.

"It'll be the best soup you ever ate. I promise. Now scoot! And don't look down."

"I won't."

His hand on Nell's leg met wiry strength he hadn't been prepared to encounter, and it bolstered his own confidence in her ability. She'd do it. He steadied the child as she made her way up the rock slowly and carefully. Once she slipped, skidding back several hard-won inches. Mark braced himself to take the weight of her fall, his heart hammering in his chest. He knew he couldn't save either of them from going over the ledge if her fingers lost their grip and she came tumbling back into his arms.

"Nell!" Jessie's face was white with anxiety despite the fact she'd stretched herself dangerously far our over the edge of the rock lip. "Hang on, baby. It's only a little farther. I'm here."

Nell choked back a terrified sob. "Only babies cry." Mark wondered if even Jessie could hear the faintly muttered childhood curse.

"Keep going." It was the tone he'd used so many times in Nam, a monotone almost devoid of expression or emotion. It was an order strictly calculated to keep raw youngsters going when they thought they couldn't. He hoped it worked as well on little girls. "I have to let go of your leg now, Nell. But just one or two more handholds and you can reach your mother. It's all a piece of cake from here."

"Chocolate cake?" came the breathless little-girl voice that made this throat ache with the pathos of its bravery.

"Double Dutch devil's food, what else? Now go!" A scramble of rubber-soled shoes, a shower of moss and pebbles, and she was up over the edge into Jessie's arms.

Mark rested his forehead against the quarry face a few moments, blinking back stinging, unfamiliar, unexpected tears of relief and gratitude. It had been the look on Jessie's face more than anything else that had jolted him out of the past, out of his stoic, habitual control. It was that look of love and pain and joy that had transfused her features as she pulled Nell into her arms. They'd done it. Together.

"Mark." She was back, leaning down again. He looked up, smiling. "How are you going to get off that ledge?"

"Damned if I know." He grinned, but Jessie's face was stiff with anxiety. Fear sparked again in her eyes, but this time it was fear for him. "Hey, cut it out, Jess. Who's in charge here?"

"I'm not sure. It can't be you. You're in the same darn position Nell was five minutes ago. So now it must be me. Take my hand," she commanded every bit as forcefully as he had.

"No." At least he'd goaded her into action. He'd been afraid she'd fall apart after the worst was over. He'd seen it happen so many times to women and men. Again he underestimated his Jessie. "I said take my hand," she shouted, sharp and staccato, as though he were an errant child.

"I don't need it, Jess. Get back. I'm coming up, too." It wasn't the wisest move he'd ever made, Mark realized the moment he started up the sheer rock face. The hand and footholds had been adequate, barely, for a thirteen-year-old child—but not for a man who stood six feet even in his stocking feet and wore size eleven shoes. Still, he almost made it. Jessie had ignored his orders, as usual. Her hand was there. Her clutching fingers brushed across the back of his, trying to get hold of his wrist. "Give me your hand!" She groaned with her effort to reach him.

"No." He wasn't going to make it. His foot slipped. If he grabbed her hand now he'd pull her over with him. His only chance lay in hitting the ledge, breaking his fall enough to land on the even smaller projection eight feet below it. Otherwise there was nothing but thin air and solid rock for another fifteen feet.

"Mark, take my hand, damn it." Jessie's voice was shrill with tension and fear.

"Can't reach it," he lied. Hell, he was falling off a damn cliff and he hadn't even told her he loved her. And he did love her. The thought didn't take him by surprise. There wasn't room for surprise, only chaotic plans, an aversion to dying before he'd been able to make love to Jessie, make love to her slowly, passionately, totally, at least ten thousand times.

"Too late," he growled. Now. But he'd tell her over and over again. If he didn't break his damn fool neck.

Mark did hit the ledge, but the crumbling granite undermined by countless seasons of freezing and thawing, wind and rain, and the tenacious weakening of clinging moss and lichen couldn't sustain his weight. He made a grab for the edge, and his fingers held for a moment, long enough to allow him to twist his body around and slither along the rock face to the small ledge below.

There his luck failed. He landed with a jarring thud that sent shearing pain up the left side of his body from knee to shoulder. His right foot missed the ledge altogether. Mark stepped backward into space, with a weightless, terrifying sensation of falling that lasted countless, endless seconds.

There was solid ground beneath his hands. And pain. He heard the twins' voices screaming, which made the pain worse. He wasn't dead, Mark decided, trying to move. He hurt too much. You weren't supposed to hurt at all if you were dead. He rolled onto his side. The pain increased, roaring through his body, blotting out sound and light. His last thought before the darkness surging outward from behind his closed eyelids settled down over all of him was one of thanksgiving. "At least I didn't break my damned fool neck."

VOICES WERE RINGING in his ears. Hands, surprisingly competent, were firmly and steadily running over his arms, his legs, his neck and shoulders. "I don't think anything's broken, Mom." Ann's voice or was it Lyn's? He had trouble telling them apart when he didn't see them. "He might have a concussion, though, or even a fractured skull." Definitely Ann. But the hands belonged to Jessie.

"No fractured skull." He was sure of that much, but his voice was weak and scratchy. He tried again. "I'm all right."

"You are not." Jessie sounded angry, very angry. Why was she yelling at him? Mark wondered in painful confusion. Hadn't he saved her child's life? What did she have to be angry about? He tried to ask her but she interrupted him. "Oh, Mark, why didn't you take my hand, you idiot?" He gave up trying to understand what was going on. Moving his head to keep the sun from spearing him in the eyes had been a mistake. His stomach churned. It took all his concentration to remain conscious. There wasn't any energy left to ask questions.

Seconds passed. He could hear Nell sob. He didn't want her to cry. "Let me up." Colonel Elliot was speaking again. Maybe it would work on Jessie, too. He must have sounded stronger, for the trembling, restraining hand on his chest was removed. He understood now; Jessie was scared. He'd scared her badly. The look on her face as he fell returned to him with stunning clarity. So unbelieving, so shocked. "I want to sit up."

"No, lie still. You'll only faint again."

"For Pete's sake, Jessie. Don't say 'faint.' It sounds so damn effeminate."

"All right," echoed from a shaky trill of golden laughter. "Lie still or you're liable to pass out again. Is that better?" They were fighting words.

Mark recognized a challenge when he heard one. He rolled onto his side although he was sure he'd tried the maneuver once before and it hadn't worked. He put his weight on his left wrist and the pain streaked up to his shoulder so fast and so devastatingly that he ended up on his face in the dirt. This time when the lurking darkness returned he didn't even try to fight it.

"MARK."

Jessie's voice again, calling him back. It was quieter now. They were alone in the quarry. The sun had moved behind the rim. It no longer hurt his eyes. He didn't feel as bad, either; the dizziness was gone. Most of the pain, except for his knee and shoulder, had receded to a dull ache. His head was in her lap. Was that why he felt better? Her perfume mingled with the smell of crushed grass and sand. What was it? Something simple and nice. Lily of the valley? Lilac?

"Mark?"

He opened his eyes. "Where is everybody?" They couldn't stay here on the quarry floor forever. "Have I been out long?"

"Only a few minutes. It seems like forever, but my watch says otherwise. Do you feel better?"

"Compared to what?"

"You're better."

He could feel her sigh of relief in the touch of her stomach against his cheek. She had a round woman's belly, not one of those flat concave abdomens that was supposed to denote femininity in today's mixed-up, crazy world.

"You scared me silly."

"Scared the hell out of myself, too. I can't remember exactly what went wrong. I think a piece of stone must have broken loose under my foot."

"Why didn't you take my hand?" Her thigh muscles stiffened under the back of his head. The hand that had been smoothing his hair halted its caress.

"Is that what you're angry about? Lord, Jess, I outweigh you by sixty pounds. I'd have pulled you over for sure."

"How do you know? I'm strong. Stronger than you realize. You could have been killed, you idiot." Jessie sniffed back a sob.

"Don't yell and don't cry. I don't feel so well again." That wasn't strictly true, but it worked. He'd done what he had to do up there. But he loved Jessie for wanting to save him. He loved her. The knowledge made him dizzy again.

"Mark." The exasperation was gone in an instant. She was all softness and caring. "What can I do for you?"

"A kiss would be nice," he said, to let her know he was better.

"Humph." But she was smiling, the first real smile in a long time. "No kisses now; later. First we have to get you out of this damp old hole."

"There isn't any way but walking." He couldn't suppress the groan of pain as he tried to sit up. Jessie held him back, gently but firmly.

"Let that be a lesson to you. Be patient, the girls are bringing a litter."

"A what?"

"A litter, like the Indians used. Nell dreamed it up. They used birch bark and saplings. We're going to try polyurethane. I hope it works. Here they come now."

She looked over his head, past him to the sloping, shallow edge of the quarry where man-made diggings met the original gradual incline of the island's interior. Mark closed his eyes, not understanding completely, trying to marshal his strength for a long, uncomfortable walk. He didn't know how he'd make it back.

In the end he didn't have to. The girls had brought the two-man boat. Nell had suggested its use as they kept anxious vigil at his side. At first Jessie had been too distracted. She couldn't see any merit to the idea. But when Nell explained that her precious wilderness primer had told how to make a sledge—and the improvisation she'd dreamed up on her own—Jessie agreed. Nothing could be worse in her opinion than spending the night in the open with an injured man.

The trip back to camp was a nightmare that took nearly an hour. Mark endured it with stoic silence. He knew he couldn't walk. He didn't want to spend the night in the open any more than Jessie. By the time he was back in his tent he was holding on to consciousness with grim determination; the boat was a ruin, and Jessie and the girls resembled the survivors of a natural catastrophe of great magnitude.

Jessie didn't care what she looked like. She was only grateful the ordeal was over. Mark looked exhausted, gray and spent, with deep lines from nose to chin. She didn't bother him, didn't fuss about cuts and scrapes; she let him rest undisturbed while she got the girls busy with preparations for the evening meal.

It never occurred to her to go back to Mark's tent and search for the radio to summon help. But he'd have been furious. Now that she'd assured herself his injuries, thankfully, weren't serious, there was no reason to suggest going home, unless Mark decided to do so. She'd promised to stick it out. She didn't intend to go back on her word.

The sun was a molten copper ball on the tip of the horizon when she crawled back into Mark's tent. The light came through the nylon in diffused shades of gold and bronze. Mark was awake, regarding the scrapes and bruises on his arms and chest with a scowl.

"I feel like hell."

"You look like it, too." Jessie wanted to keep the conversation light. She hadn't put enough distance between her emotions and recent events to be objective about them—or about her feelings for Mark. They'd deepened alarmingly in the past few hours.

"I guess it's poetic justice of a sort. I'm the one who cast the deciding vote to stay out here without a first-aid kit. So I ought to be the one to suffer."

"Mark, don't joke about it." Jessie sat the basin of warm water and the towel she'd been balancing in one hand down beside his sleeping bag. "I can't be quite so nonchalant about it yet." She regarded the small tin of medication in her other hand as if she'd never seen anything like it before. "I want to thank you for saving Nell's life."

"Jessie..."

"Don't try to brush it off. I don't know how I could have managed if something—" her voice broke, but Jessie plowed gamely on "—if I'd lost her like I lost her father."

Mark tried for a quip that just missed. "All in a day's work for us heroes."

"All in a day's work, my foot." Jessie was clearly miffed. "Mark Elliot, don't ever let me hear you say such a thing again."

"Yes, ma'am." He grinned to hide a groan as he flexed his wrenched shoulder. "I'm not up to taking on one of your temper tantrums right now."

"Oh, Mark." Jessie was instantly contrite, as he hoped she'd be. She was a sucker for the lost-puppy routine, he decided happily. "Are you sure your shoulder's only bruised? And your knee?"

"The same. All I need is a good night's sleep." *Or two or three*, he added to himself. He was going to be stiff and sore for longer than that. "Jess, do you want to go back? Call it off?"

"No way. I don't have nearly enough shots to interest *National Geographic*. Don't you trust us to take care of you, Colonel?"

"I think you can do anything you put your mind to." The look of strain around his mouth lessened somewhat.

"You're correct, sir. We can handle anything. That's settled then. We'll stick out this mission till the bitter end. Any more problems?"

"No, ma'am." Mark settled back with a grunt.

Jessie reached behind him to smooth the wrinkles out of his sleeping bag. "I brought some water to get the dirt off you. Feel up to it?"

Mark lifted his hands to regard the dirt embedded in the scratches along his wrist and palms.

"Ann and Lyn have soup ready. It smells pretty good, if I do say so myself. Nell is baking corn bread. I'm not sure how that's going to turn out." She was prattling again and she knew it, but it certainly beat crying on his shoulder. Relief and reaction had finally caught up to Jessie. Her hands were shaking again; there were huge butterflies banging around in her stomach.

"Sounds fine."

"This shirt is ruined," Jessie observed, working steadily at the one or two remaining buttons. She was dizzy, and her breathing was shallow and irregular. But this was reaction of a different sort. This was a reaction to Mark, not to his accident. She sucked in her breath sharply when the parted fabric revealed scrapes and lacerations still oozing blood. She hoped Mark would attribute it to his condition and not the effect the sight of so much of him produced on her senses.

"Lucky my pants are made of a lot heavier material," Mark observed wryly, propping himself on his good elbow to survey the damage that ended at his waistline, except for a scrape on his damaged knee.

"I've got just the thing for it."

"What's that?" Suspiciously, he eyed the bright green tin decorated with red clovers and the head of a particularly contented green cow.

"Mom makes sure we never travel without it," Jessie explained innocently. "It's just a salve, good for what ails you." She skirted the comment nimbly, hiding the tin between her knees while she sponged the dried blood from his chest and hands.

"It smells terrible," Mark decreed, wrinkling his nose.

"It works."

"Let me see the tin."

"You don't need to see anything. Trust me." Jessie couldn't hide her laughter as she pushed him gently down onto the sleeping bag. "Give me your hand."

"No. Jess, I'm warning you." Mark looked skeptical and perturbed as well as amused. It was a potent combination. Jessie wanted to lean over and kiss the question mark from between his thick dark brows. Instead, she put a generous portion of the medication on a corner of the towel and passed him the tin.

"Bag Balm? What the hell..." His voice trailed off as he read the directions. Jessie continued to slather the salve over his chest with studied efficiency. She watched his reaction from beneath her lashes. "'Veterinary use only. For superficial scratches, abrasions, windburn and sunburn—'"

"Two out of four ain't bad," Jessie giggled as enlightenment dawned on his face.

"'Apply after each milking....' Milking? Jessie, this stuff is for cows! Cows with sore—"

"Udders?"

"Or worse."

"Stop fussing. It works fine on people, too. We've used it for years. It's great for what ails you. Our vet swears by it—and so do I."

"Cow medicine." He grimaced down at his hand as Jessie worked the medication into the skin. "Ouch! You're hurting me."

"Men are such babies," Jessie said, clucking and wiping her hands before pouring a glass of tepid water from the thermos in the corner of the tent.

"Sore udders." Mark grimaced, glancing at the two pink lozenges Jessie held out to him. "Now what?"

"Pain pills. Aren't you glad I came prepared?"

"They don't look like aspirin," Mark observed distrustfully. He hesitated before allowing Jessie to pop them into his mouth.

"They're marvelous," Jessie soothed. "Trust me." Mark swallowed obediently, washing down the medication with the water she'd poured.

"Okay, what were they?"

"Do you really want me to tell you?"

"No...yes...I'm not sure, but I'd rather know the worst up front."

"They're absolutely the latest thing for menstrual pain."

"Oh, God," Mark moaned in heartfelt agony. "I'll wake up a soprano."

"Don't be silly," Jessie giggled, punching the rolled-up blanket he was using as a pillow. "There's nothing like that in them." She ticked the points off on her fingers. "They have a pain medication for your head; something to relieve pressure and swelling—that's for your shoulder and knee—and no caffeine, so you can sleep. Just what the doctor ordered," Jessie finished triumphantly, a devilish glint lighting her eyes. "Besides, they're all I've got to give you."

"You're enjoying this, aren't you?"

"No, I'm not." She rocked back on her heels, watching him closely as he settled himself more comfortably on the browse bed. "You two scared the hell out of me. Mark, promise me, no more heroics."

"It wasn't heroics, Jess."

"I know, I know." Jessie shook her head in mock defeat. "You did what you had to do."

"Always. Just like you."

Silence took possession of the small tent. The girls' voices, involved in earnest discussion, wafted in on a stray breeze. The surf was a lulling, monotonous undertone to every other sound. "I hate to admit it but this stuff's working already." Mark's voice was low, a little slurred. Jessie leaned forward to catch his next words. "I'm tired. Would the girls be offended if I don't have that soup quite yet?" He looked very serious, as if her answer was of great importance to him, but his eyes were unfocused, distant.

"Of course not. Sustenance always waits on the invalid in our household. They'll understand. Do you want anything else before I go?"

"Yes." The teasing, caressing note was back in his words. "I want you to stay." He reached up, locking his wrists behind her neck, pulling her closer but not touching. "There are so many things I want to tell you, Jess."

"Shh." She touched his mouth lightly, sweetly, with delicious restraint. "I know. There's a lot I want to say to you also."

"Tell me now." He kissed her back, deeply, hungrily, letting their mouths and tongues compensate for a lack of greater physical closeness. She rested her weight on her hands, then on her forearms as she cradled his head, spreading her fingers through the fine, thick layers of his hair, avoiding the bump on the side of his head.

"I can't. I don't have the right words yet. But you're not to worry about anything for a while. The girls and I will take care of you. It's our turn to be in charge, to shoulder the load." She hesitated, searching for her thoughts. "This afternoon had made me see so many things more clearly. I need time to sort it all out."

"Exactly. Very important things. Like you and me." Heavy lids fringed with dark, spiky lashes closed over his remarkable blue eyes. Jessie lifted her head, holding her breath.

"Mark?" Could he have fallen asleep that quickly?

"I'm tired, Jess. Kiss me again, please. I don't have the energy to pull you down here again." He let his hands fall from her neck. It wasn't a command. It was a plea. Jessie didn't hesitate a moment before complying.

The taste of his mouth was warm and exciting. Jessie let her tongue glide into the dark cavern, let her lips smooth over his, let her hands move to the steady beat of pulse at the base of his throat.

"For a minute back there on that ledge I was afraid I'd never get to touch you like this again," Mark confessed in a muffled, sleepy voice.

"I was, too. So scared. For both of you."

"Stay with me awhile, Jess."

"As long as I can." She shifted her weight to stretch out beside him.

"Mom! Mom, my corn bread is on fire!" Nell's treble voice quavered with imminent tears. Jessie sat up reluctantly.

"So soon? Will it always be like this?"

Jessie was almost afriad she'd heard him wrong. *Always be like this*. What lovely words. She was too tired, too excited by everything that had happened to analyze them now. "I'm afraid so. Never a dull moment." She leaned down to give him a peck on the tip of his nose.

"Jess." His voice held her. "Will you come back?"

She dropped a second tiny caress onto the corner of his mouth. "I won't be far. All you have to do is call. Sleep now."

He did.

Chapter Five

"It's nice having a few minutes to ourselves." Mark propped his hands behind his head, narrowing his eyes against the watery glaze of sunlight on the sea. Was he tiring of so much exposure to her and the girls? She shot him a quick, surreptitious glance. Or was he teasing her again? The small, satisfied curve of his lips suggested the latter.

Mark stretched with sinuous masculine grace, arranging himself more comfortably along the ledge of unyielding rock above the camp. He was wearing cut-off fatigues and a light gray cotton shirt open to the waist to prevent the material from irritating the scrapes and abrasions on his chest.

His eyes followed the soft curve of Jessie's bottom longingly as she rested her elbows on the ledge to focus her camera in on Nell, who was searching diligently through the tidal pool directly below their perch. His last sally didn't produce the automatic defensive apology it would have done two or three days earlier.

"You've had me all to yourself for the past hour and a half." Jessie didn't turn her head, but a bedeviling smile played swiftly across her lips.

"It's more like fifteen minutes since Nell's last trip up here to show you the lastest aquatic marvel she's discovered." Mark's tone was deliberately testy. But it wasn't totally a conversational gambit. He ached with suppressed longing. Jessie's breasts pushed jauntily against the cotton of her bright yellow T-shirt, increasing the torment.

"But, Mark, I'm her mother. It's terribly important to encourage a child in all her education endeavors." Jessie's smile widened impishly. It seemed so natural to be teasing him about her children.

"That's not what I mean and you know it." Mark grimaced. "How do people find time to do anything alone when they have children?"

Jessie laughed. "I told you it wouldn't be a cakewalk, but you didn't have to prove me right by falling off a cliff." She snapped two more quick shots of Nell examining a bright orange starfish. Nell whirled in glee. Jessie supposed the image would be blurred, but it might make an interesting print just the same. The starfish would be in brilliant contrast to her Kelly-green Windbreaker and a background of somber gray rocks and muted pines.

"Jessie, come over here," Mark wheedled in a weak whisper. "I'm having a relapse! Humor me." He groaned. She ignored him, zooming in on the twins farther along the shore as they carefully replaced a rock after studying the teeming invertebrate life-forms that called it home. They moved lightly, warily, respecting the delicate ecological balance of the tidal pool, exactly as Mark had taught them.

"You don't look that much like an invalid anymore, Colonel." Jessie regarded him skeptically, lifting the embroidered camera strap from around her neck. She covered the telephoto lens before placing the camera on the ground beside her. "I think that little ploy has served its purpose." She scooted over to where he lay, letting her eyes feast on the sharply etched curves and ridges of his body. He'd shaved that morning preparatory to returning to civilization, but the rakish, soldier-of-fortune air remainded. "You seem to be enjoying your privileged status just a bit too much for your own good. Isn't there a military term for that? Goldbricking, I think it's called." Jessie batted her lashes innocently.

"Me? Goldbrick?" Mark looked offended. "Never, ma'am. Are you certifying me fit to return to active duty?" He favored his wrenched shoulder exaggeratedly as he propped himself on his right elbow. Jessie traced an inquisitive finger lightly, daringly, over the half-healed scars on his chest. She took his palm in her hand, turning it upward to inspect those wounds also.

"Your hands do look much better," she confirmed in a serious mood. Mark hadn't been completely successful in hiding the discomfort of still-protesting muscles under his teasing facade. She'd given up trying to thank him formally for saving Nell's life at the risk of his own. He wouldn't allow it, turning aside each attempt with facetious lightness. Jessie wasn't fooled by the glib act. The harrowing experience at the quarry had affected him too deeply for easy words. She respected his reticence.

"Good as new, despite your unorthodox remedies." He made a fist to prove his point.

"No untoward side effects?" Jessie inquired, ignoring the slur on her ministrations. "As I recall, you were afraid there might be some from the pain medication if not the cow medicine." She couldn't resist the retort as she gave him an appraising once-over.

"La...la...la-la-la." Mark ran down a scale. "Nope. Still a baritone, thank heaven. Come here. Let me prove it."

Jessie rested her weight provocatively on outstretched hands, leaning over him, keeping a tantalizing space between their bodies. "I do believe you've gotten lazy, Colonel." She maintained the discreet distance, but the air was electric with a sensual current that underscored the bantering.

"I could get used to being waited on hand and foot without much effort whatsoever," Mark conceded unabashedly. "Especially by four such lovely handmaidens."

"Three handmaidens, one handmatron," Jessie corrected with a comical grimace. "I haven't been a maiden for more years than I care to remember." *Or a totally fulfilled woman,* she added to herself with a tiny secret pang of regret.

"Thank God for that!" Mark's eyes were no longer teasing. He reached out, circling one slender wrist, tugging Jessie closer. "I'm too old for maidens."

She tugged back, breaking the gentle bondage. She curled her arms around her legs, resting her chin on bent knees. "Your chauvinistic tendences are showing again," she cautioned.

"Sorry." His tone was deliberately docile as he continued. "Lord knows I'm trying, Jess. I've been the perfect patient these past few days. I've let you and the girls take over the running of this camp without a whimper. I've eaten when you told me, no matter what it looked or tasted like. I've slept on your command. I think I'm getting the idea of this partnership business down pretty well." The last words were gruffly spoken. Mark pitched the stone he'd been rolling between his fingers off into the bracken. He flopped over onto his back, resuming his contemplation of cloud patterns in the blue sky.

"You've been the model patient, Colonel Elliot." Jessie paused, cleared her throat and took a deep, fortifying breath. "I think you deserve a reward."

"Such as?"

"A kiss."

"Really?" He looked inordinately pleased.

"Really." Jessie didn't blush but lowered her chin to her knees just the same.

"In that case to hell with this partnership business. Come here, woman, that's an order."

Jessie uncurled herself from the cramped position to lean over him, waiting for his touch, waiting for him to sweep her into his embrace.

"Mom! Come look, quick!"

This time it was one of the twins. Mark still couldn't tell their voices apart. He tried to hide his irritation and his arousal. He checked his watch. "Fifteen minutes exactly."

Jessie shrugged, grinned sheepishly and crawled over to the ledge, waving in reply to the imperious summons. Mark felt his view of her backside almost compensated for the aborted kiss. He went back to studying the sky.

They'd been thrown together almost constantly the past two days as a result of his accident. The strain was beginning to tell. He'd had too much time to think, to begin to plan for a life that included Jessie and her girls. She meant so much to him already. It was hard to assimilate the depths of emotion she'd called forth in so short a space of time. He was falling in love with her. He wanted to tell her so—now, this minute. Mark managed a smile when she returned. "What is it this time?"

"A difference of opinion over the proper classification of a very ugly type of snail. Five days ago they wouldn't have come within five feet of the creature." Jessie shook her head in disbelief. "They thought you might be resting and didn't want to disturb you. I told them you'd be down to arbitrate. I don't intend to get near the thing."

"Thanks." He laughed and closed his eyes. He was used to accepting responsibility for eager young charges, but this business of teenage hero worship was something else entirely. It was most flattering.

Jessie breathed a small sigh of relief. Mark wasn't annoyed. She tried to relax. Still, she couldn't entirely forget the way the few other men she'd come in contact with had reacted to her children, looking on them as liabilities, not assets. For a time she'd been guilty of the same offense, but no longer. Mark had helped her relearn to enjoy her daughters for the unique emerging young adults they were.

He encouraged her girls at every opportunity, encouraged them to stretch out in new ways, both physical and mental, no matter how much inconvenience it caused him. They'd taken over most of the chores since his accident and did them well: chopping wood, carrying water, duties they would have balked at in everyday life but tackled enthusiastically because of Mark's interest in them and their accomplishments. The girls were learning independence. Jessie was learning tolerance and how to let go. She was glad they'd come in spite of everything that had happened.

Everything that had happened—the thought tugged at her, arousing varied and differing sensations. Not the least of which was her own ambivalent feelings about Mark. She had yearned for time to get to know him better. Now it was granted. They talked for hours as the girls took over the foraging and fishing. In the evenings she'd been content to stay quietly in the background, exchanging amused glances with Mark as her daughters practiced their feminine wiles around the campfire.

They told and retold, in differing versions, the story of Nell's rescue and Mark's fall. That exercise proved so stimulating they tried their hands at wheedling anecdotes from his life in the military. Next, they demanded tales from his days as a consulting engineer in Brazil. When he tired of that they begged for events and experiences from the year he'd spent backpacking along the Appalachian Trail until he met up with old Mr. Peavy, gave up any thought at all of returning to engineering and decided to buy *Meanderings*.

Jessie suspected with good cause that he liked those tales best himself. At least they didn't have to be heavily censured, as she assumed the others had been in deference to the age and innocence of the majority of the audience or glossed over as he did when asked to speak of his boyhood. She listened as avidly as the girls, caught up in the spell of the whispering surf, dancing firelight and Mark's mesmerizing voice.

She was giddy, nervous, strangely silly and sad by turns—all unmistakable symptoms of falling in love. The speed with which the potentially dangerous incident at the quarry had occurred served as a catalyst of sorts as far as Jessie's emotions were concerned. She was close to falling in love with Mark Elliot. There was absolutely no doubt about it. The fact had burst into her mind with laser swiftness that afternoon at the quarry edge. But did Mark feel the same?

"JESSIE. WE'RE LEAVING in another couple of hours. I want you to know how grateful I am to you for sticking it out this week, you and the girls." Mark could have kicked himself for the pious sound of his words. Jessie was silent, her eyes unfocused. She'd been lost in her thoughts for several seconds. Mark wasn't sure what had prompted him to call her back from her reverie.

"Grateful?" She returned, quick hot tears pricking the back of her eyelids. Of course that's what he was, grateful. And she'd been ready to throw herself at him.

"Yes. Jess, you're not making this easy for me. I'd like to go on seeing you when we get back to Manchester."

"But you will see me. The pictures, the spring issue."

Lord, but she could be dense! Mark didn't know whether to laugh or shake her. "I didn't mean professionally, Jess. I'm asking you—"

"For a relationship?" Jessie said in a squeaky little whisper.

"For your friendship. I want to get to know you. I've come to care so much for you this past week. It's overwhelming for both of us, I think." He reached out, imprisoning both her small hands between his large, strong ones. "I want to know you much better still, Jessie. That takes time. And privacy. I want to know your girls better, too, and your mother. Your heart and soul and body. But not all at once. Not today." Mark watched her. Jessie's heart pounded against her ribs.

"I want that, too," she breathed, smiling beguilingly. "I'd like that very much. But, Mark, do you know what this might lead to? What it entails?" She had to make sure he was aware of the pitfalls. She'd come a long way this week, but establishing a relationship with a man opened up an entirely new area of doubts and insecurities. Not only about her children. But about herself.

"It means you're worrying too much as usual, Jess. I know what I'm doing. Aren't you even going to give me a chance to prove I can fit into your world?" Mark lifted her stubborn chin, forcing her sparkling brown eyes to meet his. It was the hardest thing he'd ever done, keeping this casual, keeping Jessie from feeling threatened by the intensity of emotion beating away inside him. What if she refused? Did he have the patience to lay siege to her all over again back in Manchester where the busy demands of their lives would make being with her harder still to accomplish?

"You're just such a...a greenhorn. The girls have been on their best behavior out here...." Jessie choked off the words as Mark raised a long warm finger to her lips, resting it gently against her mouth, shutting off her protests.

"I'm a greenhorn, I admit. So were you when you stepped on that lobster boat, but you came anyway. Give me credit for the same amount of daring. I want to be with you, Jess."

"I'm glad," she whispered. "I hope it happens just that way."

"It already has. At the plant you're always so damned efficient I couldn't get near you. Out here we've made a beginning. A good one, just as I hoped we would when I asked you to come along with me. The girls like me, I think," he added a bit wistfully, surprising himself by how much he really did care for Jessie's daughters.

"You know they think you're the greatest thing since sliced bread."

"Precisely." He preened officiously, making her break into a gurgle of golden laughter. "That's half the battle, I think."

Jessie nodded shyly and stared down at her clasped hands. "Come on, let's go check on Ann's snail." He understood her hesitancy. Hell, he had reservations of his own. Would she even believe how uncertain he was himself of falling in love at his age, of considering giving up control of his life and placing it in her keeping?

"Do you know how hard it will be finding time for ourselves?" She forced herself to continue meeting his probing gaze. "The girls, my mother..."

"Lighten up, Jess. I think I know what's coming. I'll think of some way to get to you to myself. I'm nothing if not resourceful. I've been working on ways and means already."

"I should have known." He curled long fingers around the back of her neck, pulling Jessie close. This time she didn't resist the drag on her senses. "Do you ever give up?" she couldn't help asking.

"Never, and I have the patience of Job." Mark was so strong, so sure of himself that he could allow her to set the pace. He wouldn't rush her into anything. This would be best for both of them, for all of them. She lifted her mouth to his.

The kiss was incendiary. Jessie felt herself drawn closer to the hard strength of his chest. Her hands reached out to pull him closer still. With a fraction of her senses that was not involved with Mark, she heard

the girls scrambling toward them, voices raised in altercation. Nervously Jessie pulled back. Mark snorted in
irritation but jumped to his feet, helping Jessie to rise.
He moved a few inches away but kept her folded in the
crook of his arm.

"We're only being friendly." He laughed down at her
but his breath was quick and uneven. "We're celebrat-
ing our successful venture with a kiss, that's all."

The girls topped the rise, staring openmouthed at
their mother in Mark's arms.

"Mom, the boat's here," Nell informed her parent,
not seeming to notice the compromising position Jessie
felt she'd been placed in by the open embrace. "Everything's packed. I have a bucket of clams for
Grandma." She indicated her sisters with a jerk of her
thumb. "*They* said I can't take them back. May I
please?" She looked directly at the two adults for the
first time, just as Mark bent to place a quick proprie-
tary kiss on Jessie's warm, pink lips. "Mom!" Jessie's
youngest bellowed, shocked.

"Mother, really!" Ann and Lyn chorused severely,
nowhere near as embarrassed as their mother. "You
don't let us kiss boys like that," Lyn added, sensing a
potential crack in Jessie's maternal armor.

"I'm not a boy," Mark growled amiably, never taking his eyes from Jessie's stunned face. "I'm your
mother's friend. And yours. I intend to see a great deal
of her in the future. Do you ladies have any objections?"

"No, sir." They giggled obediently and on cue,
catching the drift of the situation with surprising ease.

Ann tugged on Nell's jacket sleeve. "We'll go start
loading the boat. Come on, Nell."

"But my clams! They said I can't take them, that the clams will spoil and poison us all." Nell didn't take her eyes off Jessie, but her silver-plated grin was puzzled and inquisitive.

"Bring them along, Nell." Mark's tone was authoritative, cool and decisive. "We'll get ice for them at the ferry dock."

"Thanks, Mark." She spun on her heel to confront the twins. "Hear that." Satisfied her sisters had been put in their place, Nell regarded Mark once again. "Are you going to be Mom's boyfriend?"

"Yes, I think I might qualify."

"Good."

"Boyfriend. Oh, dear. I didn't mean for this to happen yet."

"Jess..."

"I know. 'Lighten up.'" Jessie managed a lopsided smile.

"You've finally got the hang of it. Now tell me." He spun her around into the welcoming circle of his arms. "Didn't I handle that well?" he prodded, fishing for compliments unashamedly as he kissed the sunburned tip of her nose.

"Yes, you did," Jessie answered most sincerely, settling back into the curve of his clasped hands. "You're a natural."

"JESSIE, IF I'M NOT MISTAKEN we're supposed to be establishing a relationship, remember? When can we start?" Mark leaned his chin on his crossed hands. His arms rested on the roof of his car. The car was parked in Jessie's driveway just behind the VW that they'd picked up on their way into town.

"I'm sorry, Mark, I can't hear you," Jessie answered mendaciously, her voice muffled as she poked around under the front seat of his car. Cicadas shrilled loudly in the huge maples that lined the quiet residential street adding counterfeit veracity to her statement. "I found it." She waved Nell's misplaced survival book victoriously overhead as she silthered out of the passenger door fanny first.

"I said when will you have the time to spend time with me?" Mark repeated the query. He was wearing a khaki-colored regulation shirt and fatigues. He looked tall and fit and impressive. Just like an army poster of the perfect GI. "Why can't we have dinner tonight?"

"I have to wash my hair?" Jessie said mischievously. She hoped her humor didn't sound forced. She was as nervous as a cat on hot bricks. She couldn't even remember how it felt to have a date.

"Tomorrow."

"Uh-uh. It's the twins' birthday this weekend. Two parties, sleep-overs. They've always been in separate classes," she explained in great detail to cover the quaver in her voice. "Ann will have the volleyball team, I imagine, and Lyn most of the girls in the drama club. And I'll probably end up feeding the entire football team both nights." Jessie looked mournful and shook her head.

"Sunday, then." Mark glowered at her over the car roof. Jessie slammed the passenger door to avoid meeting his gaze.

"After two nights of chaperoning sleep-overs? You've got to be kidding." Her palms were sweating. She resisted the impulse to wipe them on the seat of her jeans. Her face was probably the same shade of coral as her long-sleeved, button-down shirt. Thank goodness her mother hadn't seemed to notice she still wasn't wearing a bra.

Mark took a deep breath. "All right, Sunday's out. How about Monday? Any objections there?"

"First day back at work?" Jessie tried, without much hope of success. "And how much longer than that can you expect me to start developing my film?" She made no attempt to hide her excitement. "I think it's some of the best work I've ever done."

"All right, Monday's out. But is this a test of some sort?"

"No. It's just a fairly ordinary five-day schedule around here. With the exception of the twins' birthday of course."

"My patience is wearing thin. Tuesday, Jess."

"Let's see. Tuesday might not—"

"Tuesday." The word came out close to a roar.

Jessie rounded the front of the car at a trot. "Mark—" she looked down at the book in her hands "—my time's not always my own. I can's just drop everything to please myself." She lifted her hands to dramatize the statement.

"So that's the problem. I thought you were trying to back out of our agreement, stand me up," Mark grinned sheepishly. "It almost worked."

"I wouldn't do that, Mark." Jessie laid her hand on his arm to emphasize her sincerity.

Mark breathed a private sigh of relief. He'd been afraid she would try to back out of the relationship before it had truly begun. "I won't make you choose between me and your family. I thought you knew me well enough by now." He should have recognized her reticence. He'd have to get over being defensive about her children, too.

"And I'll lighten up." Tension drained out of Jessie's taut form like sand through an hourglass with Mark's last remark. She felt giddy and suddenly at ease. "What time Tuesday?"

"Jessie!" Her mother stood on the front stoop below the wide, wraparound verandah of the turn-of-the-century frame house that Jessie and Carl had bought two years before his death. "Is everything out of the trunk?"

"Yes, Mother. We're all unloaded." Jessie surveyed her mother fondly. She was wearing a rose-pink, linen pantsuit and a silky gray blouse that matched her shortly cropped salt-and-pepper hair. And she was barefoot. Jessie couldn't even remember seeing her mother barefoot in the middle of the day.

"Good. Isn't it nice we all got home so close together. I dreaded spending all evening in this big old house alone. Now we can get right at it and have the washing done in no time." Marta turned back to the house, shaking her head over the felicitous coincidence of a nearly simultaneous return to Manchester.

Jessie watched her in wide-eyed fascination. "I hope she's not coming down with something. She hates to do the laundry."

"I'm sure she's fine; probably just keyed up from her trip. You didn't answer my question. What time can I pick you up on Tuesday?"

"What? Oh, how about seven? Don't you think she looked a little flushed?" she asked Mark seriously. "Her eyes were so bright. She might have a fever."

"Your eyes are every bit as bright." Mark brought Jessie's attention back to himself without a twinge of conscience at the underhanded tactics. "Your mother looked just fine," he added hastily as Jessie opened her mouth to speak. He took her hand. She responded immediately to the pressure of his fingers, moving closer as though drawn to him by a magnet.

"I can't be away too late," she cautioned.

"I promise to have you safely home at a decent hour—three in the morning at the latest. Is there anyplace special you'd like to go?"

"Anywhere at all that we can be alone together." Jessie's voice was husky, deep with desire and longing. Mark sucked in his breath. The rush of heat through his body was almost painful.

"I'll take you to the moon, give you the stars," he began whimsically.

"Mom!" Nell bounded down the steps like a small sneaker-shod tornado. The ancient wooden screen door slammed shut behind her with a crack like a pistol shot. Jessie jumped away. "Mom, my guppies've exploded. There must be a hundred babies in the tank. Come look!"

"Great," Lyn added, following more sedately in the youngster's wake. "You can feed the extras to Cecelia. Mom that cat's pregnant again."

"Oh, no," Jessie moaned, resting her forehead against the door frame of the car. "We barely got rid of the last batch of kittens a month ago. I knew I should have taken her to the vet."

"Are all the resident pets in this household female, too?" Mark asked, astounded.

"Almost," Jessie admitted. "There's Cecelia—she's a very popular lady in the neigborhood—and her mother Frances. But Frances has been spayed, thank goodness. We're not too sure about one of the hamsters. They're awfully hard to tell apart. And certainly we have male guppies. How else do you account for the population explosion?''

"How stupid of me," Mark replied faintly, but a ghost of an irritating smile tightened around the corners of his mouth.

"Jessie." Marta returned with a batch of unopened letters in her hand. "It seems we've gotten Mr. Wharton's mail by mistake again."

"Nell just had to run into the house and open all of them," Lyn supplied from her perch on the porch railing.

"Doesn't she always?" Ann seconded from the dilapidated but surprisingly comfortable old canvas porch swing by the front door.

"Enough." Jessie raised a warning hand. "The postman transposed the house numbers again, Mother, that's all. I'll run it over later."

"That one's a third notice for something or other." Nell approached to take the treasured paperback from Jessie's hand.

"Do you suppose he's actually that far behind on his payments?" Marta queried, inspecting the official-looking manilla envelope with renewed interest.

"Is it really a third notice?" Jessie couldn't help asking. "For what?"

"Jessie, I'm surprised at you gossiping about our neighbors in front of Mr. Elliot like this," Marta scolded, absently perusing the letter herself. She beamed benignly and vacantly at Mark, then went back to reading the letter. Jessie felt another wave of apprehension slide over her skin. Marta was definitely not herself.

"Sorry, Mom." Jessie rolled her eyes at Mark. Marta paid no attention, still immersed in the absent Mr. Wharton's private communication.

"Why, it's only one of those letters bugging him about renewing a subscription to a magazine. We should just toss it away," she murmured disgustedly. "Save him the guilt trip."

"Mother..."

"Is it one of those that starts out: 'Dear Mr. Whoever. It has come to our attention that you have relatives in the old country'?" Mark interrupted, reworking his Viennese mad scientist accent to resemble a Prussian military officer. Barely.

"Yes, it is," Marta nodded, pleased at his levity. "So annoying, don't you think? I'm going to toss it in the trash. If he wanted the magazine he'd have renewed his subscription before this. I'm sure Mr. Wharton would do the same for me. Thank you, Mr. Elliot."

"Call me, Mark. Please."

"I'd like that." Marta smiled impishly, suddenly looking half her age. "And you must call me Marta."

"Mother, you can't throw away someone else's mail," Jessie pointed out logically.

"Well, I'm going to. It's the neighborly thing to do." It was said with such conviction that Jessie didn't dare argue with her. "Come on, girls. We've got work to do. You can tell me all about your trip while we sort the laundry."

"That does it. She's ill. She's back to the laundry again." Jessie took a step after her mother and almost collided with Mark. "Mom, are you sure you're feeling okay?" she called anxiously.

"Why, yes, Jessie, dear. I've never felt better. What makes you ask a thing like that?"

"Nothing. Go ahead. I'll be right in," Jessie asnwered as obediently as her daughters. "I have to go in," she explained unnecessarily to Mark.

"Do I get a good-bye kiss?"

"Yes, a kiss," Jessie said in a dreamy, singsong voice. "That's what I need to get me through till Tuesday. Do you think you can manage a kiss that will hold me until then, Colonel Elliot?" Her eyes glowed, her lips parted appealingly in anticipation of such a caress.

Mark bent his head, taking her back into his arms. His hands rested low on her hips, pulling their bodies together. Jessie didn't protest, although their embrace was only partially concealed by the car. She didn't care if the whole world was looking. "Now that's an order I won't have any trouble obeying."

"Is MARK GONE, Jessie?" Marta called as her daughter floated into the house a few minutes later.

"Yes, Mom. He had things to check over at the magazine. How was your trip?" Jessie stared at the tremendous pile of laundry in the middle of the kitchen floor, then at her barefoot mother in its midst. "My goodness, we'll be at this till midnight."

"Nonsense, Jess. It won't take more than a couple of hours." Marta ladled Tide with a heavy hand into the venerable Maytag, slamming the lid.

"Mother, sit down. Leave that for the girls," Jessie ordered propelling her mother toward the kitchen table with loving firmness. "Are you feeling yourself?"

"I've never felt better. Why do you ask?"

"Because you're acting very strangely, running around confiscating the neighbor's mail. You hate to do laundry—" Jessie gestured "—and you aren't wearing any shoes."

"You aren't wearing a bra," Marta replied tartly. "That's strange enough for you."

"Oh," Jessie sputtered, the wind effectively taken out of her sails. "I didn't think you'd notice."

"I may be old enough to qualify for Social Security and a Senior Citizen discount at the movies but I'm neither blind nor senile, Jessie. Of course I noticed. And I saw you kissing Mark Elliot out there behind his car. That's the same way you used to behave with Carl— sneaking around corners... staring off into space."

"My Lord, does it show that much? Do you think the girls suspect? Oh, Mom. What if it's true? Do you think I might be falling in love with him? Is that possible?" She dropped a soiled beach towel back into a pile of clothes, not realizing she'd given the statement veracity merely by voicing it aloud.

"I think you'd better tell me all about it," Marta suggested, resting her chin on her hands. Jessie outlined her feelings as succinctly and as lucidly as she could manage. Marta seemed to understand. "Far be it from me to pass judgment, but Mark Elliot doesn't seem like the kind of gentleman who'd kiss a 'friend' like that."

"But all he asked me to be is his friend."

"Maybe I am reading too much into it," Marta admitted. "Or maybe I can spot the symptoms more easily because I'm in the same condition myself."

"You're in love? With a man?" Jessie croaked, grabbing the back of one of her prized pressed-oak kitchen chairs for support.

"No, with a baboon," Marta answered tartly. "Of course, a man. Is that so hard to believe?"

"No, certainly not," Jessie lied. Her father had been gone nearly a dozen years and her mother had never expressed an interest in another relationship. "It's just so out of the blue, that's all. I'll need a little time to get used to it. Who's the lucky fella?" She hoped her voice sounded normal. Marta looked as happy, as easily hurt as the twins would be.

"Hiram Parker. Do you remember him?" Jessie shook her head. "No, I suppose you don't. He had children closer to your brother's age." She flicked her hand across her forehead. "My wits have gone begging. Tim and Helen send their love. They want to know when you're coming out to visit." Jessie's older brother was line foreman in a large farm machinery plant near Lancaster. He also farmed her mother's small acreage on shares. The earnings helped his growing family of five and supplemented Marta's income nicely.

"I thought we'd go home for Thanksgiving if that's all right with you," Jessie replied absently, piling blue jeans back into a duffel to take to the Laundromat for washing in a heavy-duty machine. It would save hours of time and wear and tear on Jessie's overworked washer and dryer.

"I might be busy over the holidays, dear," Marta returned coyly, rising from her seat to help Jessie steady the duffel. "Hiram and I are considering getting married then. Here in Manchester. He lives in Florida now. We'll be going down there for the winter." Her hazel eyes were full of concern as she watched Jessie closely, trying to gauge her reaction to the news.

"Married!" It was Jessie's turn to sink into a chair, still clutching a pair of Nell's jeans. "Move to Florida!"

"Yes, dear. You aren't angry with me for deserting you and the girls, are you?"

"Mom, don't even think such a thing." But she was, a little. She'd never thought of her mother wanting to have a home of her own again. She'd been such a comfort, such a help to Jessie for so long. Had Jessie been selfish to assume they'd be together forever?

"I can't help but worry, Jess. It's all so sudden and so wonderful. I feel like a twenty-year old again. But I'm worried about you and the girls."

"Don't be. We'll just miss you so terribly, that's all. Hiram Parker must be some kind of man to sweep you off your feet like this." Jessie strove to move the subject along as smoothly as possible. The whole situation would take a lot of adjustment regardless of her assertion to the contrary. If her laugh was strained and high pitched, Marta pretended just as hard not to notice.

"He's such a wonderful man. He was a nice boy and he's grown into a wonderful man," she repeated.

"This is all so sudden." Jessie looked heavenward as if for divine confirmation. "Imagine. We've both been alone for so long, lonely so long," she added more softly, cocking her head at Marta's round petite figure. Her mother nodded shyly. "And bingo, just like that we each find somebody! Both of us," Jessie finished on a lighter but still wondering note.

"I didn't find Hiram," Marta explained, delighted to fill Jessie in on the details. "We'd lost track of an old, old friendship, that's all. He'd been living in California for years. His wife died, oh, about three years or so ago. I didn't know it until the night of my alumni banquet. Lettie reintroduced us."

"How is Aunt Lettie?" Jessie inserted, kicking dirty socks into a separate pile as she jumped off her chair, already infected by her mother's glowing happiness and her own inner joy.

"She's fine." Marta dismissed her sister's well-being as a topic of conversation with a wave of her hand. "Where was I? Oh, yes. Hi Parker was the best-looking boy in school. We dated for a year, then broke up just before I met your father. He was a soldier home on leave from the war. I never could resist a man in a uniform."

"Mom! You didn't marry Dad on the rebound?" Jessie didn't like the idea at all.

"Certainly not, silly. I loved your father to distraction from the first moment we met, but I've always had a soft spot for Hi. He was quarterback of our high school football team, you know."

"No, I didn't know." Jessie's voice was muffled as she transferred the wet clothes into the dryer. Its monotonous rumble counterpointed their words from then on.

"I have his picture right here," Marta revealed, going to her handbag, which was still resting on the kitchen counter above her suitcase. "Naturally, he's changed a little—but haven't we all?" The paunchy grandfather of eight smiling broadly into the camera bore only a slight resemblance to the rangy youth in the odd-looking old-fashioned football uniform that Marta pointed out in her yellowed yearbook.

Jessie shook her head, bewildered by the rapid turn of events and her own internal upheaval of the past week. "You weren't even going to go to that class reunion. If you hadn't, you wouldn't have found each other again."

"It's eerie, all right." Marta made a clicking sound with her tongue against her teeth. "It's downright scary how happiness can rest on such a fragile foundation sometimes, isn't it? Oh, well, no matter how it came about, I'm going to work hard to build it into something strong and lasting. Tell me you're happy for me, Jessie, honey.''

"How can you think otherwise? I'll admit I was taken aback by this whole thing. But if you love him, we'll love him.''

"I'm so glad,'' Marta whispered with a little catch in her voice. A merry giggle pealed across the room. She was close to laughing and crying at the same time. Jessie brushed an errant tear from her eyes as well. "We're as bad as the twins, Jess. Get us away from this house, the dishes, worrying about how to pay the bills and the laundry—'' she made a face at the floor ''—and we're as silly as teenagers.'' She giggled again, cupping her hands over her mouth to stifle her glee. "How are we going to tell them?''

"Who?''

"My granddaughters.''

"We aren't, at least I'm not. Not yet,'' Jessie said more seriously. "Mark and I...we're...friends. I'm not sure where this relationship is going. Let's keep these our little secrets. Would you like that?''

"Yes, I would—'' Marta agreed, nodding reflectively ''—for a few days, anyway, to get used to the idea myself. It's been a whirlwind romance so to speak. Hi is coming up at the end of the month to meet all of you. And pop the question officially, I hope,'' she added wistfully. "If he doesn't, I may have to,'' she added with more of her usual verve.

"If he's got any sense at all, he'll ask you right away. I'm sure I have a bottle of champagne from a client around here someplace.'' Jessie pondered a moment, then stepped up on a small stool to reach the top cupboard. Stretching her arm into the far corner, she brought out a bottle of vintage New York State champagne. "Drat, it's warm." She looked down at her mother, aggrieved.

"Why wouldn't it be warm, stuck away up there in the cupboard?" Marta shook her head at Jessie's apparent loss of sense. "Put it in the fridge."

"I'd better pop it in the freezer; it's quicker. Wait here while I unearth the wineglasses," she directed, preparing to hand the bottle to the older woman. "We'll drink a toast to our new friends before the girls get back from whatever it is they're doing."

"Is Mark your lover?" Marta asked bluntly.

"No," Jessie confessed, shocked. She stepped down off the stool. She was relieved the activity made eye contact inadvisable. Mark would be a tender, caring lover, she had no doubt. But her lover? "We're just friends."

"Well, then we'll drink to your friend, Mark, and to my lover," Marta said complacently, but deviltry sparkled in her hazel eyes.

"Mother!" Jessie's startled gaze flew to her mother's cherub face. Her mouth dropped open in disbelief.

"Forget about chilling this stuff, Jess," Marta stated firmly, rescuing the wine from Jessie's slack grip. "Just get the glasses. We'll put some ice in them. You look as if you need a good stiff belt."

Chapter Six

Jessie slipped through the screen door, the full, pleated skirt of her lemon-yellow shirtwaist whispering against her stockinged knees. "Hi," she greeted Mark, a bit breathless from her dash downstairs. She closed the screen pointedly behind her, blocking his entrance into her home. "You're early," she stated, a tinge of accusation in her tone.

"Only a minute or two. You're ready to go, I see," Mark returned, craning his neck to look over her shoulder. "You've got a beautiful old house here, Jess. What are you hiding in it?"

"Nothing," Jessie insisted, splaying her hands protectively along the sage-green wooden frame.

"You told me you've done a lot of restoration on it. I'd like to take a look inside." He was teasing again. Jessie had missed that honey-rough edge to his voice nearly as much as she'd missed the man it belonged to during the past hectic days.

"Oh, no, you wouldn't," she replied feelingly. "Not today, anyway."

Mark cocked his head, lifting one hand to rest on the wooden frame by her cheek. One brow crawled toward his hairline; fine laugh lines fanned out from his marvelous blue eyes. "That bad, eh?"

"Definitely. You can't imagine how long it takes to get everything back on an even keel after two sleepovers." She lifted the back of her hand to her forehead, fluttering her lashes in imitation of a suffering silent-film star. "The kitchen will never be the same. Nor will I."

"Must have been some parties," Mark said with what sounded like a note of envy in his raspy baritone.

"They were. Ann's volleyball coach stopped by to be sure everyone was going out for the team." Jessie made a fist, pumping it skyward in imitation of a perfect serve. "Her speech was so effective that after she left they started an impromptu game in the family room. Thank goodness, they used one of those sponge balls, or it would have been Armageddon."

Mark whistled in admiration. "You didn't have a coronary? I guess I won't be having to tell you 'lighten up' anymore, will I, Jess?"

"I think I did handle it very well," Jessie replied in a self-congratulatory way. "Not quite a natural at it yet, but I'm trying. Ann's developing a mean spike, if I do say so myself," she added in a thoughtful tone. "Let's see, what else happened? Oh, yes. I have it on good authority that both parties were an unqualified success because the football coach called at midnight both nights to make sure all his boys were in before curfew."

"Did you get any sleep at all?" Mark's gaze searched her flushed, happy face for signs of fatigue.

"Some. Sunday we all crashed. Monday seemed to go every which way; the twins are avid to get their driver's licenses, so we got started on the preliminaries. I can't believe so much work piled up on my desk at A & M.

I'm just getting things back under control today. And I got the first batch of negatives developed. They're great! I don't care if I have to toot my own horn. They're good...." Jessie's voice died away. She looked down at her hands, unsettled by Mark's intensity, but her eyes snagged on the long stretch of flannel-covered legs planted firmly on the porch.

"How do you do it, Jess?" He reached out to lift her chin with a tapered forefinger. He leaned closer, placing both arms on the door frame to block her escape.

"Lots of women do it on their own, Mark. I'm not special," Jessie demurred, raising her eyes to the level of his chin. She was flustered by his praise, his nearness, the clean scent of him in her nostrils, the heat of his body radiating out to warm her through the fabric of her dress.

"Oh, yes, you are special, Jessie Meyer. Very special." He moved closer, his mouth inches from hers. The front of his crisp oxford shirt brushed the tips of her breasts through the thin batiste of her dress. "Raising three children alone, working full time for Abrahms and Mahoney, moonlighting for *Meanderings*...."

"I have my mother's help," Jessie began but dwindled to a halt. She wouldn't have her mother to be a buffer or a companion much longer if she married Hiram Parker. What would Mark think of that development? Could she tell him? She could and probably would. It was a comforting thought. But his overpowering nearness drove those cogitations from her brain in the twinkling of an eye. Was she already drifting past the safe delusion of friendship? Was she on her way to loving him?

"Jessie, I'd like to take you someplace where we can be alone, to talk."

"I'd like that." Jessie got the words out with barely a squeak. "Someplace quiet and not one bit crowded."

"I know just the spot." Mark took her hand, preparing to lead the way down the brick steps, along the mossy herringbone-patterned walkway to his car.

"Wait a moment." Jessie tugged him back. "We're leaving now, Mom," she called through the screen door.

"I didn't hear Mark drive up." Marta's voice came down the hall. "Hello, Mark."

"Hello, Marta," he answered the unseen greeting politely.

"Have a good time, Jessie, dear. Don't be worried about getting back late. The girls and I will do just fine without you. Jess!" The older woman's tone was suddenly both muffled and excited at once. "I've found where the ants are coming from."

"Hurrah," Jessie called back. "Where?" She shot Mark a half-impish, half-rueful look.

"From under the living-room couch." Marta's voice grew fainter still. "Aha. I found it. The lost pizza that almost started the riot Saturday night." Her voice returned to its normal volume and timbre. "There's a full column of the industrious little beggars all the way to the kitchen sink."

"The spray's on the back porch, Mom."

"Good night, Marta," Mark called over his shoulder, urging Jessie down the steps. "I'll take good care of her."

"Yes, you do that" came the faint reply. Obviously Marta was fully occupied with her ants.

"Don't be late, Mother," one of the twins cautioned from a vantage point above their heads.

"We expect you home at a decent hour," her sibling added in a schoolmarmish tone. Stifled giggles issued from an upstairs window. Two heads appeared briefly to enforce the directive with waggling fingers.

"Yes, my dears. I'll be good as gold." Jessie laughed, waving up at the girls. "Go help Grandma get rid of the ants. She found your lost pepperoni pizza, Lyn."

"She did! Bobby Lester didn't eat the whole thing, then. I told you so." She tweaked Ann's hair. "'Bye, Mark."

"'Bye." Both teens disappeared from view.

"Good-bye, girls," Mark spoke into thin air as he opened the passenger door for Jess. Yet another voice delayed their departure. Mark thumped an impatient hand on the roof of his car.

"Where are you two going, Mom?" Nell queried from the macramé hammock strung between two old maples in the side yard. It was one of Marta's most ambitious winter craft projects and incredibly uncomfortable to Jessie's way of thinking. Nell didn't seem to mind. She hung over the edge, dangling a book in her hand, defying the laws of gravity. "Should I wait up for you?" she suggested helpfully, keeping her balance by some miracle of acrobatics.

"No, miss, you will not wait up for your mother," Mark responded, leaving no room for argument. "That's an order." Jessie could feel the back of her neck getting warm. She wished they could be on their way without any further adieus.

"Yes, sir," Nell replied equitably enough, flopping back into the hammock's folds. "Have a good time, Mom." The pregnant Cecelia leaped gracefully onto Nell's stomach and curled up against the girl's warmth.

"I feel as if I've run the gauntlet." Mark let out a long sigh of relief as he settled Jessie into the seat.

"I warned—"

"Don't say it, Jess," he cautioned darkly, slamming the door. "It's got to get easier. The novelty of my showing up on the front porch will have to wear off sooner or later."

Jessie didn't answer, letting the warming glow his comment produced deep in her middle spread out and envelop her like a glowing cloud. Mark took her hand in his. They drove through the familiar residential streets in silence.

Jessie rolled her window down. The air was cool, typical late summer weather with a hint of fall in the air. She leaned her head against the seat rest, closing her eyes. Tiny butterflies played tag in her stomach, but she wasn't nervous. Not really, only pleasantly stimulated by thoughts of the evening ahead.

The radio was tuned to a station that played soft classical music. When was the last time she'd gotten in a car and the radio didn't blast her out of the seat the moment she turned the key in the ignition? Too long. The strains of a Chopin nocturne lulled her into a state of languid peace. She was barely aware when they crossed over the canal into the old manufacturing district.

"Why, it's the magazine," Jessie said, slightly confused, as she glanced up at the three-story brick building. "I thought we were going out to dinner."

"We are. At least you are. You wanted some place private and quiet, I think you phrased it. You've got it. I live upstairs, didn't you know?"

"No, I didn't. I spend very little time here," Jessie reminded him.

"I know, part-time help. Well, the place is cheap," Mark expanded in mock seriousness. "The utilities are paid and I needed something to do with my hands. I spent three weeks with my sister when I first moved up here. It was fun being part of a family again but nerve-racking and more than enough incentive to spur me on to a place of my own. Here we are.'' They'd bypassed the magazine's small, eclectically decorated offices and reached a side door in the long, drafty corridor that led to the printing plant. Jessie seldom ventured beyond the composing room when she dropped off slides of her work, so she wasn't surprised she'd never noticed the big metal door with its small, wire-mesh-enforced glass window that led to Mark's home.

She also wasn't surprised to see the bare-stud wall at the top of the second flight of stairs. There were thick pink mats of insulation stuffed between the wooden supports, attesting to Mark's determination to make himself a comfortable home in the drafty factory loft. What did surprise her were the double leaded glass doors set about two-thirds down the length of the wall.

"They're lovely." Jessie ran her hand over the satiny finish as Mark held one open for her to enter.

"Aren't they? Found them up here with a bunch of other stuff when old Peavy sold me the building. Seems the original owner was a textile manufacturer."

"What else in New Hampshire?" Jessie interrupted, stepping over the threshold.

"He'd planned on building himself a house befitting his standing in the community. He never got it done."

Inside the loft was one long, narrow room situated to take the biggest advantage of the view out over the river canal.

The floors were bare golden oak polished to a high sheen. The walls were bare, too: mellow sandblasted brick that echoed the colors in the brass-framed hunting prints hanging with military precision along its length. The off-white kitchen was to Jessie's left, the sitting room directly ahead. The ceiling where they stood was low. It was a sleeping loft, Jessie guessed and found she was correct when she stepped into the living area and saw the open staircase leading up into the shadows.

"Mark, it's a lovely home. The old cotton baron's loss has certainly been your gain," Jessie said in genuine admiration. She liked the colors, all earthy and warm. It was very like him: simple, direct, strong. The furniture was straight-lined and deep-cushioned. Jessie realized just how tired she was when she couldn't stop herself from slipping out of her too-tight heeled sandals to sink down onto the tuxedo-styled sofa in deep contentment.

"Would you like something to drink while we're waiting for dinner to finish up?" Mark bent over the back of the sofa to drop a quick kiss on top of her head.

"Gin-and-tonic if you have it."

"Coming right up."

"I didn't know you cooked," Jessie observed, scooting around to watch him moving with sure grace within the small confines of his kitchen.

"I can in a pinch. Don't expect miracles, though. It's a curried lamb-stew recipe I picked up from a friend in the Middle East. Dessert is an incredibly expensive Amaretto mousse I ordered from a bakery downtown. It's worth every cent; I guarantee you'll love it."

"I will." Jessie accepted the frosty glass from his hand. Their fingers brushed, and Jessie's middle tightened in pleasurable anticipation. She doubted if she'd taste a bite of their meal no matter how delicious it was. All she could think about was Mark: his hands, his lips, his body. Jessie shook her head to clear her mind of the

erotic vision. "Tell me what you've done since we got
back." She swallowed a hasty mouthful of gin-and-
tonic, cursing the inanity of the remark but it was the
best she could do.

"Nothing compared with your weekend, I can as-
sure you." Mark grinned at her from the other end of
the couch where he'd stretched out with his feet on the
glass-topped coffee table. "Catching up on the back-
log, paying bills, roughing out the article for *National
Geographic*." He hadn't tried to touch her after that one
butterfly kiss. "I'm looking forward to your prints.
Would you like another drink or shall we eat?"

"Let's eat. I'll tell you my mother's big news over
dinner."

"Your mother's news? Sounds intriguing." Mark
uncoiled his rangy frame with unhurried grace, reaching out a hand to assist Jessie up from the sofa.

"Do I have to put my shoes on again?" Jessie asked.

"Not as long as I can take mine off, too." Mark
stepped out of his suede loafers and kicked them under
the coffee table.

"Deal." Jessie laughed, leading the way to the small
maple pedestal table under the high, uncurtained windows. "Didn't this place go out of business during the
Depression? I think I recall Carl's parents speaking of
it occasionally."

"Yes. It was empty until after the Second World War.
That's when old Mr. Peavy took it over and converted
it for his magazine."

"Can't I help you serve?" Jessie offered when Mark
disappeared into the kitchen.

"No, ma'am. It's all right here." He returned almost
at once with a serving cart laden with thick crusty bread
and butter, salad and the savory stew. It looked deli-

cious, smelled delicious and, Jessie knew, would also taste delicious.

"What's your mother's big news?" Mark led the conversation back as Jessie guided her fork into the stew a few moments later.

"She's getting married!" Jessie brought her earnest gaze level with his as a piece of lamb remained suspended on her upraised fork. "Can you believe that?"

Mark raised a dark brow in acknowledgment of the momentous announcement. "Yes, I can. Your mom's a terrific lady."

"Of course she's terrific, but to fall in love in six days. To have a love affair—" Jessie broke off, stuffing the lamb in her mouth. What a gauche thing to say. Her mother's love life was none of her business.

"I think it's great," Mark said softly. "I wish her every happiness. Who's the lucky guy?" Mark kept on eating his meal but he didn't taste a bite. He didn't have any trouble believing her mother had fallen in love in six days. It wasn't taking him much longer to fall in love with Marta's daughter.

"He's an old high school flame." She was answering his question and Mark tried to pay attention to her words, not merely to the sound of her speaking them. "He's coming up soon to meet us all. I'm sure he'll propose. I'm going to miss my mother very much." Jessie gave a wistful shake of her head. Mark watched her, entranced by her hair. It was pinned in a loose coil on top of her head. She'd highlighted the deep brown of her eyes with a coral shadow. A deeper shade of coral accented her cheekbones and the sweet inviting curve of her mouth. The makeup enhanced and refined her soft features, but in his eyes she looked just as good without it.

"I take it she'll be leaving Manchester?" Mark asked, trying hard to keep up his end of the conversation. He sensed Jessie needed to talk about her mother's unexpected romance, perhaps work through a few points in her own mind.

"His home is in Florida. I'm sure they'll spend at least the winters there. He has children. I'm not sure how many." Jessie frowned. "Three, I believe. And eight grandchildren. So they'll want to spend time with them and my brother's family."

"You're having trouble taking it all in, aren't you, Jess?" Mark refilled her coffee cup. She wasn't aware she'd emptied it.

The dark rich mousse appeared on her plate as if by magic while she mulled over his last remark. "Yes, I am. I hadn't thought about Mom leaving me and the girls. Naturally, I'm aware they'll be gone before I know it or want it to happen. But I always thought we'd be together."

"She has a right to her own happiness, Jess." Mark laid his fingers over hers where they rested on the table. Outside, the sun must have set, because the sky had faded to a dusty rose. Jessie stared up into the empty sky crisscrossed by high white vapor trails.

"Nobody deserves happiness more. She left her home and came out here and held us all together after Carl's death. I think it's just the shock. It's funny how things work out."

"If my nieces hadn't thrown a tantrum that day, none of this would have turned out as it has."

"We wouldn't have come to know—" She'd almost said "love" but shut her lips tightly before the near escape of the word. "We'd never have become friends.

And my mother wouldn't have gone home to her class reunion to find Hi again. How odd."

"Not odd. Damn lucky," Mark said in a husky rasp. He stood up and led her back to the couch. "You look tired. Curl up over here." His manner was tender.

"Dinner was lovely." Jessie smiled, but inwardly she was aware all at once of the deep flame in his fascinating blue eyes. He pulled her down beside him. "The dishes, Mark," Jessie said, flustered, regretting the inanity the moment it left her tongue. It had been a long time since she was alone with a man who excited her as much as Mark. She wanted their evening to be special, but what should she do next?

"Leave them. I've missed you, Jess. It's been a long five days." He laid his arm along the back of the couch, and she cuddled against him so naturally. Mark held his breath, controlling his impulse to gather her closer still. Her hand slipped into his. He cradled it to his chest. "I've thought of nothing but being with you every minute."

"I've missed you, too." Jessie swallowed against the truth of that admission. It sounded so simple, but it wasn't. The emotions she'd experienced in the days since they left the island were profound and complex.

"How could you have time to miss me? The birthday parties, your job, your mother's news and your photographs. There couldn't have been time for me," he protested but sounded pleased at her avowal nonetheless.

"I did miss you," Jessie said quellingly, sparks kindling in her eyes. "Are you doubting my word, Colonel Elliot?" She drew herself to her full height inside the circle of his arms.

Mark pulled her head down to his and brushed his lips over hers with gentle restraint. Jessie had brought so much to his empty life, including the awareness of that emptiness. He wondered if he would ever find the words to tell her so.

Jessie's mouth blossomed under the pressure of his. Her tongue flicked out, tasting his skin, inviting him inside the moist darkness. When Mark pulled her tight against him, she relished the loving pressure of his arms. The kiss was endless yet over far too quickly for either of them.

"I still feel just like the kid in his dad's Chevy," Mark confessed with a nibbling string of kisses along the side of her neck. "All strung out when you're around, never quite knowing what to do or say. It's awful."

Jessie shook her head, laying it on his shoulder. "I don't want to be that young anymore." He smelled nice, of spicy soap and some subtle cologne. "No monumental upheavals with every decision that has to be made. No terrifying changes in my mind and body from one day to the next. No fumbling in dark cars, sneaking in after curfew." Jessie stiffened. Good Lord, what had made her say that?

"Did you do such things, Jessie, sweet?" Mark's hands were on the top buttons of her dress. He smiled down into her wide brown eyes, acknowledging the sensual undercurrents in her statement and requesting so much more.

"Mark, where are we going?" She broke off as his palm slipped lightly inside her dress, tracing the swelling curve of her breast.

"I don't know, Jess. Not anyplace you don't want to go. But it's going to be a wonderful trip."

"I think what I feel is so much more than friendship...." She wasn't expressing herself well at all. But suddenly she wanted very much to be far more than just his friend. Jessie's heart hammered against her ribs.

"I wanted us to become friends, Jess, for us to be comfortable together. I want you to trust me, to be sure of me. I'd never hurt you, Jess. I couldn't. I meant what I said back on the island, that I want to know your mother and the girls. Everything about you. But now with you here in my arms all my good intentions seem to have disintegrated." The rest of her buttons parted under the persuasion of his fingers. His eyes blazed a trail; his hands followed, down over the pouting swell of her breasts, the lush roundness of her waist, the curve of her thigh nestled against his on the rough surface of the couch.

"Jessie, would you believe me if I tell you I think I'm falling in love with you?" The words came out without conscious thought. Mark ceased his tactile exploration of Jessie's scented softness. Now he'd done it. God, why couldn't he keep quiet? He hadn't even intended to make love to her, although he wanted that as much as he'd ever wanted anything in his life.

"Maybe it's just puppy love," Jessie whispered, trying to keep her voice even and light but the combination of his exciting caress and the words defeated her good intentions. "Emotions that belong to the kid in the Chevy."

"No, damn it. It's not, Jess." Mark's words were harsh, so at odds with his gentle touch. Several pins had come loose from the swirl on top of her head and long curls slipped over her shoulder. Mark reached out as though he couldn't help himself, twisting a curl between his thumb and forefinger. "It's not like that. I

began falling in love with you in bits and pieces last
week on the island. Since I dropped you off Friday
night it's been happening in big chunks. But tonight all
I planned was a quiet evening alone. I won't rush you,
Jess.''

"You're not rushing me. My mother told me I had all
the symptoms of falling in love. She was right, as usual.
Oh, Mark, I'm not sure how to act, what to say. There's
never been any man in my life but Carl. It's all so new
and strange. I want to please you." Somehow the decision had been made between them without words having been spoken. "Falling in love again is—"

"We have all the time in the world and no reason to
worry about anything at all." His hands returned to
shape the ripe curves of her breasts. Jessie felt her nipples respond more eloquently than any words to the
glory of his touch. She didn't think she could get
enough of him. With delicious restraint Mark stood up,
kissing the tip of her nose, pulling her up with him.
"You'll never be sorry, Jess." The words were as old as
lovers, but Jessie understood the sincerity behind them.

He led the way up the carpeted stair. Their clothes
came off quickly between seeking kisses and lingering
caresses.

Mark turned back the sheets on the big, old iron bed
and followed Jessie down onto the firm mattress. Their
bodies were gilded by the low gleam of the bedside
lamp. Mark's legs were long and rough against the
smoothness of hers. His weight pushed her into the
mattress. She liked the heaviness of him, the thrust of
his ardour against her hand when she lowered it boldly
to embrace him there.

Mark groaned. "I've wanted you so badly all these
days. But I was afraid to tell you so, to show you, for

fear I'd frighten you off." His tongue tantalized a dusky nipple. His hands gentled her, circling lower to settle on the delta of her femininity.

Jessie clung to him with arms and legs that seemed possessed by a will of their own. She explored his lean, rangy strength, dazed by the return of passion and desire she'd thought buried forever under the ashes of her mourning for Carl. But her passion wasn't dead; it had only been sleeping. Mark had awakened it for her. There wasn't an inch of him she didn't want to know as well as she knew her own body. When he entered her at last, Jessie ceased to think coherently at all, only to feel. Every cell of her being was alive to the joyful mastery of his body.

Mark rested within the snug heart of her. How good she felt sheathing him with gentle feminine strength. He'd needed Jessie for so long, it seemed, possibly forever. She was the woman of his dreams, all those private fantasies of five thousand lonely nights. She was a feeling, caring woman who would love him to his dying day, a woman who would be a partner and a lover and the mother of his children.

He moved within her, the warm moistness of her clutching at him, sending rippling shudders of delight all through him. Jessie, his love. She complemented each movement of his body with an answering beat of delicate passion.

Mark almost forgot to breathe. He was getting dizzy; the pulse beating in his head quickened with his physical response. Beneath him the tempo of Jessie's sighs escalated. She seemed to splinter in a series of trilling shudders that communicated themselves to his soul. His body, his mind, his heart combined in a triumphant explosion as he was pulled into the vortex of desire with her and they came to rest beyond its swirl together.

"Jessie, I do love you," Mark said long moments later. "And you love me; you've proved it with your heart and your body." Jessie raised her passion-darkened eyes to his. "I want to marry you when you're ready. I want to love you and care for you the rest of your life."

Jessie closed her eyes against a rush of joy so strong it almost deprived her of the power of speech. He loved her. Mark loved her and wanted to marry her, to spend the rest of his life with her. "Happily ever after" could happen the second time around.

"I love you, too, Mark. I have for days and days. I can't fight you any longer. I don't want to. I want to spend the rest of my life with you." Tears pricked behind her lashes, tears of joy and happiness. "But the girls..."

"I think they'll accept me," Mark stated with patently false modesty. Jessie's reservations weren't going to stop him now. Next thing she would be telling him that he didn't have to marry her, that she would understand why he didn't want to be saddled with a whole harem of females.

"Yes, I imagine they will. I've never seen them take to anyone as quickly as you." Was there the tiniest hint of pique in her soft words?

"Are you worried that they'll suspect what we've been doing here tonight?" Mark smoothed the frown from between her arched brows with a gentle, callused thumb.

"No...I mean only a little." Jessie could feel the beginning of a blush heat her skin. "Do you think they'll guess?"

"If you blush that hard every time someone mentions my name, they will. Do you mind?"

"It's unsettling," Jessie responded with innate honesty and an embarrassed little gurgle of laughter. "I believe the twins can judge between a mature commitment and casual sex. At least I hope so. I've tried very hard to give them values," she added with a slight hesitation as she pondered her words. Could any teen make that complicated a moral judgment where his or her own parent was concerned?

Mark took his time answering, respecting her reservations. He tangled his fingers in the auburn waves of Jessie's hair where it had come uncoiled and lay like a scattering of autumn leaves against the pillowcase. "I believe they can and will. You're doing a fine job with them, Jess. You'd prefer that they not know we've become lovers at all, wouldn't you?"

"Yes, but not for that reason." Jessie caught his roving hand and turned her lips into the palm. "Because of the upheaval my mother's leaving us will cause for them." Mark moved against her, unable to control the jolt of passion the erotic nipping caress sent arcing through his body. "And because it's all so new and wonderful." Jessie shot him an upward glance. She could feel him gathering himself within her. "I want to keep you my own precious secret for a little while longer. Will you do that for me?"

"You're in control of this relationship where the girls are concerned. I trust your judgment. But for now, Jess, I can't get enough of you. Will you love me again?" He began to move within her. Jessie felt the urgency of his desire catch her up in a cyclonic slipstream with a speed she couldn't comprehend.

"I've never made love like this...twice in such a short time, not ever." Her words were wispy with wanting and needing, her eyes aglow with a desire to give in return.

"Then we're learning about love together," Mark said jubilantly, "because neither have I."

"JESS, WHAT TIME IS IT?" Mark's voice was thick with sleep. Jessie smiled into the darkness, glancing at his bedside clock.

"Are you too tired to turn over and look for yourself?" she chided lovingly.

"No, just too lazy," Mark confessed. "What time is it?" His hand reached out, circling her wrist. "You aren't leaving?" Mark rolled over, curling her into the S-curve of his body, planting a kiss on the ivory slope of her shoulder, glowing pale in the moonlight from the high, uncurtained windows of the loft.

"I'll have to leave soon."

"When can we be together?"

"Oh, Mark, I don't know when I can get away again." Was he going to become possessive so quickly? "My schedule, Mom's wedding."

"I don't think I worded that request very well," Mark chuckled. His breath sent renewed shivers of longing sailing along Jessie's nerve ends. How was it possible to desire a man so much, to have loved him so totally and still want him again as if they had yet to share the joining? "When will you marry me?"

"Marry you." Jessie echoed his words; she liked the sound of them. "Soon," she whispered, sealing her promise with a kiss.

"Too long." Mark couldn't repress the pride or arrogance in his words. She loved him. Jessie was willing to risk her heart again with him. He knew instinctively how difficult it had been for her to reveal her feelings. He admired her for it. He couldn't love her any more deeply, but he was proud of her. "I want to keep you with me. I want to learn everything I can about you. I want you to grow sleek and fat with our child." The words came from the most private, guarded recesses of his soul.

Jessie stiffened within the crook of his arm. *Grow sleek and fat with our child. Oh, God.* Jessie rolled against Mark in the darkness, praying she hadn't heard him correctly. "What did you say?" she questioned in a small voice, her nails scoring half-moon indentations on the back of his hands where they rested below the swell of her breasts.

"I'd like to have a child with you, a boy, maybe. But you're already so good at girls that I'd like us to have one of them just as well. I didn't have a family for a lot of years, Jess. Part of that I couldn't help, but part of it was my own fault. Now I see, being with my sister and brother, being with you and the girls, I see what I've been missing. Does that make sense?"

"It's just so sudden, Mark," Jessie hedged. "I can't quite take it all in yet." She wasn't good at communicating her inner feelings. How could she tell him she loved him and wanted to marry him in one breath, and then deny him a child with the next? Who would have thought a man forty-six years old would want a child? She should have guessed any man as good at parenting as Mark would have a nesting instinct equally as strong. Jessie felt a tide of panicky torment rise within her. She didn't want any more babies. Not even Mark's. "I'll have to think about that, Mark." She tried to sound nonchalant, unalarmed.

"Yes, I suppose you will. I sprang it on you pretty quickly, didn't I? I'm sorry. But I never thought I'd find you out there in this big lonely world, let alone make you love me. I just blurted out one dream too many. We'll talk about it later, all right?"

"Yes, we'll talk about it later," Jessie agreed cowardly. She was glad of the reprieve. *One dream too many.* Only he'd told her that one a little too late to save her heart from breaking.

How could she tell him she didn't want any more children? Even in her own ears it sounded cold and callous, so unnatural. She loved her daughters to distraction, but she was so much more comfortable with them now—despite the problems inherent with three teens—than she'd ever been when they were small. It sounded so infeminine, so unmaternal, to voice those convictions aloud. It was unthinkable to say them to the man who had just asked her to bear his child out of love.

"Will you stay with me a little longer, Jess? Then I'll take you home." Mark's voice was a sleepy rasp in her ear. He kissed her hair lightly.

Jessie nodded silently. Yes, home, with her mother, her daughters, where everything was familiar and safe. There the pain of her heart cracking in her breast couldn't be heard over the beat of rock music and the bickering of sibling rivalry. Home—that's where she belonged. There she could lick her wounds in solitude and think of some believable explanation for refusing to marry the man she loved.

Chapter Seven

"Jessie! Open that door this instant!" Marta kept her voice deliberately low, although she wasn't sure why she bothered. The twins were sealed in their room listening to someone, or something, called Motley Crüe; Nell was in front of the family-room TV rooting for her favorite batch of superheroes. Jessie was incommunicado. She hadn't spoken an unnecessary word in the past two days. It was enough to try the patience of a saint. And heaven knew, Marta didn't consider herself even re- motely eligible for that honor. "Jessie!"

Thirty-five years of conditioning paid off. "Just a second, Mom. I'm coming. You know as well as I do that I can't develop these prints of the trip with the door open."

"I'm tired of standing out here" came the unyield- ing staccato reply. "We'll talk through the door."

The subtle threat brought results. "All right, all right." Jessie's head appeared around the edge of the door to her darkroom. In actuality, the room was a converted pantry off the kitchen with a twelve-foot marble counter that had evolved from a weighty, un- sightly white elephant into a valuable work space five years ago when Jessie took up photography seriously.

"I wanted to get this first batch of prints drying before—"

She stopped abruptly, noticing the mulish look on her
mother's cherub face. Jessie opened the door revealing
her jeans and sweatshirt-clad figure. Dark hollows
shadowed her great brown eyes, fine lines bracketed her
usually smiling mouth. Marta frowned harder. "What's
on your mind, Mom?" Jessie's clouded gaze slid away
from her mother's appraising, sympathetic eyes.

"You're on my mind. You've been since the night
before last when you dragged me away from the Car-
son show to pick you up at Mark's magazine. Sneaking out of the building in your stocking feet, in the
middle of the night—"

"It wasn't even twelve-thirty," Jessie corrected with
an attempt at a smile. She couldn't defend the charge of
not wearing her shoes. She had been barefoot. And
she'd been running away.

"Why didn't Mark bring you home? It was too late
for a woman my age to be traipsing all over Manchester. You scared me half to death."

"Mom, we've been all through this. Mark and I...we
had a...a disagreement."

"It had to have been more than a disagreement to
bring on an attack of the vapors like you had. Jessie,
you're the world's worst liar; you always have been.
That's why you never got away with anything as a kid.
Now 'fess up. Did you two have some kind of fight?"
Marta's voice was loving but acerbic, a habit of hers
when dealing with a sticky problem.

"We didn't fight at all, actually." Jessie waffled,
scrutinizing a series of eight-by-ten color prints strung
on a wire line over the marble counter. "What do you
think of these?"

Marta closed the door firmly behind her, shutting out any distractions that might have saved Jessie an explanation. "Mark must have spent a great deal of time with the girls that week. He's in every shot, isn't he?" Marta made the observation pointedly, returning to the attack with her next breath. "I want to know what upset you so badly that night, Jess."

"Damn, these prints do have a green cast." Jessie cocked her head, pretending to study the prints as she sorted through her jumbled thoughts for an answer that would silence her mother's probing. "Can't you see it?"

"They look fine to me."

"Well, it's there nonetheless," Jessie mumbled in desperation as Marta's snare tightened. "I'd better reduce the magenta filtration on the filter pack. I'd love to be able to afford an enlarger that would do it automatically."

"You could do it at the magazine as you have before. Mark understands why you like to choose your shots from completed prints instead of negatives or slides. He thinks it's a good idea. Why do you think he invested in all that expensive new equipment when he took over *Meanderings*?" Marta's voice was gently chiding. "Nothing ever happens easily for you, does it, Jessie, honey? Is it because you're trying too hard to make everything come out right in the end?"

"No." Jessie was emphatic. "I've learned to lighten up considerably. At least I thought I had." Her tone was a mixture of croaking laughter and hidden tears. "I just can't face Mark yet."

"I suppose it would be awkward meeting the man when you've refused to accept his calls and messages for the past two days."

Blinking hard, Jessie adjusted another negative under the secondhand print enlarger she'd scrimped and saved for. With the speed of thought her mind converted the complementary colors and orange wash of the negative into a fuzzy, out-of-focus image of Nell whirling in glee, the bright starfish clutched in her hand, a streak of gaiety against a bleak background. "I can't talk to him now, Mom. I don't know what to say to you or Mark. I need time to figure out exactly what I'm going to do."

"That's logical. Couldn't you tell him that and put the poor man out of his misery?" Marta perched one ample hip against the counter as she studied a print of the twins with Mark rekindling the banked campfire while early-morning mist swirled in ragged streamers around them. "What happened, Jess?" Marta's concern was evident.

"I'm so mixed up. I've made a mess of everything," Jessie said truthfully. "Mark asked me to marry him," she concluded with a sniff. No need to say anything about the precious hours they'd spent in each other's arms.

"And you ran away?" Marta squawked. "Jess, that's fabulous! I mean that he asked you to marry him."

"I thought it was fabulous at first. But everything's happened so fast. I guess I can't handle whirlwind romances as well as you." Jessie tried a lopsided smile but it slipped off her lips. When she spoke again her voice was hard with repressed sadness. "It won't work for us, Mom."

"Won't work? Jessie..." Marta halted abruptly, clearing her throat. Her next words were quiet, more subdued. "Jessie, did you say no because of me?" The only illumination in the windowless pantry came from a red safelight above the bleach bath that stabilized the prints against further exposure to light. It distorted even Marta's soft, familiar features, but there was no mistaking the pain in her words. "Because I've gone and fallen in love like a silly old fool? Because I'm deserting you and the girls?"

"Stop talking like that, Mom. We'll miss you terribly, but you're only going to be as far away as the telephone." Jessie put every ounce of conviction she could muster into her words. She would miss her mother terribly but not enough to jeopardize her chances of happiness with Hi.

"I'll stay if you need me," Marta promised with quiet certainty.

"We'll be fine. And I'll work things out with Mark. I'll find the words to tell him somehow." Marta settled stubbornly on a stool in the corner, her back to the floor-to-ceiling painted pine cabinets that had been one of the house's chief selling points when Carl and Jessie bought the rambling old Victorian.

"Work what out, Jessie? If I know what the problem is, maybe I can offer a solution. Aren't you sure of your own feelings?"

"I'm sure I'm falling in love with Mark Elliot," Jessie said with simple conviction. "I'm also sure it would be a terrible mistake to marry him. That's why I sneaked off."

Marta snorted with disdain at that convoluted reasoning. Jessie was in love. Whether her stubborn daughter realized that she'd be miserable without Mark in her life was another problem. "It can't be because of the girls." She let the inflection of her voice rise a fraction, making the statement just less than an outright question. All the response she got was another watery sniff and a negative shake of Jessie's head. "I didn't think so. Look at him in those pictures. I'll bet everything I own he'd be a wonderful father."

Jessie sniffed louder, giving up any attempt to appear as if she weren't crying. "That's just it. He wants to be a father. He asked me to marry him and to give him a child of our own."

"A baby!" Marta sounded as taken aback as Jessie had been that night in Mark's arms. "You're too old for babies," she blurted with a lamentable lack of tact.

"I know that," Jessie responded, slightly miffed despite her own similar conviction. Marta didn't need to sound so shocked. But wasn't it exactly the tone of voice Jessie had used when her mother told her she was having an affair with Hi? "I'm not quite thirty-six. These days that's not so old. I could have another baby. I'm not afraid physically, if that's what you're driving at. Lots of women have babies at my age."

"I'm aware of that," Marta said with a shake of her short salt-and-pepper curls. "I did myself. But I also didn't have three teenagers already. It's just such a surprise. If anyone could bring it off, you could. It might be nice to have a little one around the house again," she concluded thoughtfully.

"I still have the cradle and the high chair," Jessie said softly, pulled to memories of the babies she'd held in her arms and nourished at her breasts. Perhaps she had been too hasty that night. Mark's baby—the thought was compelling.

"Of course it wouldn't be fair to have just one more child." Marta had decided to play devil's advocate.

"What do you mean?" Jessie questioned sharply, sensing a trap. Her brain was already overruling her heart; all of her reasons for not wanting another baby came rushing back with renewed strength, clamoring for recognition and agreement with her logic.

"A child shouldn't grow up alone. The twins will be going off to college in less than two years. Nell will be in high school and then away on her own, too. I've never believed in an only child myself. You'd owe it to the new baby to give him a brother or sister. No child should be raised alone."

"Two babies?" Jessie dropped her head into her hands, panic fluttering in her middle. "Two pregnancies, two infancies with colic and baby shots and ten more years of pediatricians...nursery school...Mom, I can't do it."

"Then you'll have to tell Mark so. Don't you think he'll understand, honey? He's a great guy. He loves you, I'm sure he does. He'll understand," she repeated for emphasis. With Jessie's next words, Marta's carefully constructed argument blew up in her face.

"I don't think so." Jessie's voice sounded scratchy with pain and she felt as lost and forlorn as dead leaves skittering before a cold November wind. She saw the pain of Mark's rejection in her mind's eye. "I don't think he'll understand or forgive me. Because telling him the truth will kill his dreams."

JESSIE'S LIFE was domestic chaos.

Mark was familiar with chaos in its more dangerous forms—the directed furor of a guerrilla attack, the controlled mayhem of huge construction sites—but the prospect that greeted him at the bottom of Jessie's basement stairs was something else entirely. It was as if a Norman Rockwell illustration for the *Saturday Evening Post* has suddenly gone awry.

No attempt had been made to conceal the utilitarian function of the big old low-ceilinged room. An electrician's trouble light spotlighted the gathering of the Meyer clan just to the left of the stairs.

The twins and Nell were perched on the bottom step as they watched their mother's head disappear into the depths of an old chest-type freezer. Jessie's pleated plaid flannel skirt in muted tones of brown and orange rode high on her thighs. She was still dressed for work. High heels accented the long sweep of her legs. Mark's breath caught in his chest. How he wanted to reach out and smooth his hands over the soft curve of her bottom. Or he would have wanted to, he corrected mentally, if he hadn't been so damn mad at the woman.

Marta fluttered into his line of sight, holding the lamp cord for a short, balding man to poke a screwdriver haphazardly into the innards of the freezer. Jessie straightened abruptly with a sack of frozen food in her hand. She cursed quietly and effectively, but the oaths didn't carry a sting, censored as they were for her avidly listening teen audience.

"Nell, get this stuff upstairs." Jessie raised her voice to carry over Marta's and her companion's murmured consultation behind the freezer. "Ann, Lyn, don't just sit there. Do something. Take this steak to the Petersens' and beg for freezer room." She whirled around. Mark watched as the color drained from her face, leaving it barely brighter than the long-sleeved, ivory silk blouse she was wearing. "Mark!" His name echoed across the room.

"Problems?" He was proud of the ordinary, everyday tone of his voice. He didn't feel ordinary. His hands were sweaty and his heart was beating hard against his ribs. Why had she run from him? She loved him; she had told him so, had proved it with her body's response to his. What had he done wrong?

Mark grinned down at the twins staring up at him from the steps. For the first time his smile failed to captivate a Meyer woman. The girls stared sharply back, aware of the tension emanating from their mother's taut form.

"Hello, Mark," they responded politely.

"We'd better go do what Mom said." Ann nudged her twin.

"Mark, it's good to see you." Marta sailed into the breach as Mark moved to allow the twins to pass him on the stairs. "I'd like you to meet my fiancé, Hiram Parker. Hi, this is Mark Elliot, the owner of *Meanderings*."

Jessie had confided in her mother. The slightly guarded look in Marta's eyes, the studiously noncommittal set of her mouth told him so.

"Nice to meet you," Hi Parker boomed. He rose from the floor with some difficulty. The two men shook hands. Mark's tall, imposing figure dwarfed Hi. "Nell came down for ice cream a few minutes ago and found this old girl on the fritz."

"Lucky Nell's got such a sweet tooth. Nothing's melted but the ice cream and the strawberries. The girls will make quick work of those." Marta smiled with comical gravity.

"Can't seem to find the problem," Hi said.

"Let me take a look at it," Mark offered. Hi backed off obligingly.

"No, let's just get it unloaded. I'll call the repairman first thing in the morning." Jessie's voice was shrill with strain. She was close to the end of her rope. She had no more idea of how to explain her behavior to Mark than she had when she left the loft.

"It's no trouble, Jessie. We have plenty of time," Mark said.

Jessie resisted the urge to rub her hands together in dismay. She couldn't resist the inclination to meet his sparkling-blue gaze. A ripple of apprehension coursed the length of her spine. He was angry, and deep in those cobalt-reflecting depths she sensed his pain.

"We didn't have anything special planned tonight," Mark added.

Jessie shot her mother a beseeching look, willing her to contradict Mark's mendacious statement. Marta studiously ignored her offspring. Jessie gritted her teeth.

"How did you find us down here?" Marta asked conversationally.

"I followed the commotion."

Marta laughed. There was no way she could stay angry at the man who'd saved Nell's life. Jessie felt her base of support crumble.

"Everything looks okay back here. What about the plug?"

"Checked first thing," Hi answered smugly.

"And the socket?"

"The socket?" Marta glanced at her beloved with a hint of disapproval.

"It can't be the socket. I just had this basement rewired three years ago," Jessie snapped.

"Never hurts to double-check," Hi said equably. He unplugged the trouble light, handing the plug to Mark, who was by then on the floor behind the freezer. He inserted the plug. Nothing happened. Hi snorted, reaching for the end of the extension cord so Mark could plug the freezer into it. The faithful old motor hummed to life.

"That does it. Good work, my boy."

"You'd have found it yourself in a minute or two." Mark extricated himself from his cramped position, brushing the dust off his pant leg.

"Ready to go, Jess?" She looked as if she were going to take off on him again. Mark tried to school the anger and irritation out of his voice.

"The electrician," Jessie began lamely. "That plug is dangerous."

"It's only a loose wire, I suspect, Jess," Hi said. "I'll look at it later. Your mother will show me where the fuse box is. I'll be careful. Don't want to get electrocuted before we tie the knot." Only Marta managed a genuine chuckle at his joke.

"You two run along. I didn't know you had a date tonight," Marta said archly. She eyed her daughter sharply.

"It must have slipped her mind," Mark inserted quickly.

"Let's go, Jess."

"The girls will help reload the freezer. No need for you to stick around. Run along, you two." Marta waved as she turned to lead Hi off into the gloomy basement to locate the fuse box.

"I'd rather not go with you, Mark," Jessie began as Mark took her arm.

"You don't have much choice." He led her toward the stairs. "I want to know why you ran out on me. I've waited four days. I'm out of patience."

The twins were making strawberry milkshakes out of the melted ice cream. The kitchen was a mess. Jessie wished Mark could have seen it at its cheery, country-style best, not with a day's worth of dirty dishes and after-school snacks littering counter and tabletop.

"Will you be gone long, Mom?" Nell's small gamine face was serious as she spooned softened black-cherry ice cream into her mouth.

"No, I won't. Do your homework before you watch TV." School had started the day before and Nell still wasn't reconciled to her loss of freedom.

"I hate refrozen ice cream." She smiled up at Mark.

"Me, too." Mark didn't try not to grin. She was such a cute kid. She could have been his—another piece in the jigsaw puzzle of his most secret dreams become reality. He'd love Jessie's daughter as much as he would love the babies she'd give him.

Mark ushered Jessie into his car with scant ceremony. "I'm not going to argue with you here. We're going someplace where we can talk without interruption."

Jessie didn't answer, just stared sightlessly out the window as residential streets gave way to rural roads. "Where are we going?"

"A place I know." He swung the car off the highway down a rutted, pine-bordered lane. At the end of it the skeletal remains of an abandoned farmhouse stood outlined starkly against the purpling sky. It was mute testimony that New England's rocky soil and unforgiving climate had claimed other people's dreams as well as her own. Jessie shivered at the unhappy comparison.

"Look, the trees out here are beginning to turn," she ventured. "Summer's gone. Winter might come early this year." It had certainly taken up residence in her heart, regardless of the date on the calendar.

"Quit stalling." Mark's hands were tight on the steering wheel, his voice rough and uncompromising. His knuckles showed white against the dark interior of the car. "Start talking, Jess."

"I am talking." She attempted to lighten the heavy atmosphere inside the vehicle. Mark only pinned her with an unnerving stare.

He was aware he wasn't going about this the right way. He was frightening her. But the pain inside him wouldn't submit to reason. He hurt, and it was Jessie's fault. She'd shattered fragile dreams that he'd protected in the depths of his soul for over half his life.

"It isn't easy for me to begin," Jessie continued in a small voice. "Could we take a walk around the farm? Or is it posted for trespassing?" she inquired as an afterthought.

"It isn't posted." He opened the door. Jessie did the same, too restless to sit still any longer. Her mind churned ceaselessly with opening gambits to explain her behavior.

They scrambled up the rocky rise to the house, silent, side by side but separated by several feet. It might as well have been several miles as far as Jessie was concerned. She plunked down on a lopsided porch step. Mark leaned his shoulder gingerly against a surprisingly sturdy railing.

"What happened that night at my place, Jess? I've racked my brains for what I said or did to hurt you so badly you'd run away from me while I slept." Mark dropped onto the balls of his feet, bringing his face level with Jessie's guarded features. "I love you, Jess." He took her face in his hands, but his kiss was harsh, possessive, fueled by the raw pain and hurt pride that had festered in him for four long, puzzling days.

Jessie was taken by suprise at the barely leashed violence. She jerked back, out of his arms. Her lips felt bruised. She was frightened and resented the weakness. A tiny bloom of anger flowered inside her, giving her courage she hadn't possessed a few moments earlier. "Mark, don't."

He released her immediately, looking down at his hands in stunned disbelief. Jessie scooted farther along the porch step. "I'm sorry for everything that happened that night at your place, Mark, but don't take out your anger at me that way. It won't change anything."

"Good Lord, Jess, I don't know what got into me. I'm sorry." He stood up, moving back to lean against the post. "I won't touch you again."

"That's what I'm afraid of," she said sadly, but so softly she didn't think Mark even registered her words. Jessie crossed her arms on her bent knees, tugging her skirt straight, resting her chin on her hands. She had only herself to rely on. How very lonely that made her feel. "I can't marry you, Mark. It just wouldn't work." She shrugged her shoulders inside the soft gabardine jacket she'd grabbed on her way out of the house. "I'm wrong for you."

"What the hell kind of cockeyed justification is that?" Mark exploded in quiet fury that was all the more spectacular for its rigid control. Jessie had never seen him this angry. It was a facet of his personality she'd been unaware of during their days on the island. He had a temper, too, just like hers, only held on a tighter rein.

"I can't ask you to give up your dreams." She wished she could explode in righteous indignation. It would be far easier to keep from breaking into tears that way. She tried again to speak around the lump of misery lodged tightly in her throat.

"Jessie, you are my dream," Mark interrupted vehemently. "Spending the rest of our lives together, watching the girls grow up into fine young women, raising children of our own. It's what I've always wanted."

"That's it." Jessie swallowed a sob. "I don't want to have a baby, Mark, not any babies at all, not even yours." God, how cold and hard it sounded, even to herself. Jessie began to panic. She couldn't explain her feelings coherently or logically. Mark was falling in love with the woman she was today, not the strained and overtired mother of three young children she'd been ten years ago, that she would be again.... How could she make him understand that?

"You don't want to have a baby with me?" Mark sounded as if she'd hit him in the stomach with a baseball bat. He shoved his hands into the pockets of his sweatshirt, pulling the fabric out of shape.

"Yes." Jessie's voice was strained but held a note of defiance despite the breathless quality. "I can't marry you because I don't love you enough to give you a child." That was even worse. That she loved him enough to deny herself the glory of his love was far closer to the truth.

Crystalline shards of silver ice appeared in the depths of his blue eyes. Mark jerked Jessie to her feet, his strong fingers digging into the soft flesh of her upper arms. His eyes compelled her to meet his angry gaze. He'd never in his life felt like such a fool. Wasn't she the same Jessie he'd fallen in love with on the island? Was this bleak-eyed woman anything but a complete stranger? He thought he'd known her so well. He'd woven so many fantasies around her quick laughter and infectious smile, her wit and capacity for caring.

"I want a home and a family, Jess," Mark said tonelessly, burying his anguish under a layer of cold anger with the strength of tempered steel. He was forty-six years old and his heart was breaking. He was a class-A fool. "You're the only woman I've ever asked to marry me, do you know that? I want you to bear my child and you're turning me down flat."

Jessie drew herself up with dignity. She reached out to cup his face in her cold, trembling hands. "I'm doing what I feel is best for both of us. I need a life for myself, Mark. I've been a mother since I was only a little older than the twins. I can't do it again, no matter how much I love you." She knew she was making it worse. He didn't even appear to be listening. He'd turned inward, nursing his pain, relying on his own resources, refusing succor like a wounded animal. "Mark, I'm so sorry."

How stilted and selfish she sounded. If only she'd coalesced her wants and needs for the future into a blueprint plan that she could spread out before him. Perhaps then he could understand. "I have dreams, too, Mark," she whispered brokenly. He didn't hear her plea.

"You really know how to hit a guy where it counts, don't you, Jess?" Mark's laugh was a primitive sound that sent a shiver down her spine. "You've made me feel like a man half my age, like a happy, damn fool kid. You've dredged up all the old dreams I'd almost given up on. Now you sound like a woman twice your age: old, stodgy, mired down, afraid to take a chance on a new life." He was being needlessly cruel but he couldn't stop himself. He'd never loved any woman as he loved

Jessie. She was special. So were her daughters. She was good with them; he'd seen that on the island. She was a wonderful mother. He could make her happy, make all of them happy. Was it so wrong to want to have his own child with her?

"Please, Mark, you have to understand...." Jessie tried again to find a logical progression to her thoughts. All she could feel was pain: his pain, her pain, their pain. Mark dropped his hands from her shoulders and turned away with an abrupt, jerky movement unlike his usual unconscious grace. Jessie's hands went automatically to massage the spot where he'd held her arms so tightly.

"Forget it, Jess. At least we found out before it was too late. I don't believe in divorce." He was walking away from her at a rapid rate. Jessie broke into a trot to keep up.

"Neither do I. Can we still be friends?"

He stopped but didn't turn around. Jessie held out her hand but dropped it at the continued sight of his broad, unyielding back. "I don't think so, Jess."

Jessie didn't believe she could hurt any more, but those words sliced deep into her heart. "I'm sorry, Mark. I hope someday you'll understand how I feel, why I'm doing this." He didn't answer but started forward again. He passed the car. Jessie halted at the rear bumper, unsure what to do next.

"Mark, where are you going? Please stop." The note of tears and panic in her voice infuriated Jessie but seemed finally to penetrate Mark's detachment.

"I'm going to walk back." He dug in the pockets of his slacks and tossed the key ring toward her. Her hand reached out reflexively to gather it in. "Leave the car at that convenience store down the street from your place.

Just stick the keys under the front seat. It'll be all right till I get back.''

A breeze stirred the curls of Jessie's hair. She pushed them back impatiently, blinking furiously to keep from crying. She couldn't cry. The girls would detect any trace of tears the moment she walked in the door. There would be no time for tears until the cold small hours of the morning. ''Mark, we're miles from town.... It'll take you hours to walk back. I can wait—''

He cut her short. ''Don't bother. I need the exercise. And I don't think I want to be that close to you again just yet.'' His tone held a note of finality that Jessie didn't have the courage to challenge.

Was this how it felt to have a broken heart, Jessie wondered a little wildly as she watched the man she loved trudge away out of sight down the pine-bordered farm lane. This aching, splintery feeling inside was even worse than what she'd experienced after Carl's death. It was as if she'd amputated a part of herself and was watching her life's blood seep into the ground at her feet.

''You made a good, sharp break of it, Jessie girl,'' she complimented herself acidly. ''He won't even trust himself in the same car with you.'' She dragged open the door and got inside, dropping her head wearily onto the wheel. A month ago she'd been contemplating slipping quietly into middle age, convinced she'd never be lucky enough to love again. She had been that lucky. She'd found a new love, but there still wasn't a happy-ever-after ending waiting around the corner. And losing love a second time, Jessie was learning, was far harder than she'd feared it might be in her worst nightmares.

Chapter Eight

The misty late-October darkness wrapped around him. It was chilly, clammy, the gloom barely relieved by the inadequate wattage of a dim light above Jessie's front door. A stray swirl of breeze stirred the dry maple leaves still hanging from the trees; a dozen more drifted down to the thickly carpeted yard. Off in the distance a cat howled. Behind him a few late trick-or-treaters hurried home to gloat over their booty.

Mark shifted his weight, settling the heavy tricornered hat firmly under his arm. He pushed at the hot, uncomfortable wig on his head. At least the damn thing wasn't powdered, he thought irritably. Then he would have felt like a complete idiot coming face to face with Jessie for the first time in nearly eight long silent weeks. At least the fancy-dress costume made a convenient excuse for the state of his nerves. He didn't like to admit walking up Jessie's front walk and ringing her doorbell was the hardest thing he'd ever done.

The cat howled again, closer. The pregnant Cecelia? Shouldn't she have had her kittens by now? He'd have to ask the twins. They'd been his only connection to Jessie these days. A carved pumpkin grinned at him from a table that propped open the vintage wooden screen door. Mark scowled back at it as he twisted the key to the antique doorbell in the middle of the carved door.

Halloween. How besotted was he to have agreed to Kerry's idea of a costume party for the magazine's staff? *Plenty,* came the unflinching inner voice, *if you let her talk you into this ridiculous charade.* He doubted if anybody would even show up in costume. He must be out of his mind—a minuteman, for God's sake. Practical, down-to-earth Jessie would laugh herself silly.

Yet, seeing her glorious smile, hearing her happy, infectious laughter would be worth it. He'd never forgotten how miserable she'd looked when he took off that evening at the farm. God, he was stupid. Maybe a life for them together wasn't in the cards, but he shouldn't have told her they couldn't be friends. He meant to remedy that situation here and now—if she didn't order him off her porch.

The door swung open. A myriad unearthly screeches and howls filled the night. The most extraordinary figure moved forward out of the shadows created by two dozen flickering candles. Mark stared in fascination. The black-cloaked phantom was at least seven feet tall. It seemed to float along the floor. Hands reached out for him, and Mark stepped back involuntarily.

A glowing jack-o'-lantern's grinning, diabolical face topped the apparition. It spoke: "I'm sorry. You're too late for trick or treat. It's after eight o'clock, you know." The pumpkin head tilted forward to the approximate height of an eight-year-old child.

"I'll take your daughters instead." Mark tried for a light, noninvolved tone and thought he succeeded pretty well, but he wondered if it would deceive anyone but the woman muffled inside yards and yards of black cotton.

"Don't feel bad. I might have—My daughters! What the blazes?" Jessie yelped from inside her uncomfortable disguise. She couldn't see a thing. The jack-o'-lantern head tumbled forward into black-gloved arms. She thrust it toward him unthinkingly, her hands tugging to free her head from the black folds.

Mark didn't say a word. He'd grabbed the hollow pumpkin head with his free hand and watched her struggles with undisguised interest. Once she was free of the elastic neck of the cloak, her hands flew to anchor the listing swirl of auburn hair on top of her head. When she'd finished her makeshift repairs, curling tendrils brushed her heated cheeks and the topknot was still endearingly off center.

"Mark Elliot."

"In the flesh." There was a breathless quality to her lilting contralto that Mark would have given his soul to attribute to her happiness at seeing him again. Unfortunately, her frown and sparkling, angry eyes belied his wish.

"What are you doing here?"

"I'm here to pick up the twins," Mark replied stiffly, guilty again of dreaming unwisely. She wasn't going to fall into his arms, tell him in a few sentences that their fight had been a terrible mistake, that she still loved him and wanted to give him all the children he wanted. So much for self-serving daydreams. And so much for sophomoric hopes of platonic friendship. He'd had plenty of time to think about it. He'd come to a single, rock-hard conclusion: He wanted Jessie Meyer heart, body and soul.

"The twins?" she parroted, drawing her brows further into a frown. "But they're babysitting for—"

"Kerry Bay. Had you forgotten the magazine's staff party is tonight? Didn't you get an invitation?"

"I got an invitation," Jessie said dismissively. She had no intention of setting foot inside the building tonight or any other night. Not if she could help it.

"Kerry's very efficient that way."

"Really?" Kerry Bay, his receptionist? How long had this been going on? Jessie felt a stab of distress course through her body that carried the voltage of a near-lethal jolt of electricity. Eight weeks, and the pain hadn't eased a bit. She could ignore it now, sometimes for hours on end, but it was still there. How long would it take to get over him?

All her life, Jessie decided fatalistically.

"You've got a fantastic costume there," Mark persisted, moving over the threshold and setting the pumpkin head down on the hall table, where the scant remains of a crockery bowl of treats also rested.

"I can't go," Jessie shot back quickly, her breath misting in the cold air pouring into the foyer. She moved behind Mark to shut the door. "I...I have to help my mother fit her wedding dress. She and Hi have decided on the week before Thanksgiving for the wedding. I'm so busy." She broke off, looking down at her black-gloved hands. She couldn't meet his warm, searching gaze. Her eyes were level with Mark's because she was wearing a pair of sixties-vintage black spike heels to give her ghoulish creation added height. It was a Meyer tradition to greet the trick-or-treating neighborhood youngsters in some outlandish costume. This year Jessie had been drafted at the last moment when her daughters found other pressing commitments.

"I understand," Mark said quietly. She did look up then, staring recklessly into cobalt-blue eyes. Jessie shivered, blaming it on the cold foyer. He was serious. Remnants of pain clouded the depths, but far down Jessie saw a brighter flicker of amusement. Or was it anticipation, impatience to get on with life, to find a new love? Kerry Bay?

"Mother's in the family room. I'll go get the girls." She picked up the trailing folds of the cape and motioned him forward. The sharp staccato tap of her heels echoed on the wooden floor, the noise no longer masked by eerie howls and moans from hidden stereo speakers. "Mom, look who's here," Jessie said with counterfeit brightness.

Marta peered sharply over the tops of her sewing glasses at Jessie's overly merry entrance into the room. Her lap was full of folds of soft rose-gray watered silk. "Mark, how nice to see you again. Come, sit down." She patted the sofa beside her with a hand and wrist decorated with a colorful pincushion.

"How are your plans coming?" Mark folded long buckskin-clad legs under him, settling on the sofa close by Marta's plump, smiling form.

He looked comfortable enough to be planning a lengthy stay, Jessie thought. Her temper wiggled out from under the heavy depressing layers of sorrow that had weighed down all her emotions for many weeks. How dare Mark Elliot come to her house and act so casually, as if he hadn't broken her heart, stranded her five miles out in the country—so to speak, Jessie corrected honestly; after all, he was the one who'd walked five miles to retrieve his car—and now have the monumental nerve to come and pick up her daughters to baby-sit for his new girl friend. Damn his arrogance!

"I'll tell the twins you're here," she said with frosty hauteur, sweeping toward the stairs on the rickety heels.

"Don't trip in those awful old shoes and break your neck, Jess," Marta warned, heedless of her daughter's dignity, before returning to the more engrossing subject of her wedding that Mark had so obligingly initiated.

"Would it make any difference if I did?" Jessie mumbled spitefully over her shoulder at the half landing. But no one paid attention to her grumbling. She kicked off the shoes at the door of her room, hearing them land against the closet door with two satisfying thuds. The black elbow-length gloves met the same fate. In stockinged feet she stalked down the hall to the twins' room. It looked like a demolition zone, as usual.

"Mark is here to pick you up and take you to Mrs. Bay's," she said. Ann was primping in front of a rejuvenated dressing table rescued from the back room of the Salvation Army store and stained a dark oak. Her eyes snagged Lyn's for a brief, guilty moment—the other girl was lounging on her bed—then sidled away.

"She said she'd send someone over to get us. Then we wouldn't have to drive the VW home so late at night."

"How nice of her," Jessie answered with only the merest trace of acid etching her words. She searched her brain for a clear image of Mark's employee who'd become so important to her in the past few minutes. Only a hazy recollection of a very thin, very young brunette came to mind.

"She's probably afraid we'd run over some little trick-or-treater." Lyn waved pink enameled fingers above her head to hurry their drying. "She's seen how Ann drives."

"Very funny." Ann stuck out her tongue. "Kerry's okay, but those kids of hers are real brats. Why do you think we're both going over there?"

"How old are they?" Jessie plunked down on Ann's unmade bed. Suddenly she felt as if her age had halved and the twins had somehow doubled theirs. Lyn finished blowing on her nails. "Nathan is four, almost five, I think. Peter is two. He isn't potty-trained yet. Do you know Kerry? That's what she told us to call her," she added hastily as Jessie opened her mouth to protest. "She got married when she was only seventeen. That's just a year older than we are now."

"She's twenty-three," Ann added helpfully, as if her mother might have forgotten how to add.

More than a dozen years younger, Jessie calculated mournfully. No wonder Mark was pursuing Kerry so hard. She was everything, obviously, he'd found lacking in Jessie. The perfect age to give him a baby.

"Well, I for one certainly don't want to get tied down that young. Just like Joan Grayson," Lyn said with assumed worldliness, capping the bottle of nail polish with exaggerated care to protect her handiwork.

"Imagine having a baby at our age," Ann murmured, styling brush poised above her wisp of bangs.

"Who's Joan Grayson?" Jessie rallied her maternal forces, dragging her mind away from the tall figure sitting downstairs, no doubt discussing guest lists and wedding favors chattily with Marta. She still wanted him, needed him so badly it was a true physical pain that tightened her diaphragm and made her breath come in short, hurting gasps.

"Oh, didn't I tell you already? Joan Grayson's a girl in Lyn's drama club. She's a senior and she's going to have a baby at Christmas time," Ann went on dreamily. "Isn't that romantic? The father is in the service. They're going to get married when he gets out of basic training or after graduation or sometime."

"Or sometime? No, that is not romantic," Jessie said in a strangled tone she hoped they attributed to sternness and not to incipient panic. "It's a very serious situation with consequences that will affect all three of them for the rest of their lives. I just hope everything works out for them." The odds were woefully stacked against the young couple, Jessie knew. "I think perhaps the three of us should have another talk someday soon."

"Not about the birds and the bees again, Mom," Lyn yelped, hopping off her bed with lithe grace. "You got mixed up enough as it was the first time. Don't worry about Annie. She's only bluffing. She wouldn't even let Bobby Lester kiss her good-night at her birthday party."

"Shut your trap," Ann bellowed. "Mom, it's none of her business if I don't want to kiss that creep."

"It is my business." Jessie wished this diversion from her heartaches hadn't been so explosive a subject in itself. "I still think we should talk."

"Whenever you feel up to it, Mom," Ann teased, grabbing her letter jacket off the curved arms of a bentwood pier glass. Lyn dragged hers off a hook behind the door. Jessie wondered for the thousandth time why she'd paid a fortune to have closets put in the old house. The twins never used them. She could have saved plenty on carpeting, too. Just as many colorful pieces of wispy lingerie and dainty blouses dotted the floor. "We'll give you a few hints on how to get Mark from Mrs Bay. She's a piranha in sheep's clothing if I ever saw one."

Lyn giggled at her twin's use of such a mangled metaphor. "She'll eat a nice guy like Mark alive," she corroborated. They exchanged knowing glances. Jessie stared at them as though they'd changed again before her very eyes. They looked so grown-up; she felt so young and insecure. What would Ann and Lyn say if she told them the true underlying reason for her breaking off with Mark? Would they understand her reluctance to have more children? She thought not. Their newly found maturity was a fragile thing, a new experience. It wasn't fair to burden her daughters with a decision that must be entirely her own.

"Kerry Bay is looking for a man," Ann said bluntly in case Jessie was still acting obtuse. She pulled her thoughts back from her own inner turmoil. No, the twins were growing up fast, but not that fast. "She's a man-eater."

The conversation had gone far enough in Jessie's opinion. "That's it. No more soap operas for you two. We have no idea what goes on between Mark Elliot and Mrs. Bay." She couldn't help wondering how long it had been going on herself but refused to satisfy her curiosity and ask the question. "Don't judge her until you've learned what her life is like. Can you imagine how it must be to be left alone, completely deserted by your husband, with two tiny babies?" That much was general knowledge in the neighborhood. The young divorcée had moved into a duplex just two streets over several months earlier. Her landlady was one of Marta's bridge partners at the senior center. "You should admire how well she's coping with her problems." She probably sounded horribly pious when she was only trying desperately hard to be fair to a woman she was well on her way to disliking already.

The twins made identical grimaces. "You're probably right, Mom," Lyn admitted grudgingly. "But she's still got two of the brattiest kids we've ever had to sit with. Right, Ann?"

"Gremlins. Monsters. I can't think of a word mean enough to describe them. They're worse than Nell ever was."

"That bad?" Jessie gurgled, regaining a measure of her equilibrium now that the focus of their attention had shifted again. She was doing a good job with her children, just as Mark had so often told her. The news about the Grayson girl's pregnancy had thrown her for a minute, but she thought she'd ridden it out pretty well. The twins were levelheaded and smart. They'd be fine; she just had to learn to let go gracefully, a little at a time.

Lyn came forward to give her mother a peck on the cheek. It was something neither of them did often anymore. Jessie missed it but respected their need to assert independence in so many telling little ways. She reached up to give Lyn a quick, hard hug, blinking back sentimental tears. "Mark's a great guy, Mom. Don't let Kerry Bay get her petite little claws on him. We like him a lot. He likes you, too."

"More than he does her," Ann said with complete conviction. "I can tell. He talks about you all the time when we're over there. It bugs her. I'd bet next month's allowance on it."

"You're just imagining things, girls," Jessie scolded, avoiding their sympathetic gazes as she prepared to rise from the bed. "Mark and I have too many differences. They didn't show up on the island, unfortunately—" she sighed, bunching up a handful of the black cape "—but they did later on. It's over. You'd better go on down. Mark will want to get to the party. After all, he is the host."

"Don't look so down, Mom. We'll talk tomorrow," Lyn said in her best adult tone. "If we put our heads together, we'll come up with a plan to get him back for us."

It was time to put a halt to this fantasizing before she began to believe it was possible herself. Jessie spoke sharply to hide a suspicious tightness building in her throat. "We'll do no such thing. Whatever Mark and I might have had is long over. It never really got started. If he wants to pursue a relationship with Kerry Bay, it's none of my business and absolutely, positively, none of yours. Do I make myself perfectly clear?"

"Yes, ma'am." They exchanged a last conspiratorial look before they darted out the door and clambered down to the half landing. Jessie took several deep, sustaining breaths and followed more sedately.

When she reached the landing, the twins were making a deceptively calm entrance into the family room. Waves of competing and highly scented lotions and sprays wafted around them. Mark rose from the couch where he'd still been sitting attentively by Marta's side.

"Wow! A minuteman! Mark, you look sensational. A wig and everything," Ann enthused. "Isn't that outfit something, Lyn?"

"Great. Where's your flintlock?" she added to the complimentary opening gambit.

"At the magazine," Mark beamed. They seemed to be over their animosity toward him. He'd been working hard to reestablish good relations ever since he first discovered they were Kerry's baby-sitters about three weeks ago when he took her home after a late session at the magazine. He still wasn't sure exactly how he'd let Kerry by a few of the barriers he'd thrown up around himself, but they were definitely drifting into a more personal relationship with every passing day. "It's the only genuine thing about this costume. The gun be-

longed to my great-great-great-grandfather. I think I've
got that right.'' He paused, then shrugged expressively.
"These buckskin pants are man-made, and the home-
spun shirt is half-polyester. The hat was made in Hong
Kong." He grinned, and the twins returned the gesture. Mark glanced up as Jessie shifted uneasily on the
stairs.

The outfit might be a reproduction, but he certainly
looked marvelous in it. The dull blue fabric of his shirt
strained across the broad sweep of his shoulders; the
tight knee breeches accented muscular thighs and ribbed
stockings molded long, well-shaped legs. Jessie sucked
in her breath to speak. "I'm sorry, Mark, but they have
to be home before midnight. Tomorrow is a school
day." She folded her hands primly across her middle.
She didn't let any tinge of softness creep into her tone.
If he wanted to play house with a woman a dozen years
younger than she, not two months after he'd broken her
heart, he was welcome to her. But Jessie wasn't going to
aid and abet his already highly refined seduction techniques by sending her daughters to watch the other
woman's children until the wee hours of the morning.
She pinned Mark with what she hoped he'd recognize
as a quelling, disapproving glare.

He seemed totally unconscious of the subtle threat.
He included Jessie in his entrancing grin. Her heart
flipped over in her breast, and unwillingly an answering smile tugged at the corners of her mouth. She ignored it, concentrating her attention on her ragged
heartbeat. It was the first sign of life the damned thing
had shown since the night she'd left Mark stalking off
across a deserted pasture, driven his car home, shut
herself in the bathroom, turned the shower on full blast
and cried her eyes out.

"Don't worry, Jess. I'll have the twins back safe and sound by the witching hour. Halloween isn't a good night for fairy princesses to be out that late." The girls preened under the blatant flattery. Marta chuckled indulgently from the sofa. Nell was the only Meyer woman absent or she'd have been fawning all over him, too. Thank goodness she was off being pleasantly terrified at the Manchester Men's Club annual Haunted House.

"I'm sure you will." Jessie hoped she'd managed just the right note of condescending lack of interest—like a grand duchess, which she felt she resembled somewhat in the huge, enveloping cape, at least now that she'd abandoned her pumpkin head.

She started forward with her nose in the air, made it to the third step from the bottom and pitched forward when she stepped on the hem of the billowing costume. A startled squeak pushed past her lips as she grabbed for the banister and missed.

Mark was there in an instant, cradling her in his arms, saving her from an embarrassing and painful fall on the uncarpeted foyer floor. Without a moment's hesitation he swept her high into his arms, striding back into the family room. It was over in a matter of seconds. Marta jumped up from her seat, scattering wedding dress, thread and scissors onto the carpet.

"Jessie! My Lord, what a fright! I told you not to wear those awful old shoes. You could have broken your neck, or worse."

Jessie didn't ask what could possibly be worse than breaking your neck, she already knew. Being held in Mark Elliot's arms was painful and exhilarating. It showed her too plainly what she'd lost. She couldn't believe how marvelous the touch of him, the scent of him, the strength of him, felt to her. Until this moment she hadn't admitted even to herself how much she missed him, how much she still loved him, would always love him. Or how great the differences between them really were. She loosened her stranglehold on his neck, wiggling in his arms. "Put me down, Mark, before we both fall," she said with unnecessary vehemence. "I'm fine, really."

"It's those shoes," Marta repeated distractedly.

"I'm not wearing any shoes," Jessie said sharply, kicking one foot out from under the concealing folds of the black cape. "See?"

"Are you sure you're all right, Jess?" Mark asked. His breath tickled her ear, stirring the errant copper curls. He wasn't even breathing hard, although he held her high against his chest. His heart beat steadily and reassuringly against her side—as it had that night in his bed.

"I'm fine. Put me down and I'll prove it." Jessie's voice cracked with strain and repressed desire, but her fundamental reservations hadn't changed. He wanted babies; she didn't. There was no getting around that fact.

"You guys look just like George and Martha Washington." Ann giggled nervously, the color beginning to return to her face. "Except Mom's taller and not quite as fat as Martha."

"And Mark doesn't have wooden teeth," Lyn couldn't resist adding.

"Thanks," Jessie said scathingly, pinning her daughter with a chilling maternal glare.

"My teeth are one of my best features," Mark mumbled under his breath. Jessie unwisely turned her head, to be impaled by his gaze as he lowered her protesting form to the sofa. The room narrowed down to the space of his arms, everything receded into the background, leaving Jessie alone with him in a pool of enchanted silence. The seconds stretched out endlessly until Mark spoke again, breaking the spell. "You have gained a few pounds these past weeks, haven't you, Jess?"

She glared up at her rescuer. "As a matter of fact, Colonel Elliot, I've lost six pounds, thank you for noticing." She'd been too miserable to eat.

"Should I call Dr. Perkins, honey?" Marta leaned over the back of the sofa after carefully depositing her upended wedding dress on the armchair.

"No! For heaven's sake, Mother, I'm fine. I didn't even hit the floor." At the moment Jessie wouldn't have minded being blessedly unconscious. "Stop fussing, all of you. Mark, you'd better be on your way. You don't want to be late to your own party."

"I suppose that wouldn't be quite the thing, would it?" He didn't seem to notice the shattering sarcasm Jessie had tried hard to inflect into her tone. He seemed different somehow, she thought wistfully, more sure of himself. This was how she wanted to remember him, tall, imposing, totally in command of himself and the situation around him, not the hard angry shell of himself he'd been the night they'd parted so angrily and so painfully.

"Don't forget they should be home before midnight," Jessie said softly, still caught up in her musings.

"Midnight it is." He gave her mother one of his special smiles. "I'll check up on her then, Marta." He might have been talking about Cecelia and her kittens for all the emotion in his voice.

"That won't be necessary," Jessie said, pushing herself up against the arm pillows. He must have gotten over her pretty quickly to sound so unconcerned after practically saving her life. That last klutzy performance on the stairs had been just the thing to cure him, obviously. He was probably thankful to be rid of her. "We don't stay up that late. Girls, do you have your keys?"

"Yes, Mom." Another smug glance passed between the twins. Jessie would have liked to get up off the couch and slap their smiling, satisfied faces, but the damned black robe was all bunched up around her legs; she'd probably fall flat on her face again. She didn't intend to compromise her dignity any further. She contented herself with a withering stare.

"I've been expecting you at the magazine to okay the proofs I've chosen for the spring issue, Jess," Mark ventured as he accepted the dropped tricorner from Lyn. "Can you make it after you leave Abrahms and Mahoney tomorrow?" He couldn't keep the hint of challenge out of his voice, even though he tried. "I want to get it into production." He attempted to inject a note of humility into the last statement, hoping Jessie would rise to the bait.

"Is five-thirty okay?" she answered, capitulating more quickly than he'd bargained for. She wasn't resigned to being thrown back into his company. Wariness was now obvious in her great brown eyes. Mark wanted to kick himself for bringing back that defensive, defeating attitude.

"Fine." He wanted to ask her out to dinner after she okayed the proofs but stopped himself in time. Their last dinner date had ended in his bed. He had a lot of thinking to do before he started anything with Jessie

Meyer again. They had plenty of problems to solve between them, and now there was the added complication of Kerry Bay. He must have been out of his mind the past few weeks, or merely very, very lonely to have let his relationship with Kerry go as far as it had.

"I'll be there." Jessie heartlessly denied another leap of her pulses. It was reaction to her near-fall, not to Mark's asking her to the magazine. This was strictly business, nothing more. It had to be done. It was better to get the meeting over as quickly as possible. It would be shock therapy, so to speak. She'd beard the lion in his den and cure herself of loving him once and for all. "It shouldn't take long."

"No, it won't take us long now," Mark replied cryptically. Jessie blinked, wondering if she really did see the telltale teasing glint in his cobalt eyes. "Good night, Jess, Marta."

"Good night, Mark, thanks for saving *my* daughter this time."

"All in a day's work for us minutemen." He made a creditable sweeping bow with a flourish of the tricornered hat. The twins giggled and sighed romantically. Marta shooed them out the door with loving laughter.

"You're a fool if you don't take that man back," she said, shutting the door solidly behind them before returning to the family room to pin her daughter with a gimlet stare. "He's still in love with you."

Jessie just flopped back on the pillows and groaned.

Chapter Nine

The following day was the longest of Jessie's life. There wasn't a thing left on her desk at Abrahms and Mahoney after two-thirty in the afternoon. She doodled her way through half a steno pad, changed the ribbon on her typewriter and the batteries in her calculator. She watered the plants, dusted the windowsill and checked the clock every three minutes. All in all, by the time five o'clock rolled around she was a nervous wreck.

She even began to wonder if she shouldn't wear her hair down. It would make her look younger, she reasoned, make it less apparent that she was almost old enough to be Kerry Bay's mother. She sneaked into the washroom, unpinned the shining knot of auburn curls on top of her head, fluffing it out on her shoulders to study the effect. It didn't work. She did look younger, perhaps, but shy and less sophisticated, too. It wasn't a good trade-off. She needed all the self-confidence she could get. It would be confusing to start changing herself now. She was too old and too set in her ways to start making over her life.

Yet maybe that was the problem. She was too set in her ways.

As she repinned her hair, Jessie tried again, for the thousandth time, to talk herself into accepting the idea of giving Mark a child. It was a futile exercise. She knew herself too well. She'd fought hard for her serenity and maturity. She loved Mark as much as ever, even more now that she'd given up his love. But she was also aware that agreeing to have a baby would only create more problems than it solved.

She adored her daughters, but her dreams had gone in other, less maternal directions now that they were older and more independent, directions that were only beginning to take form and substance in her thoughts. How could she make Mark understand so fundamental and private a decision when it involved him so intimately? It was hard to find the right words even for herself.

It was best if the subject never came up. The disillusion in Mark's eyes the night they'd broken off their relationship had seared its image into her memory. Granted, last night when he came to pick up the twins, he'd been almost his old self, the man she'd fallen in love with on the island. But she couldn't risk hurting him any more. Added to all the other questions and complications was the new problem of Kerry Bay. Just where did she fit into Mark's life? Was she the woman to give him happiness?

So it was probably inevitable that Kerry was the first person Jessie saw as she stepped inside *Meanderings*'s door.

The other woman looked even younger than Jessie remembered as she came forward to take Jessie's lightweight trench coat. *She is a fairy child grown up,* Jessie thought mournfully, as the slim figure deposited the coat in a closet behind her desk. Whatever the twins' speculation as to Kerry's character and motives, the limpid green eyes she turned on Jessie were guileless and full of lively intelligence.

Jessie's heart sank into her shoes. It was evident Kerry was everything Mark subconsciously wanted and needed in a woman, a damsel in distress who appealed to a man like Mark with old-fashioned ideas of chivalry. Jessie smiled in return at Kerry's shy gesture of friendship. No matter how hard Jessie tried, she wouldn't be able to hate Kerry Bay.

"Hello, Mrs. Meyer," Kerry greeted Jessie politely. Her words were like grace notes from a crystal wind chime. She was wearing a very feminine ice-pink, high-necked blouse and a gauzy skirt in a deeper shade of pink. They weren't expensive garments, but it didn't matter. Kerry still managed to look soft and delicate, like an English tea rose.

Jessie tugged at her serviceable oatmeal tweed suit, straightening the blazer a little roughly. Kerry pretended not to notice, popping a cover on her Smith-Corona. She motioned through the door that led to the printing plant, the composing room and Mark's apartment. "Mark—I mean, Mr. Elliot is waiting for you. He said to go right in."

"Thank you, Kerry," Jessie replied in a voice that was as dry as her throat.

"Please tell him..." Kerry blushed entrancingly. Jessie wondered if it was possible for Kerry to control a supposedly involuntary reaction so that it exactly matched the shade of pink in her blouse. Dusky curls danced around a pixie face as thick lashes lowered over the green eyes for a fraction of a second. "Please tell Mr. Elliot I'll mail the quarterly tax reports you sent over. And I'll lock up on my way out."

"I'll be happy to pass on the message," Jessie said, and meant it. At least she'd have one coherent sentence to speak. Her pulse beat so hard in her temples she was sure Kerry could hear the echo all the way across the room. Her palms were damp. She took a firm grip on her shoulder bag. Somehow she hadn't planned on being alone with Mark. They'd had so little time alone before. She always fantasized their meetings in company, except when memories of that magic night she'd spent in his arms worked their way past the filtering sensors of her brain.

"Good night, Mrs. Meyer. I think you've done some excellent work on those shots for the spring issue." The compliment was added as a shy rider to the parting remark.

"Why, thank you, Kerry. My daughters are three of my favorite subjects," Jessie said, pleased.

"I particularly like the one of them all foraging with Mark." This time she didn't try to correct the familiar use of his name. It was all too clear to Jessie that, although Kerry might appear young enough to be one of the twins' classmates, she was definitely a grown woman. Kerry Bay was sizing up the competition. What remained to be seen was how much of a threat she perceived Jessie to be.

Kerry's eyes traveled dismissively over the tweed suit and amber blouse Jessie wore. It was evident she didn't consider Jessie too much of a problem for the time being. She smiled beguilingly. "It must be very helpful having such photogenic subjects to work with." Somehow Jessie didn't think she meant the girls.

"It certainly doesn't hurt. Good night, Kerry." Jessie sailed through the swinging doors with her head high. She truly wished Kerry Bay had been the two-leg-

ged she-wolf the twins envisioned. She could fight a
woman like that much more easily. Kerry roused too
many conflicting, sympathetic feelings in Jessie. They
had too much in common: two women alone, raising
their children, in love with the same man. They couldn't
be enemies.

Jessie didn't intend to fight anyone for Mark's love.
She'd given it up of her own free will; no one had taken
him from her. On that distressing and deflating note she
came face to face with the man of her dreams.

"Has Kerry left?" Mark knew the moment he spoke
the words that they were the wrong ones. The soft look
of happy anticipation on Jessie's face died away, leaving her eyes cool and watchful, a faint line between her
brows.

"Yes, as a matter of fact, she asked me to tell you
she'll mail the quarterly tax reports and lock up on her
way out."

"Thanks." Damn it, he'd been worrying that Jessie
and Kerry might meet this way; he'd planned to be there
to run interference. Now it was too late. Mark wondered what had passed between the two women in his
life. How was he ever going to explain his protective and
confusing feelings for Kerry Bay to the woman who held
his heart in her keeping?

"Well?" Jessie didn't try to disguise the sharp edge
to her voice. She'd attempted to prepare herself for
Kerry, but it hadn't been enough. The lovely doll-like
creature with her great luminous green eyes, peaches-
and-cream complexion and quiet, gentle voice had given
Jessie's self-image and self-esteem a rude jolt.

"Well?" Mark followed his own thoughts. Should he
confess all of it? Tell Jessie how Kerry made him feel
wanted and needed those first bad weeks after he and

Jessie had broken off. How her youth and blatant sexual interest in him had bolstered his sorely bruised ego? No, he'd better not; Jessie wasn't looking very sympathetic at the moment. She probably wouldn't even believe him if he told her that his relationship with Kerry had so far been platonic—for reasons he preferred not to analyze more closely.

"Mark." Exasperation tinged her tone. "The mock-up, where is it?" Good Lord, couldn't he get his mind off Kerry long enough to show her the proofs? Jessie's temper raised its sleeping head. She felt like giving the aggravating, infuriating man before her a good hard shake. "Mark, I'm speaking to you."

"What? Oh, the mock-up." Mark gave her a thorough searching glance, then laughed, seeming to throw off the spell that enveloped him. Jessie eyed him cautiously. "It's over here on the board. We've got some of the best stuff you've done yet, Jess. I don't think we'll have any problem at all selling the story to *National Geographic*." He held out his hand and Jessie took it reluctantly, all too aware of the vivid reminders his touch had evoked the night before. Today was no different. Her temper died; her breath stuck in her throat. She had to send a frantic and direct message to her brain to get her lungs working again. Mark, apparently unaffected by her malaise, drew her toward the long, angled storyboard and mock-up of the article.

"What do you think, Jess?"

"Oh, it does look good. It really does." Jessie let her eyes roam over the shots he'd chosen. Most of them were favorites of her own: candid shots of the twins; Mark at the woodpile and the fire; Nell with a grin as big as all outdoors, fishing. Only the study of her youngest daughter and her starfish was absent. Jessie tried hard to hide her disappointment. It was, for her, by far the most interesting and evocative photograph she'd ever taken. "This is marvellous, even in this rough stage. This issue is going to put *Meanderings* over the top." She spun around in excitement, to find Mark only inches away.

"I think so, too. I'm going all out with this issue, Jess." Enthusiasm spilled out along with the words. "I'm going to double the run, make a big push at advertising, publicity, the works. I'm putting every cent I've got into it. And I've got a cover that will sell it all by itself."

"You do?" Jessie said numbly. His arms were on either side of her, almost as if he were blocking her escape. That was silly, she wasn't going to run away. Or was she? Jessie backed against the storyboard, taking a deep breath. Her nostrils filled with the invigorating, heady scent of his skin. Her bag slid down her arm, dropping onto the floor with a weighty thud. Mark ignored the distraction, but Jessie leaned forward, welcoming the excuse to break the heated regard of his gaze.

"Leave it, Jess," he ordered. His arm reached out to take her hand again. "Come with me. The cover mock-up is in my safe. I wanted it to be a surprise." She might have been a robot programmed to the sound of his commands, at least to the timbre of his voice. She stood passively in the middle of the room while he opened the safe and took out an ordinary manilla folder. As he spread it open on his desk, Jessie moved forward as though she'd been pulled by invisible strings.

She knew what she would see. It was Nell and the starfish. The print was of excellent quality, attesting to Mark's more sophisticated equipment. It was a kaleidoscope of color and texture, shadings of light and dark. But who had told him it was her favorite shot? "My mother," Jessie breathed. Mark didn't pretend to misunderstand.

"Last night. I told her I wanted the cover to be full of life and energy but I hadn't chosen a format or a subject as yet. She told me she considered this the best work you'd ever done. When I got back here, I took a second look at it; then everything just seemed to fall in place. Marta was right, Jess. Look at Nell. She's everything I want our kids to be: alive, energetic, in love with life and learning about life." He saw the stricken look on Jessie's face.

Mark rounded the corner of the desk in two swift strides. "I meant New England's children, Jessie, not the children I want to have with you." There was the faintest hint of sadness and resignation in his tone. Or was she only superimposing her own regrets on his words? "Don't look so frightened, Jess. That's over and done with. I won't hound you about it again."

"You didn't. I'm sorry." She let the heartfelt apology hang in the air between them a moment before continuing. "This is the kind of future we want for all the children." Jessie ordered her thoughts back to the cover, injecting a note of enthusiasm into her voice. "It's a sensational cover, Mark. It says exactly what you want it to. It shows her joy in life, in discovering nature. It's all there. Congratulations."

Mark's hands reached out to circle her waist, spinning her off her feet. "Jess, you took that shot, not me. All I did was blow up the negative and arrange the wording on the cover to least interfere with the imagery you created. We make a hell of a team." He let her slide down the taut, corded length of his body. "We do make one hell of a team. I've missed you, Jess." His voice was low and rough, barely above a whisper. His mouth swooped down to stifle her instinctive protest. Jessie held back a long moment, stiffening in his embrace before giving in to her natural, inevitable response to his touch. Jessie leaned into his embrace with no further restraint, hungry for the sensations only Mark could produce in her.

"I've missed you, too, so much. I've wanted to be with you so often." His mouth parted hers, his tongue entered to search out the satiny moistness. "Mark, don't stop...." What was she saying? He was involved with another woman and she was asking him, telling him, to make love to her. Next she would be speaking things that should never be said aloud. She'd lost her mind. "Mark, we can't..."

"Shh, Jess. Just let me hold you a minute. I'll come to my senses, I promise. But, God, how I've missed being with you and the girls." His hands framed her face, tangling in wisps of coppery hair.

Why did that simple fragment of speech snag so stubbornly on her consciousness? *Being with you and the girls.* Why did it suddenly make everything right? She couldn't understand, but then, nothing at the moment made sense. There was very little reality at all beyond the touch of Mark's hands through the thin silk of her blouse, the taste of his kisses on her lips, the heat of him burning through layers of fabric and skin to sear her soul. "This isn't right, Mark. Not anymore. We haven't solved anything... I don't believe in casual...liaisons."

"This isn't casual." Mark pressed her more tightly against the desk and his desire for her was blatant. Jessie felt the stirrings of feminine power deep in her middle. She burned from the heat of her apprehensions changing into need and then lingering on in the molten glow of renewing passion. "We can discuss our problems, Jess. We've hurt each other too much to have done that before today. Now maybe we can start to talk—but later, in my loft, after I've held you and loved you enough to think coherently. Say you'll come with me, Jess."

Several buttons of her blouse opened under the persuasive attack of his long tapered fingers. His hands played along the lacy froth of her ivory-toned chemise. Again, she wasn't wearing a bra today. He concentrated his attention on her breasts, his hands moving, circling with lazy deliberations over contracting nipples. Jessie groaned against Mark's lips. She knew she should deny him what he asked, at least insist on conversation before making love to him again, but her body refused to listen to her logic. She kissed him back, arching into the warmth of his callused palms, glorying in the resurgence of her love for him. "Yes, I'll stay a little while. But we do have to talk. Loving you again won't make our problems go away. I'm afraid it will only add to them."

"I'm beginning to understand your reservations..." Mark never finished what he was going to say. Jessie had heard it, too. The door to the corridor had slammed shut behind hurrying footsteps that were headed directly for the composing room.

"Damn, another infernal interruption." Mark stepped away, sending a stirring rush of cool air over Jessie's bare breasts. He slipped the thin silk straps back over her shoulders. She whirled away, her fingers flying to restore order to her clothing, her heart beating high and hard in her throat. Mark ran his hand through his hair distractedly and put a few more steps between them.

"Who could be coming back to the magazine this late?" She voiced her thoughts aloud.

"Mark, thank God you're still here."

Jessie turned at the fraying edge of hysteria in Kerry Bay's lilting voice. She stood silhouetted in the doorway of Mark's office.

"I don't know what to do." A tiny, melodious sob broke from Kerry's lips. She almost ran the last few steps across the room to hurl herself into Mark's arms.

"Kerry, what's the problem? Is it the children?" Mark sounded as bewildered as Jessie felt. "Has something happened to your children?"

"No." The negative was more an interpretation of Kerry's frantic gestures than an utterance. "They're with my landlady."

"Did you wreck your car?" Mark glanced over at Jessie with a purely male appeal for deliverance from a crying female. She'd know what to do. Kerry's sobbing whirlwind intrusion into his reunion with Jessie had been a shock.

He hadn't meant to seduce Jessie here and now—in truth, he wondered if he wasn't the one seduced—but he could have made things right with her if only they'd had more time. Now he was back to square one if the obdurate, uncomprehending look on Jessie's face was any indication of her mood. It was all going to go haywire again. He'd never get a chance to tell her what he'd been thinking of all these weeks. Not if she reacted like this.

Kerry's tears were soaking his shirt front. Mark dragged his attention back to her. "Kerry." He spoke as severely as her unsteady condition allowed. "Try and tell me what happened."

"The IRS." More sobs. Kerry burrowed deeper into the front of his shirt.

"The IRS?"

"Yes," Kerry wailed. "This notice was in the mail." Still sobbing, she waved the registered letter under Mark's nose. "I'm being audited by the IRS."

"Is that all?" Was there just a suggestion of impatience in his raspy baritone? Jessie's ears pricked up. Could it be that Kerry's clinging-vine loveliness was beginning to get on Mark's nerves? His long, strong arms wound around Kerry protectively. She lifted her face and gave him a smile that would have blinded Jessie if it had been turned in her direction. It wasn't. It was meant solely for Mark's benefit.

"What am I going to do, Mark? David took care of everything. When he left me I was so angry I even burned a lot of his things. How will I explain that to the IRS? How will I ever afford to pay any more money to the government?" Genuine horror seared through the crystal chimes of her voice.

Jessie felt real sympathy for Kerry's plight for the first time. An IRS audit had sent much stronger people than Kerry rushing in gibbering panic into her office at Abrahms and Mahoney. "They aren't gangsters, Kerry," she said kindly, moving over to the storyboard. Jessie scooped her bag off the floor and rummaged inside for a tissue to offer the weeping woman. "The IRS tries to be fair. They'll give you time to find your records. Couldn't you contact your ex-husband?"

"I don't know where he is for certain." She gave Jessie a defiant stare, pride firming her doll-like features, giving her a great deal more maturity. "He couldn't take it any longer," she explained defensively. "No work, no prospects for getting any. I'm not sure where he went or where he is. California, I guess. He sends checks for the kids in care of his parents whenever he can. Oh, God, they'll want to see those, won't they? I didn't keep receipts. Mark?" She started crying again.

"The deposits will be in your checkbook, Kerry. Try and get hold of yourself," Mark soothed. He looked beseechingly at Jessie once more.

Poor man. Jessie swallowed a giggle, surprised at herself as her anger bubbled away at the look of quiet desperation in his eyes. It did serve him right. Damsels in distress were notorious for being unable to extricate themselves from their dilemmas. Didn't Mark know that? His education in that respect was sadly lacking. He'd be marvelous at playing Saint George and the dragon; he'd give Robin Hood a run for his money when it came to fighting off the sheriff of Nottingham's men. But the IRS? With his princess sobbing on his shoulder? Jessie sighed. She knew what she had to do.

"Let me take you home and sort this out, Kerry. It's my business, you know. And your house is barely two blocks out of the way. Mark will see that someone gets your car back to your place."

"You'll help me?"

"I'm a CPA, remember? I'll help you all I can with the examiners. It won't be so bad, you'll see."

"Jess, would you?" Mark's gratitude was heartfelt. His smile almost made up for Jessie's renewed heartache—almost, but not quite.

"What are friends for if not to help each other in emergencies?" Jessie felt like a hypocrite. Taking charge of the high-strung Kerry and her tax audit wasn't the basis she'd envisioned for reviving her relationship with Mark.

"Jessie..." Mark seemed to hesitate. He glanced down at Kerry again, almost as if he didn't quite know how she got there, hanging on his jacket lapels, or what to do with her next. "We still have a great deal to discuss."

Kerry's head popped up. She was suddenly attentive to the conversation.

"I think we've said all we can today," Jessie replied, with a pointed look at Kerry, still adhering tightly to Mark's jacket. "Things haven't changed, not really." But they had. And not for the better. She must have been crazy to believe they had. That's what being in Mark's arms did to her reason—obliterated it.

"Jess." He looked as if he were about to give her an order. She wasn't going to stand for that. Jessie cut off what he'd been going to say.

"We'd better be leaving, Colonel." It worked. Mark set his jaw in a tight line. Jessie smiled with cool politeness. Kerry's arrival had saved her from a grave loss of common sense. She couldn't carry on a purely physical relationship with Mark, her emotions were far too deeply involved. It had been a close call. "My car's out front, Kerry. Are you ready to go?"

JESSIE TURNED from her unseeing contemplation of the bleak mid-November day. The trees were bare, the sky low and dark with moisture. It was raining now, but a short while before it had snowed. It would snow again as the temperature dropped at the end of the short afternoon. Outside, the cold east wind carried a tang of salt and the sea. Winter was ready to settle in with a vengeance.

"Bam, bam, bam. Gotcha, ya sleazeball." Jessie stared in horrified fascination as Kerry's towheaded older son spread his sturdy legs, steadied the plastic toy pistol with cupped hands—the same way she'd seen a thousand television cops and detectives do it—and calmly laid waste to half the familiar inhabitants of "Sesame Street".

"Nathan! Stop that this instant." Kerry's lovely voice had a tendency to climb shrilly when she admonished her children repeatedly. Possibly, Jessie thought from the vantage point of longer experience, because Kerry wasn't prepared to back up her directives with appropriate disciplinary action. Children had a sixth sense about such things and exploited any weakness to the hilt. Four-year-old Nathan and two-year-old Peter were nearly out of control, in Jessie's opinion.

"I'm tired of 'Sesame Street,' Mom. Make it go off. I want to watch 'The Dukes of Hazzard.'"

"I can't make it go off," Kerry said patiently, putting down the dog-eared legal pad she'd been writing on. She uncurled herself gracefully from the sofa and tugged at the cap pistol in Nathan's hand. "No more shooting."

"I bet you can't count to ten before the Count does," Jessie challenged, sliding a pencil into her topknot as she moved back into the circle of warmth and light in the middle of the living room.

"Can too," Nathan rejoined obstinately, but he gave up custody of the toy. "Wanna listen?"

"Sure." Jessie turned off the lisping rendition as she concentrated on making sense out of Kerry's checking account. "Fine, Nathan. You're a smart boy," she said, appropriately praising when Nathan's piping voice stilled momentarily. Hadn't lost her timing yet. Jessie congratulated herself.

The closing theme from the children's show wafted across the room. Forgetting his homicidal tendencies of a few moments earlier, Nathan sang along. Then shortly he bounced down onto a ratty corduroy cushion and began to take an interest in the ritual greeting of "Mister Rogers."

"You make that look so easy, Jess," Kerry said wistfully, lifting Peter into her arms. It was a refrain Jessie had grown used to hearing during her several visits to Kerry's home.

"Make what look easy?" Jessie answered distantly as she made the last entry on her checklist of details to be worked out before Kerry's appointment with the IRS agent.

"Dealing with children."

"Lots of practice. And it doesn't get easier, I'm sorry to say, only more familiar. You're doing fine. I think we've got this thing beat." Jessie changed the subject abruptly. She didn't like to be told how good she was at mothering. It made her think of Mark, how he'd shown her she could enjoy her girls again. Thinking of Mark and how she'd hurt him made her sad even after three more weeks of not seeing him. The pain of missing him wasn't less. If she was totally honest, it had increased considerably.

"How much is it going to cost me?" Kerry bent her head to nuzzle Peter's soft dark hair.

"That's the best part. Not a thing." Jessie grinned at the hopeful look Kerry darted her way. "Unless I'm very mistaken and I'm not—the IRS will end up owing you money. Kerry, you didn't take half the deductions you're entitled to." She let exasperation show in the timbre of her voice. "There's day care for the boys, interest on your loans. Why didn't you have a competent tax person do these returns for you?"

"I thought I couldn't afford to have it done professionally," Kerry confessed with a rueful shrug of her shoulders. "David took care of all our finances. He made it look so easy I just thought I could keep on doing what he'd always done." Easy tears filled Kerry's eyes, but she blinked them back.

"I see," Jessie said crisply to avoid the waterworks, but she smiled to soften the sting. She was so used to fending for herself she'd forgotten how terribly bewildering those first years after Carl's death had been.

"I've never wanted to be a liberated woman." Kerry cuddled the toddler, who responded with a wet, sticky kiss. "I just wanted to stay home and take care of my babies, never bother with taxes and insurance and having a career. I guess I'm just a throwback to another generation." She laughed a little sheepishly.

"Mothering and keeping house is the most demanding, underrated, lowest-paying job in the world, Kerry. Don't let anyone ever tell you differently. When you have to add being breadwinner to the other responsibilities, well, not so many men could do it."

"You're sounding awfully feminist today, Jess." Kerry laughed brightly and Jessie joined her, albeit reluctantly.

"I am, aren't I? Sorry. It's just that few women can enjoy the satisfaction of being full-time homemakers anymore. Especially in an economy like ours. It's very sad."

"Yes, it is. I never thought of it like that. So few ordinary families can afford to be one-paycheck households any longer." Kerry looked down at her son with a thoughtful expression.

They weren't friends exactly. Not yet. Jessie doubted they ever would be as she watched Kerry with her son. She was too soft and unassertive to appeal strongly to Jessie's independent nature. But she could give credit where credit was due. Kerry was coping the best way she knew how in a situation far more difficult even than the one that had faced Jessie seven years earlier. Carl had always supported Jessie in her educational and personal endeavors. David and Kerry obviously hadn't had that kind of relationship. Now she was a single parent surviving the best way she knew how. That similarity forged a fragile bond between the two women.

"Mom, when are we going to eat?" Nathan piped up from in front of the TV, never turning his head.

"Cookie," Peter seconded in his piping baby voice. Nathan, with his chin propped on his pudgy hands, must look a great deal like his absent father, Jessie decided. He certainly didn't resemble his petite, fine-boned mother. Peter, on the other hand, was definitely Kerry's child from the top of his curly black head to the soles of his slender pink-toed feet. He'd be a lady-killer someday.

He would be like the child Kerry would have with Mark someday.

"Are we really finished, Jess?" Jessie nodded mutely. "Great, I have a dinner date."

"How nice." Jessie's good humor had disintegrated under the stress of her musings. Now an icy blast of suspicion assailed her.

"Mark was going to take me somewhere special this evening," Kerry lamented, "but Mrs. Mollicut couldn't come out to sit with the boys. May I warm up your coffee, Jessie? It looks cold.''

"No, no, thanks." It wasn't her coffee that was cold, it was her heart. "No more coffee. I have to be going. There are so many things to do before the wedding Saturday." So far Jessie had avoided the subject of Mark Elliot by the simple expedient of ignoring any remarks Kerry made about him. She wasn't about to start discussing him now. Jessie began stuffing cancelled checks and receipts back into the shoe box where Kerry kept them in a random order that she claimed was a system uniquely her own.

"I'm sure you do have a million things to finish up. I've missed the twins' baby-sitting."

I bet you have, Jessie affirmed in silent spite.

"Mrs. Mollicut, my landlady, has been a real lifesaver. I'm afraid the boys make Mark nervous. But she has a virus and couldn't keep them all night." Kerry blushed, but it wasn't quite as captivating a reaction as it usually was, or perhaps Jessie was less inclined to be charitable after the telling personal statements.

"I'm sorry your plans have been spoiled." Jessie got the words out of her mouth with an effort.

"Yes...Jessie could I ask you something? Something personal?"

Jessie's hands tightened on her attaché case with hurting force. Good Lord, wasn't it enough she'd volunteered her time to untangle Mark's new love's financial difficulties? Did she have to play mother confessor to the couple's problems with their love life also? It was too much. "I don't think I'm the right person."

"I thought you and Mark were friends. He constantly refers to that week you spent on the island. He spends more time talking to the twins when they're baby-sitting than he does to me." An inkling of pique tempered the soft words. "You two are the same generation...closer to the same age...."

"What is it, Kerry?" Jessie resigned herself to a painful few minutes. She wondered if this little question-and-answer session would count toward qualifying her for martyrdom.

"Mark seems perfectly healthy to you, doesn't he?" Kerry wasn't looking directly at Jessie any longer. She seemed to be paying great attention to the view from her living-room window. Peter was engrossed in mashing into the carpet a chocolate chip cookie his brother had brought him from the kitchen. Nathan had returned to watching "Mister Rogers" with a handful of cookies for himself. Jessie and Kerry might have been alone.

"He did take a nasty fall on the island but..." Anxiety streaked through Jessie like cold lightning. Had Mark suffered some complications from the accident that he was hiding from her?

"No...I don't mean that kind of physical," Kerry shook her head. "I know about the fall.... This is different. I mean," she plunged ahead, aware of the quelling look on Jessie's face. "I realize at his age...men slow down...but surely before...he must have been a fantastic lover." Her words ended on a wistful sigh.

"I..." Jessie couldn't seem to get anything past the constriction in her windpipe. "I don't know what you're referring to."

"Mark seemed so passionate at first.... Then...well, I don't understand what happened. Perhaps I'm not desirable enough?" Kerry obviously hadn't paid any attention at all to Jessie's reaction to her confidences. She only wanted a sounding board for her own thoughts. The horrible suspicion that Mark had told

Kerry about their affair died aborning in Jessie's thoughts.

"You're a lovely, loving young woman, Kerry. I'm sure that's not the problem at all," Jessie managed to croak.

"I've rushed him, I suppose. I mean older men probably don't like the woman to take the initiative. The first night he brought me home, well, it was star shine and moonbeams. I'm afraid I got a little carried away...." Kerry let the sentence trail off with delicate if delayed tact. "It was just like with...my ex-husband. And Mark seemed to want everything I've been missing. A home, a family, someone to take care of. I have to make up my mind, Jess. You've got your life so much in control. What should I do?"

"Kerry, I don't know how to advise you on this." That was the biggest understatement yet. Jessie's mind was in turmoil. Had it gone so far that Mark was ready to propose to Kerry?

"Mark could make my life so much easier, and I could give him a home, babies of his own." Jessie suddenly understood the meaning of the old cliché about feeling a knife twist in one's heart. She had to fold her hands in her lap to keep from pressing them against her breast to try and contain the pain.

"Mark Elliot will make a wonderful father and husband. I know that without any doubt." Jessie's voice was low and strained, devoid of emotion.

"But I'm not sure anymore. I've been talking to David, Jessie. I got his new number from his mother. He's changed, I think. Or maybe I have. I don't know. A few weeks ago everything seemed so simple. I still find Mark terribly exciting despite the difference in our ages. Perhaps I'm imagining this thing about his physical limitations? Perhaps tonight...after tonight, I'll be able to tell more about my own feelings...."

Jessie thought she was going to strangle. There wasn't any oxygen left in the overheated little room. Mark was going to spend the night here with this woman. "I have to be going, Kerry. I'm sure you and Mark will work this out."

"We'll see," Kerry said sweetly. "Mark will be here any minute. Won't you stay and have a glass of wine with us? He's bringing everything but the candles. He offered to cook for us here after I told him Mrs. Mollicut couldn't watch the boys. Still, I would have liked to see his place."

"His place?" Jessie's tone was unnaturally high and sharp. "He was going to cook you dinner at his place?" The bastard!

"They say he has the most adorable loft above the magazine." Kerry was clearly puzzled by the abrupt change in Jessie's attitude. "He's quite a cook. He's doing some exotic lamb dish. Jessie, are you choking? I told you not to drink that cold coffee. Do you want a slap on the back?"

"I'm fine," Jessie lied, holding up a restraining hand. *Curried lamb stew*. How could he? Her temper surged into control of her thoughts and her tongue. "I've heard he does that dish very well."

"And he's bringing dessert, too, Amaretto mousse. Doesn't that sound romantic? Oh, there's the doorbell."

Amaretto mousse! The fink. Jessie struggled into her coat and pulled on her gloves over hands shaking with temper.

"Mark, come in." Kerry's greeting floated blithely into the void in her thoughts. "Jessie's still here. We've finished up the stuff for the IRS. Wasn't she wonderful to have stuck by me these past few weeks?''

"Jessie's a trooper.'' Mark sounded as disconcerted as Jessie felt to see her in Kerry's apartment. He was carrying a large covered wicker hamper in one hand and a bottle of wine in the other. His thick, red-plaid wool jacket complemented the mahogany darkness of his skin. His hair held droplets of half-melted snow, or was it half-frozen rain? Jessie's thoughts skittered around the edges of her brain refusing to dwell on anything too long for fear she'd shatter into anger or tears. She wasn't sure which emotion was closer to the surface.

"How've you been, Jessie? We've missed you at the magazine. There's an assignment I'd like to talk to you about...."

Both the boys had jumped up at Mark's entrance. Now they came surging forward, creating a distraction that allowed Jessie to find her handbag and her attaché case under cover of its noise and movement.

"I don't think I'm going to have time for any free-lancing for quite a while," she mumbled. When she looked up again both children were firmly affixed to Mark's pant legs. Kerry was laughing, taking the hamper and the wine. Mark bent down to pick up the smallest boy and run his hand through Nathan's hair in a father-and-son gesture that left it standing up in short tufts all over his head.

"Please, stay for a glass of wine, Jess," Kerry invited, smiling in happy anticipation, as if she'd made up her mind about her future in the few short moments since Mark's arrival. Jessie felt despair settle like a lead weight in her middle.

"No, I'm afraid I can't. Mother needs a last fitting on her dress. Hi, her fiancé, will be here tomorrow and the spare room isn't ready. Nell has so much homework these days...." Jessie gave up the attempt to make excuses. "But thank you for asking." Kerry shrugged and turned toward the kitchen to deposit the hamper.

"Jess, about that assignment." Mark wasn't smiling. He was deadly serious. Jessie couldn't see that. All she could see were the happy children in his arms. The children she'd refused to give him. Why shouldn't he be here, with Kerry, a woman who could make his dreams come true?

"No, Mark. I really am far too busy. Please, get someone else for it. I have to go."

"Good-bye, Jessie." Kerry stuck her head around the kitchen door before Mark could answer. He moved a step closer to Jessie but she sidestepped him agilely as she headed for the door.

"Jessie." Peter still clung to his shoulder, sticky cookie-covered hands in his dark hair. Mark jerked his head back instinctively. Nathan's shrill little-boy voice cut off what he was about to say as he bounced excitedly against the tension of Mark's outstretched hand.

"Higher, higher, Uncle Mark. I want to jump higher. Lift me up. Way up."

"Thanks for the invitation to your mother's wedding, Jessie," Kerry called across the room. "I'm sure Mark will be there to help me with the boys. I doubt if Mrs. Mollicut will be up and around by Saturday."

"What? I...sure I will." Mark looked almost trapped, or was that her own imagination painting the dim afternoon light in shades she still so desperately wanted to see? Mark at the wedding. Jessie hadn't counted on that. There'd been no invitation addressed to him in her mother's spidery scrawl.

"You're both very welcome." Why had she tendered the verbal invitation to Kerry at the beginning of the week? Naturally, she would assume she could bring a guest, and naturally, it would be Mark Elliot. It would be a fabulously ironic joke if she hadn't played it on herself.

"Jessie, we have to talk." Mark's tone of command didn't phase Jessie at all this time. She was too numb for it to penetrate. She shook her head, moving toward the door.

Kerry's melodious voice drifted back to Jessie as she shut the door far too quietly behind her. "Mark, this mousse looks absolutely sinfully delicious."

Chapter Ten

"Mrs. Parker...Mrs. Parker...Mother!" Jessie let a note of amused, tolerant exasperation slip into her voice.

The newly married Mrs. Parker swung around from the tray of assorted cheeses, olives and pickled onions she was inspecting with a critical eye. "Mrs. Parker? Oh, that's me!" Marta's laughter was as bright as the sweetheart roses in the bouquet on the kitchen table. "Don't tell Hi I didn't even blink an eye when you called me that. He'll be insulted. I'll have to get used to it in a hurry."

"I don't think it will take you all that long or be that difficult a task," Jessie said as she uncovered the plastic wrap from a tray of meats provided by the supermarket's deli counter. "This stuff looks so good. I'm starved. I think I missed lunch."

"I know you did. You were hanging crepe paper bells in the living room when the rest of us ate lunch." Jessie's brother and his family, along with Marta's sister, Lettie, had arrived from Pennsylvania the day before and were bivouacked in nearly every room. Her house was filled to overflowing, but the addition of so many helping hands had made the last minute wedding preparations go more smoothly. The private candlelight ceremony had been lovely.

"Jess, are you okay?" Marta cut in on Jessie's thoughts. "You've beginning to look a little peaked to me."

"I'm fine, Mom, just daydreaming about the wedding. And don't say that. Do you know how hard I've worked to lose twelve pounds?" Jessie frowned severely, hurrying to change the subject. She didn't look her best, she knew; although the teal-blue silk dress was especially becoming to her coloring. She just hadn't been sleeping or eating well. Dieting and the press of Marta's wedding preparations was as good an excuse as any for her malaise. Mark Elliot, of course, was the reason.

"You look better with a little more meat on your bones," Marta pronounced. "Hi was telling me so just this morning."

"I have plenty of meat on my bones," Jessie said belligerently. "And Hi is notoriously prejudiced toward well-endowed ladies. Now, where's the champagne for toasts?"

"On the back porch. Why take up room in the fridge when it's only a few degrees above freezing out there?" She handed the hors d'oeuvre tray to Ann as she wafted through the kitchen on three-inch heels amid a cloud of perfume. "Put this on the dining-room table, honey, to the left of the cake," Marta instructed.

"You made the prettiest bride, Grandma. But where did you get that awful apron you're wearing?"

"In the bottom of the linen drawer. I don't intend to spend my wedding reception trying to hide a stain on my dress," Marta retorted sharply, glancing down at the all concealing, faded cotton garment. "I'll take it off before I leave the kitchen."

Jessie kicked the back door shut with her heel as Ann made an undulating exit through the swinging door to the dining room. "What was that all about?" She held a bottle of champagne in each hand. A third was tucked under her left arm.

"Nothing. I'll call Tim to open those." Marta stuck her head through the dining-room pass-through to summon Jessie's older brother. He appeared in the kitchen moments later looking ill at ease in a vested suit and tie. Jessie was so much more used to seeing him in faded denim work pants or worn jeans and T-shirts. He was as tall as Mark, but broader, heavier. He reminded Jessie so much of their father, with his long, serious face, beaked nose and slightly prominent ears. Tonight he looked very handsome in his sister's eyes and she told him so.

"You always did take after your father," Marta added to the compliment.

"And you were the prettiest bride in the world," Tim responded in kind. "After Helen," he added as an afterthought. Jessie's sharp-tongued sister-in-law was entertaining the Reverend Armstrong in the living room. The minister's Down East accent never failed to captivate the other woman, and when the Reverend had an appreciative audience, it broadened out to the consistency of good chowder.

Tim dealt with the wine efficiently and in a few moments he was rewarded with three satisfying pops. "A toast, ladies," Tim proposed expansively as he poured three brimming glasses from the tray on the pass-through ledge. "To many long happy years for Mom in her new life."

"To your new love and your new home in Florida," Jessie added. Marta put down her half-empty glass with a ringing chime of crystal on wood.

"Oh, Jess. I'm going to miss you all so." Marta's eyes looked suspiciously bright with unshed tears.

"Mom, for heaven's sake. We've been through all this." Tim remained silent. He'd gone over the same ground with his mother earlier. He'd let Jessie handle this round. He continued to fill champagne glasses.

"I don't know if I'll even like Florida," Marta began the now familiar litany.

"You'll have plenty of time to adjust, spending your honeymoon in California visiting Hi's children." Jessie cataloged points as she took an empty dark green wine bottle from her brother.

"That's the problem. What will his children think of me? I barely remember them from the years they still lived in Pennsylvania."

"You'll knock Hi's kids off their feet. Don't tell me you've forgotten how old Rudy Parker used to make excuses to come over to our house when he knew you were baking pumpkin pie?" Tim broke in patiently. "Aren't you spending Thanksgiving at his place in La Jolla?"

"Yes, we are," Marta answered thoughtfully, seeing Tim's point.

"I rest my case." He grinned, passing Jessie the second empty bottle.

"But his daughter's..." Marta trailed off, biting her lips.

"They'll love you because they can't help but see how happy you've made their father," Jessie replied firmly. She stepped forward, winding her arms around Marta's plump, silk-clad shoulders to give her a hug, avoid-

ing the matching silk roses nestled in the small veiled hat
she wore. It made her mother look a little like pictures
of the Queen Mother, Jessie decided, except that Marta's hat was far more sedate.

"Hi is going to be the center of your life from now
on, Mom, but we'll always be there for you," Tim affirmed gruffly. He added a second giant bear hug to
Jessie's gesture of reassurance. "It's the best thing that
could happen to you."

On those words the groom pushed open the swinging door and stepped into the kitchen. "Uh-oh, am I
interrupting a family conference?" His voice was so
kind and so filled with happiness that Jessie couldn't
restrain her smile.

His dark old-fashioned tux jacket strained a little over
the black cummerbund stretched across his paunch. The
bald spot on top of his head caught and reflected the
overhead lights. It was plain to see Marta considered
him the most handsome man in the world.

"Just a little filial advice to the bride," Jessie said
with a laugh.

"I think Mom has a case of the honeymoon jitters,"
Tim said jokingly in a dry voice.

"I have no such thing," Marta returned in a huff.
"Don't be silly, you two. I may be your mother but I
can still teach you a thing or two about life. Hi Parker,
take this champagne out to the cake table and don't spill
it on the carpet. We just had it cleaned."

"Yes, my dear." He shuffled over to the tray. "Anything else I should be seeing to, my love?" Marta giggled and gave him a playful, admonishing shake of her
finger.

"Only having a good time," Jessie ordered. "Now shoo, both of you. This kitchen is beiginning to resemble Grand Central Station."

When they were alone again, Marta gave Jessie a level stare. "I still don't know about spending the next three weeks with his children."

"They'll love you, especially in that hat."

"Jessie, don't be facetious." Marta's tone was stringent but she looked pleased at the compliment. "It is a lovely hat."

"And you're a lovely person. We'll discuss this again when you get back from California."

"I am looking forward to the trip. We've had so little time alone together these past two weeks..." She let the sentence trail off. "Jessie."

Sensing a lecture on her sidetracked love affair with Mark, Jessie hurriedly busied herself hunting for a plate of fresh vegetables and herb dip in the overcrowded refrigerator. "Mom, the girls and I will be fine alone," she finally answered into the weighted silence.

"I'm not worried about the girls now, Jess. It's you. Have you settled anything with Mark?"

"There's nothing to settle. Nothing's changed between us." That wasn't true. Kerry Bay had changed everything. At least to Jessie's way of thinking.

"Mark loves you."

"Oh, Mom." Jessie placed the tray on the table, pretending to study the colorful array calmly, unemotionally. "He cares about me, yes, but I don't think he loves me or we wouldn't have so much trouble communicating our feelings."

"Love doesn't always make you glib and articulate, Jessie. Often it makes it extremely difficult to say what's most important to you. He loves you." It was hard to refute Marta's logic. But Jessie tried.

"You never see the man but you say that. It's only because you're looking at everything through rose-colored glasses."

"Don't be silly," Marta chided with an agitated swoop of her hands. "It's obvious to a blind man."

"It's obvious he's having an affair with Kerry Bay." There, she'd said it. Jessie didn't think she could feel any more miserable about it, but saying the words aloud tore a fresh wound in her heart.

"Are you positive?" Marta looked momentarily taken aback. She fiddled with her wedding rings, then untied the apron strings and slid the garment off her shoulders.

Jessie nodded mournfully, rearranging radishes in precise geometric designs on the platter. "Yes. He cooked dinner for her last Tuesday night: curried lamb and Amaretto mousse."

"Damning evidence." Marta snorted but she looked puzzled as she shoved the apron onto a towel rack under the sink.

"He spent the night with her afterward," Jessie whispered past the lump in her throat. "I'm sure of that."

"On whose authority?"

"Kerry said..." Jessie spun to face her mother. "What does it matter? He cooked for her. For me that's proof enough. I should know. That's his specialty. He's got it down to an art. His seduction techniques are highly developed." She couldn't keep the bitterness out of her voice and didn't try.

"So are his survival techniques." Marta evidently wasn't going to pursue the matter further. She looked past Jessie, through the window-sized opening in the wall. The shuttered doors had been folded back to facilitate serving the forty or so guests assembled in the living room. One tray of champagne glasses remained, the pale amber liquid dancing with millions of tiny bubbles. "Look at the poor man." Marta made a clucking sound with her tongue against her teeth.

Jessie obediently turned her head but kept her eyes squeezed shut. She knew what she'd see. Mark, surrounded by Kerry's beautiful children and their mother smiling up at him with adoring, worshipful green eyes. "Kerry's boys are very attached to Mark."

"I'll say," Marta replied caustically. "They're crawling all over him."

Jessie opened her eyes. The tableau she'd been expecting was there all right, but there were subtle differnces in the scenario. Nathan was tugging none too gently on Mark's pant leg, his face screwed into an unattractive childish grimace as he made his obvious displeasure at not being allowed to sample the three-tiered wedding cake abundantly clear. Peter, even more obviously needed his diaper changed—there was a suspicious dark patch on the sleeve of Mark's well-tailored, dark gray, pin-striped suit and the back of Peter's navy-blue rompers. Kerry did have a dreamy, distant look in her eye but she was staring past Mark as though lost in thoughts of her own, far removed from her surroundings and the man at her side.

Tim's equine face appeared in the pass-through once again, blocking Jessie's view. "Hey, Mom, Jess, come on. I want to get some Polaroids of you and Hi with the cake before you cut it. I know Jessie is official court photographer, but at least you can take these instant shots along to California and show them off to the Parker clan.''

"That's a marvellous idea, Timothy. I'll be out in a moment." Tim made a face at the use of his seldom-heard baptismal name but obligingly disappeared from the opening with the second tray of goblets.

Jessie made a grab for one of the glasses of sparkling wine before it got out of reach. She downed it in one long swallow.

"Better watch how much you imbibe, my dear," Marta said as she left the kitchen. "You know how low your tolerance to alcohol is."

"I'm perfectly capable of holding my liquor," Jessie answered. Then she smiled. Brilliant bursts of effervescence were going off behind her eyes. If she closed them it was as good as a fireworks display on the Fourth of July. She decided to have another glass of champagne and inspected the three bottles sitting on the counter.

Two were definitely dead soldiers. The third held a scant few ounces of the starry liquid. Jessie refilled her goblet and sipped more slowly at the sparkling wine. Glass emptied, she picked up the vegetable tray and headed into the dining room. Armed with the champagne's false courage, she felt able to face Mark and Kerry for the first time. She couldn't hide in the kitchen all night. People would notice.

She never had a chance to test her newfound resolve for Kerry pushed open the painted door from the far side. "I'm glad I caught you, Jessie. Is there anything I can do to help?" she asked, catching sight of the tray.

"No, thank you, Kerry. Everything's under control." Jessie tried to be as polite as possible. A wayward hiccup punctuated her words. The champagne seemed to have gone straight to her head, probably because of her empty stomach.

"It was a lovely ceremony," Kerry went on. "I love candlelight weddings. David and I had a small ceremony very similar to your mother's." Kerry smiled softly to herself.

Jessie narrowed brown eyes at the younger woman, blinking once or twice to bring her into focus. Had Mark asked her to marry him? That possibility would account for the dreamy look in her eyes. Pain streaked through Jessie with the speed of light. She needed another glass of champagne. It was an effective over-the-counter anesthetic. She leaned around Kerry's slim figure and called her brother's name. "Tim, bring me another glass of champagne, will you?"

"Will do, Jess." Tim handed her the glass through the opening and gave her a curious look. "Are you sure you're all right? Never known you to be such a toper before tonight. Better watch the stuff. It's potent."

"Oh, shut up and go take your pictures," Jessie muttered with a brilliant hazy smile to take the sting out of the words.

"Sure thing, Jess." Tim swung his perplexed gaze in Kerry's direction, seemed to make a connection that had eluded him before and disappeared back into the noisy gathering of laughing guests.

"I thought I'd tell you how I made out at the audit yesterday," Kerry said.

"I'd forgotten about it," Jessie said truthfully, but not very tactfully. "How did it go?" She tried to inject a note of genuine interest into the question to cover her lapse of manners. Another hiccup made her cover her mouth with her hand.

"Very well. You were right, Jessie. I'm going to get several hundred dollars back plus interest. Isn't that marvellous?"

"It certainly is." Jessie stared down at her glass. It was empty again.

"I'm going to use the money to take a trip. Mark's offered me an advance on my salary."

"How nice."

Kerry seemed ill at ease. She glided over to the table where Marta's bouquet still rested. She picked up the cascade design of pink sweetheart roses and baby's breath, breathing deeply of the sweet, delicate fragrance. "I've been talking to David again this week." It wasn't what Jessie had braced herself to hear. She shot Kerry an almost sober glance.

"Your ex-husband?"

Kerry nodded shyly. "He wants us to come and visit him. He hasn't seen the boys since Peter was ten months old. He has a job in San Francisco, a nice apartment...."

Jessie began pleating the skirt of her teal-blue shirtwaist, then made herself stop the nervous gesture. She was having trouble keeping track of her thoughts. It seemed Kerry was talking about seeing her ex-husband again. But what about Mark?

"I've learned an awful lot about myself these past couple of months. You've been a big help, Jessie."

"Me?" Jessie was genuinely surprised by the last twist the conversation had taken. A little more of the fuzzy champagne haze cleared from her brain.

"Yes, you. You've shown me just how successful a woman can be alone. I've looked at my own behavior a lot differently lately. I still don't want to be assertive and domineering...." Jessie thought she detected a gentle note of criticism in the words, but ignored it. "But I realize I didn't contribute in my relationship with David. I let him shoulder all our burdens. I wanted him to take care of me. That was wrong. Marriage should truly be a partnership. I didn't hold up my end of the bargain. I wasn't there for him when he needed me."

Jessie found herself stirring the herb dip with a serving spoon. The room revolved slowly around her whenever she looked up, so she concentrated on the green-speckled dip. Kerry was telling her something very important but all Jessie could understand was that Mark was going to have his heart broken again. His name on Kerry's lips halted her useless agitation of the sour-cream-and-chive concoction.

"Mark's been marvelous to me these past weeks. I don't think I can ever repay him for his kindness." Jessie looked up in time to see the enchanting blush steal over Kerry's high well-defined cheekbones.

Jessie dropped the spoon. A dollop of sour cream landed with a slight plop on the teal-blue silk, just above her heart. She tucked in her chin to stare at it mournfully. They were lovers and now Kerry was going to leave him to be reunited with her ex-husband. Poor Mark.

"He's such a wonderful, caring, gentle man. He'd take care of me for the rest of my life. But suddenly... I'm not sure that's what I want any longer. And I think I should explain...."

"He is a gentle, caring man." Jessie said into thin air. "And passionate." She could have bitten off her tongue once the words were out.

"Well, yes..." Kerry agreed, nonplussed. "I only hope..."

"Kerry, I have to get this sour cream off my dress before the stain sets. How stupid of me to be so clumsy." Jessie continued to ramble as she dabbed at the stain with a paper towel from the holder near the stove. She had to get away from Kerry. She needed fresh air to clear her whirling brain.

"I'll help," Kerry offered.

"No, please excuse me." Jessie made a move for the outside door but never got more than a foot from the counter before the swinging door opened again.

"Grand Central Station," Jessie muttered to herself. Before her, Mark held Kerry's youngest son in a gingerly fashion.

"Poopie, Mom." Peter grinned, showing a mouthful of tiny, sharp white teeth.

"Oh, Petey. Why didn't you tell Mommy you had to go potty. I thought you were a so-big-boy now," Kerry scolded, shaking a pearl-tipped finger under the child's nose. He grinned unrepentantly.

"Gross," came the succinct reply. Nell had drifted in to survey the scene. "I'll show you where you can change him, Mrs. Bay," she said politely, catching Jessie's eye. She was dressed in a pair of violet, slim-legged dress pants, a lacy pale-orchid blouse and angora pullover in a darker shade of orchid. She was not quite as ready to dress up as the twins in their complementing thirties-style jersey dresses but looked very grown-up all the same.

"Thanks, Nell. You look very nice in that color. So grown-up." Kerry echoed Jessie's sentiments easily, taking the little boy from Mark's arms. "How old are you now, Nell?"

"Thirteen and a half. Almost," Nell added the conditional rider.

"Old enough to baby-sit, are you?" Kerry inquired meaningfully as Nell preceded her out of the kitchen.

"I sure am."

"Whew," Mark said with real feeling. He surveyed his wet sleeve with a jaundiced eye.

Jessie turned back to the counter. "You'd better go back with the others. Mom and Hi will be cutting the cake as soon as I get out there with the camera." Jessie looked around distractedly. "Good Lord, where is my camera?"

"I believe I saw it on the mantelpiece," Mark replied, moving several steps closer.

"Yes, you're right." Jessie darted to the left, side-stepping his tall, imposing figure. She stopped short. "Oh, darn, I forgot this damned stain." The pleasant daze of alcohol was wearing off. Jessie wished she had another glass, but the bottle was empty.

"Let me help." Mark's voice was a raspy baritone that acted so potently on her senses. Immediately the half-dizzy feeling returned.

"Anything else to go out to the buffet table?" Lyn asked from the pass-through. She gave Mark a friendly smile.

"Just this tray." Jessie pointed to the offending veggies. She wasn't about to touch it again. Mark scooped it up, handing it to Lyn. "I'll be out in a minute to take the pictures. I have a spot on my dress," Jessie explained with exaggerated care.

"You should have worn that awful old apron, not Grandma," Ann said wisely as she joined her sibling at the opening in time to accept the dish of herb dip from Mark. "She was right about getting something on her dress." She eyed her mother's stained gown leniently.

"Move your corsage over to cover it. Nothing will show in the pictures that way."

They were gone. Suddenly, in a house filled to bursting with people, Jessie was totally alone with Mark.

"We have to talk, Jess." He was tired of playing Mr. Nice Guy. Jessie needed a firm hand on the reins. He'd figured that out. She'd run him ragged otherwise.

"Not now, Mark. There are so many things going on," Jessie answered the challenging statement repressively.

"Someplace private," Mark plowed on. "Now." There was so much they needed to settle between them. His patience was at an end. "Lead the way."

"Yes, sir, Colonel. Will my darkroom do?" Jessie mumbled contrarily but her eyes sought deep into his. Mark kept his gaze deliberately non-committal. He wasn't going to take the chance of scaring her off again or setting off her unpredictable temper, either. That had happened too often in the past. He had to work fast. He couldn't count on more than a few minutes alone with her.

In the converted pantry Jessie switched on a dim overhead bulb and went directly to the mirror over the deep, old-fashioned double sinks. She began to unpin her corsage but her fingers felt like sticks of wood.

Mark brushed her fingers away and pulled out the balky long-shafted florist's pin. "Where do you want this?" His gaze was bold and heated. Silver flecks were shot through the blue depths. Jessie felt the swirling currents of desire between them. Fascination snagged her will, held her still, when she knew she should be running for the living room as fast her legs would carry her.

Jessie licked dry lips. "Just move it to the other side
To cover the stain." She wished her voice didn't sound
so breathless and whispery.

Mark's fingers brushed the skin of her throat as he
pushed aside the collar. Jessie shivered in pleasurable
anticipation. She'd missed his touch so desperately. She
wondered miserably how long it would take her to adjust
just to living without it. Probably the rest of her life.

"There." Mark stepped back to survey his handiwork. "All hidden. No one will ever know how careless you were." Was there strain in Mark's voice despite
the light tone of the quip? Jessie wanted to believe there
was. And not because he was embarrassed to be alone
with her. His fingers lingered on the swell of her breast
for a fraction of a second longer. A fine tremor coursed
through his hand.

Jessie took a deep breath. She had to know. The
question was eating a hole inside her. Kerry had hinted
she was assertive and domineering. Well, she would be.
Jessie came out with it point blank.

"Are you Kerry Bay's lover?"

"What?" Mark seemed genuinely surprised. His
finger brushed over the petals in her corsage with deliberate restraint. His eyes widened a moment, then
narrowed in contemplation.

"Why do you ask that, Jessie?"

"Because I care about you a great deal. If Kerry can
give you what you want—a home, your own children,
love—then I won't stand in your way." Jessie didn't feel
particularly gallant as she said it. She felt like crying.
"But don't keep doing this to me, Mark, please." She
snapped her mouth shut before she gave herself away
even more. She hadn't said she still loved him but she
might as well have.

"Doing what?" he queried softly.

"This..." Jessie waved her hand agitatedly between them, blurting out the word in pain and growing anger. He couldn't be that dense. He was baiting her. "Being so close...touching you..." she ended lamely, dropping her gaze to the knot of his discreetly patterned gray-and-black tie.

"Do you mean saying 'I love you,' then asking you for commitments you can't make?" Mark's voice was even and low, but his words demanded an answer.

"Yes." Jessie's chin came up. Pride gave her the courage to continue. "Oh, Mark. I'm not noble. I can't stand it any longer. Do you love Kerry?"

"I do care for her as you said," Mark replied with equal honesty, "but not in that way, Jess."

"You aren't sleeping with her?" If he was sleeping with Kerry it would mean he was committed. She knew him well enough to be sure of that. Causal sex wasn't his style. She was scared to death to hear what he had to say, but equally afraid not to ask.

"No." The answer came directly on the heels of her question.

"You didn't try to seduce her with curried lamb and Amaretto mousse?" Jessie was suspicious now. That teasing, sparking glint of private amusement was in his eyes. She bristled. "'Fess up."

"I was afraid you'd figure that one out." Mark looked down at his hands. Somehow they'd captured and held Jessie's small, pale ones. She felt so good. He was having trouble concentrating on anything but her, but time was running out. Someone was probably looking for her already.

He took a quick deep breath. It was heady with the fragrance of her hair, piled in soft curls on top of her head. There were roses and baby's breath twisted in the shining mass. Her skin was soft and cool. "Kerry seemed to expect it of me," he said with patently false innocence. He had to keep this stage of the proceedings as light as possible, but it was the hardest task he'd ever set himself. He needed Jessie in a responsive mood for the second, most important stage of the negotiations.

"Mark Elliot, you don't expect me to believe she seduced you?" Spirit returned to light Jessie's expressive face from deep within.

"Well, not exactly," He grinned sheepishly. One dark brow quirked upward, meeting a wave of thick black hair on his forehead. "I thought I needed to change with the times, Jess. And I was hurt." His words were serious now. "I admit I needed the ego boost. I could have made love to Kerry numerous times, but you were always there before my eyes. I couldn't do that to her or to myself. It made me so damn mad those first few weeks, having you there between us like a ghost. Maybe that was part of the reason I let it go on so long. I don't know." He shrugged broad shoulders. The rustle of his fine wool suit was loud in the quiet of the old pantry. "Then Halloween night, when you tripped over your own two feet—"

"It was that damn cloak," Jessie said, defending herself.

"It doesn't matter. I only knew I had you in my arms again. It was no use trying to pretend any longer that I was over you."

"Then Kerry started having problems with the IRS," Jessie said, drawing her own conclusions.

"She needed support. Her dependence was flattering but physically, things just never worked out—so to speak."

"Details," Jessie pressed boldy, sensing an advantage.

"Maybe I am too old to make love in the back seat of cars?" Jessie seriously doubted that, but didn't voice the conviction aloud. "I did intend to spend that night with Kerry, to lay my own demons to rest, to get you out of my system."

"But..." Jessie prodded hopefully.

"Peter developed a croupy cough and Nathan had nightmares.... Kerry lets him sleep with her when he cries at night. I figured there wasn't room for both of us in her bed," Mark added laconically. "Psychologically speaking, don't you believe that's damaging for a small child, Jess?"

Jessie didn't answer. What precisely was he trying to tell her.

"Kerry's young and vulnerable. She needed help and guidance. I'm a sucker for damsels in distress. I probably always will be," Mark admitted with endearing honesty.

"An officer and a gentleman," Jessie said musingly, the anger dying out of her tone.

"I've come to the conclusion that I'm too old to take on Kerry and her problems. I want a woman who I can relate to in more than a physical way, who looks at the world the way I do." He had to talk fast. He never got more than ten minutes alone with Jessie. With all the extra people in the house tonight, the odds were against even that long. "Jessie..."

"Mark—" Jessie pressed a finger to his lips, forestalling what he'd been about to say "—it won't do either of us any good to drag this out further. I love you, I probably always will, but I haven't changed my mind. I've made peace with myself. Perhaps I didn't articulate my feelings very well on the subject, but I still don't want to have more children...."

Mark pulled her close, avoiding the corsage on her breast but fitting their lower bodies together so intimately that Jessie gasped. "That's what I've been trying to tell you, Jess. I have—"

"Jess! Where are you? Mom and Hi want to cut the cake. We need you for the pictures." Tim's voice cut across Mark's words.

"Damn it!" Jessie had never heard him swear quite so forcefully before. He released her. "We've got to do something about all the interruptions in this house, Jess. I didn't even get a chance to kiss you. We'll discuss this later." It was Colonel Elliot speaking again. Mark ran a agitated hand through his dark hair, waving her ahead of him out of the old pantry into the brightly lighted kitchen and the duties that awaited her there.

THE NEXT FORTY-FIVE MINUTES passed in a kind of blur for Jessie. It was almost as though someone had smeared Vaseline on her camera lens, giving everything that hazy out-of-focus look that was usually referred to as romantic. To Jessie it was merely confusing.

At one point, during a lull in the festivities while Tim was rearranging the living-room furniture to accommodate dancing to the big-bands' stereo records he'd chosen to honor the newlyweds, Jessie noticed Mark and Kerry were gone. She felt a sharp tug of anxiety around her heart.

Had Mark changed his mind about the lovely young woman? Had something occurred other than the fact that Kerry had caught Marta's bouquet—thrown from the half landing—to push Mark back into her arms? Something like the fact that they hadn't settled anything back there in her darkroom? Was Mark simply fed up with competing for her attention?

Two more glasses of champagne hadn't done anything to curb her overactive imagination, Jessie decided self-derisively as she chatted near the cake table with Aunt Lettie and Reverend Armstrong. What had Mark been going to tell her when they were interrupted? There were so many possibilities that she surreptitiously refused to let her heart or mind dwell on the most wonderful discovery of all.

He still loved her. He wanted to work out the differences. That meant compromise in Jessie's book, and for her there could be no compromise on the issue of having a baby. Her spirits plummeted again. She had another glass of champagne.

Jessie was dancing with Hi to an old Glenn Miller record when Mark materialized at her new step-father's shoulder. He dwarfed Hiram, who graciously relinquished Jessie into the younger man's arms. Mark pulled her close. His suit jacket was still cold from the November night air and a few melting snowflakes dotted the dark wool. Jessie wondered vaguely when it had started snowing. Held tightly against his chest, Jessie could feel the heat of his body reach out to enfold her.

Out of the corner of her eye, Jessie caught sight of her mother in the arms of the Reverend Armstrong. Tim and Helen moved slowly beside them. In a corner of the couch pushed up against the bay window, the twins kicked off their shoes and curled up, giggling merrily, maybe at the choice of music or maybe for other more private reasons. Jessie wondered dreamily if they'd been sampling the champagne behind her back. She'd have to have a talk with them in the morning about the dangers of alcohol, she decided before giving up to the purely sensual pleasure of being held in Mark's arms.

"I missed you," she said in dreamy contentment.

"I had to take Kerry and the boys home. It was past their bedtime. Seems like they've lost their regular babysitters of late." He glanced over at the twins.

"Their idea of playing Cupid," Jessie murmured, enlightened. "Did it work?" She cocked her head and searched the rugged contours of his face.

"It didn't hurt," Mark admitted with a grin. "Guerrilla tactics, pretty ingenious. A twelve o'clock curfew for a man my age is pretty offsetting." He changed the subject, "Kerry's going to have a long day tomorrow."

"Really?" Jessie didn't care about Kerry Bay any longer, but curiosity died hard even when you were tipsy on champagne.

"Really." Mark looked down at her indulgently. He pulled her closer, ignoring the interested glances of Jessie's relatives and offspring. He'd have to get used to it. Privacy was going to be a scarce commodity in their marriage. "They're leaving for California to visit the boys' father."

"Flying?" One word replies worked best, Jessie had found. Her tongue didn't seem to have as much trouble with them.

"Driving. I have to give the girl credit. She's trying hard to grow up in a hurry. Enough of Kerry. We've done all we can for her. Jessie, marry me. Now. Right away."

"Kerry caught Mom's bouquet. She should be first," Jessie said, musingly picking at a speck of lint on his lapel. The stereo moved into "Moonlight Serenade," Jessie's favorite Miller classic. She started to hum along.

"It's possible she could be," Mark said. "At least at the rate of progress I'm making. I wish her and David luck. They've got two strikes against them already, but if they're both willing to try, who knows?"

"I think Kerry is. Is that why you didn't break it off with her sooner? I thought..." Jessie gave up trying to put her musings into words. In his way, too, Mark had been helping Kerry mature. All these deductions were too difficult. She was too tired. A nagging memory tugged at her; had Mark asked her to marry him again a few moments ago or was she dreaming? She really should ask him to clarify the matter.

"I know exactly what you thought. *I* thought we'd settled that matter out in the pantry. Jessie, are you drunk?"

"A little, but happy, mostly." The matter of Kerry Bay was settled as far as she was concerned. Mark would always be a sucker for a small, helpless woman. She wouldn't want him any other way. He was a good, caring man. And as long as his attentions to other women were strictly avuncular...

"Jessie, you haven't answered me." Her head was on his shoulder. His arms were riding low on her waist. Their weight was heavy and comforting. Jessie nestled closer, her arms around his neck. She ignored the interested, watchful eyes of her offspring, her mother, her stepfather and her brother.

"Will you marry me, Jess? You still haven't said yes." There was a note of pleading in his low, rough voice that Jessie couldn't resist.

"But we haven't solved everything—"

"We will. We'll work on it together. I still want a baby with you, but I can understand your feelings, too. If you change your mind later I'll be the happiest man on earth. If you don't, I'll still be happy because I have you and the girls. Maybe I can't give up my dreams just yet, not altogether, but having you in my life will give me other dreams to cherish. I need you, Jess. I need the girls in my life. I love you more than anything else on earth. Does that answer enough of your questions."

"Yes." It did. Maybe he hadn't been quite as eloquent as he wanted to be, either, but she understood. "Yes, I want to marry you and be with you for the rest of our lives."

"Thank God." Mark's embrace was fierce and elated but gentled almost at once. "Kiss me, Jess."

Jess glanced around. They were alone—for the moment.

"Whatever you say, Colonel," she replied with an impish grin. She reached up on tiptoe, clutching the lapels of his jacket with both hands, pulling him slightly down to meet her questing lips. The night stood still as his lips met hers, as his tongue touched hers.

"Mom! Not again!" Ann and Lyn stood in the foyer doorway, hands on slim hips.

"This kind of thing has got to stop," Ann said with mock severity.

"We need to have a long talk about kissing in dark corners. All about the birds and the bees." Lyn nodded to her sister judiciously; then they both burst out laughing.

"What's so funny?" Mark sighed, postponing for another few minutes the kiss he longed for with every fiber of his being. He couldn't help smiling at the twins' obvious merriment.

"Mom always gets it all mixed up," they chorused in unholy glee. Jessie could feel her face turning a dull red.

"Don't worry about that anymore, you two," Mark growled, holding Jessie firmly in his strong, loving grasp. "I've had lots of experience stealing kisses in dark corners. From now on, I'll be in charge of your mother's education. You can leave everything to me."

Chapter Eleven

"I don't know about allowing the girls to stay out all night, Jess." Mark's blue eyes were serious. His mouth set in a firm line as he surveyed his wife across the kitchen table. Jessie continued to load film into the camera.

"It's the junior/senior prom. They always last all night. It's part of the ritual. First dinner and the dance, then a movie and bowling or roller-skating or whatever. Breakfast is at sunrise. Don't you remember?"

"No. We didn't do such things back in the old days." Old days? Wasn't he still in his prime, for heaven's sake?

"Uh-oh, now I get it. Have the twins been teasing you about your age again?" Jessie commiserated with false sympathy. Her husband looked absolutely marvelous to her, but it wouldn't do to tell him so.

"Not exactly," Mark said with a grin that was a tad sheepish. "They just mentioned how distinguished I look with all this additional gray hair. When did that happen?" He ran his fingers through the thick dark pelt, now sprinkled here and there with a silvery shade.

"I noticed a few more after Nell sprained her ankle cross-country skiing that weekend in February, and possibly one or two more after Ann had that fender bender with your car last month."

"You ended up with a couple after the fender-bender episode yourself, old girl," Mark pointed out. "Actually, aside from Nell's ankle I thought the winter survival weekend went quite well."

"It did. I never thought I'd spend two nights in a snow cave and almost enjoy it." He loved it when Jessie teased him that way. The easy camaraderie that had grown up between them went a long way toward making up for all that he'd missed or denied himself for a lot of years. She was a friend and a lover, the best of both worlds.

"You mean you'd try it again? I've been thinking it would make a great article."

"I've got some great shots. Do you think *National Geographic* would be interested again? I can't believe how well they paid for my stuff. We could carpet the living room."

"Are you implying that *Meanderings* doesn't pay well?"

"Well, you'll have to admit you're not in the same league with *NG*. But my loyalty is with you. You can have first crack at my work," Jessie offered magnanimously.

"Just leave out the shot of Nell hobbling about on crutches made out of ski poles."

"At least she learned a lesson about following directions, and there wasn't any lasting harm," Jessie added with a fond smile.

"No one told me this parenting business would age a guy so fast."

"Oh, yes. I did try to warn you. Repeatedly," Jessie said with a laugh. "You just wouldn't listen to me." It was as close as they seemed to come to mentioning anything about starting a family of their own. Jessie had tried all winter to bring herself around to Mark's way of thinking on the subject but she couldn't. They'd been so busy at first settling into their new life together that there hadn't been the opportunity to discuss the matter at length. Then it had been tax season...and the launching of the successful spring issue of *Meanderings*. Even the winter survival weekend, supposedly private and intimate, ended up including Nell when the Peavy girl came down with chicken pox two days before they were scheduled to leave for the National Forest Systems wilderness campground in the White Mountains.

"We've only been married five months. Is it too late to plead temporary insanity?" Mark reached out to tap Jessie on the tip of her nose. He hated to see her frown. She still did it far too often to suit him. She was his now; so were the girls. He'd never enjoyed any challenge in his life so much as making them happy, fitting into their lives.

"Yes, far too late. I think you're well and truly caught, Colonel Elliot." Jessie smiled, snapping her camera shut as she danced away from his outstretched hands and look of imminent retaliation for her sauciness.

"Come here. I haven't had you to myself all day."

"Can I help it Ann's formal needed to be hemmed at the last minute? You're lucky Lyn didn't demand I lengthen hers. I'd still be at it. Mom's the seamstress in this family. I'll be glad when they get back from Florida. Have I thanked you properly yet for giving Mom and Hi the use of your loft this summer?" Jessie widened her eyes suggestively as Mark moved closer.

"Not properly," he insisted, with a meaningful glance that promised much.

The doorbell's chime interrupted Jessie's response. "That must be the twins' dates," she said with a sigh of disappointment.

"What do you know about these boys, Jess?" He had no idea who the escorts were, but it was his fatherly duty to screen the applicants.

His wife laughed and shook her head at his serious tone. "They've gone to school with the girls all their lives. I didn't ask for security clearance. Lighten up."

Now it was his turn to feel a little foolish. "Still, you can't be too careful. I know how seventeen-year-old males think."

"You do have a remarkable memory for a man your age. Tell me, what do most seventeen-year-old males have on their minds?"

"Almost seventeen-year-old females," Mark replied ominously. "I don't know if I like it."

"Most fathers don't, I'm told. Don't be so worried. You've always told me the twins were the most level-headed teens you've ever met. Trust them. I do."

Mark caught her around the waist, gazing deep into Jessie's serene brown eyes. His heart swelled with love and pride in his new family. "I trust them, too."

Jessie was thankful for the ease with which Mark had slipped into the role of father to her girls. He filled up such a big gaping hole in their lives. Not that there hadn't been clashes, but they'd accepted him so readily that most disturbances barely rippled the surface of their existence. With his help she'd been able to look on sibling differences of opinion and occasional rebellion against authority more evenly, more objectively than she had as a single parent.

"What bothers me is that they're even old enough to go to a junior/senior prom," Jessie confessed wistfully.

"That's because you don't look much older than they do," Mark offered gallantly. "You should be going along, not sitting home with your nearly ancient husband."

"Bored with married life already, Colonel?" Jessie only half-joked as she searched his features for an answer.

"No, cabin fever I think. This must be the first really nice weekend we've had this spring."

A small plan began forming in Jessie's brain, but she didn't have time at the moment to put it into execution. "Let's meet the girls' dates."

"Inspection?" Mark brightened.

"Introductions," Jessie said, cautioning him sternly.

"Yes, ma'am," Mark grinned unrepentantly and, grabbing her hand, led the way to the foyer.

Jessie paused in the entryway long enough to greet the boys and introduce them to Mark. They looked gawky and ill at ease in their rented dinner jackets and stiffly pleated, stark-white shirts.

"God, I remember how they feel," Mark whispered as they entered the room.

"Me, too," Jessie said with a giggle. "They asked my advice on what flowers to choose." She'd suggested pale yellow carnations to enhance Lyn's Victorian gown and baby-pink roses for Ann's Scarlett O'Hara-style formal. They'd agreed, and matching corsages and boutonnieres rested on the hall table. "I remember my prom date doing exactly the same thing with my mother," Jessie whispered to Mark. "Some things never change."

A rustle of satin behind her made Jessie turn and stare. Were these lovely women her little girls? They took Jessie's breath away. She raised her camera and snapped the scene through a mist of emotion. The tableau dissolved with the speed of light.

"Mom," the twins chorused in unison. "Don't go taking a role of film. It's embarrassing."

"Okay, but how about one or two for your grandmother?" Mark gave Jessie's shoulder a meaningful squeeze.

"Mother's privilege." Jessie spoke lightly to hide the lump in her throat. Mark watched over her shoulder. She kept her word and refrained entirely from photographing the awkward young men as they dealt with the tricky business of pinning on corsages.

"How about a shot of you and Mark with them, Mom?" Nell suggested as she bounded down the stairs in scruffy blue jeans and an old sweatshirt that was a size too small. She'd grown over the winter, slimming down, developing the beginning of the lush, full curves bequeathed her from Jessie and Marta. "I'll take it," she offered, holding out her hand. "Come on, Mom. Stand over by *them*." She still never referred to her sisters by their given names if she could get away with it. Mark took most of her adolescent outbursts in stride. Jessie wasn't quite as low-keyed but she thought she'd handled this daughter's transition into womanhood in much better fashion than she had the twins'.

"It'll be a nice print for Grandma," Ann said graciously, smiling at her date to show him he wasn't being left out. "A family portrait." She moved under the protection of Mark's outstretched arm never knowing the simple statement more than made up for any difficulties he might envision in molding a place for himself in their lives. They were a family, his family.

Lyn joined her twin. Mark pulled Jessie close to his other side. "Just one shot, Nell, so make it good," he advised.

"Yes, sir!" Nell had taken a fancy to military jargon over the long winter. She conversed with him as though they were fellow officers. She plagued him unmercifully about his career in the corps. Lately she'd even voiced a preference for studying military science as a career. A West Point poster showed up in her room that Jessie didn't quite know what to make of. She seemed to think the phase would pass, though Mark wasn't so sure.

Photos out of the way, the twins left amid a flurry of last minute good-byes and instructions from both Mark and Jessie.

"Whew! I'm glad that's over," Nell observed dryly from her sprawled posture at the foot of the stairs. "I'm spending the night with Sharon Peavy. Mark, could you drive me over? We're going to watch old John Wayne movies on cable. I'll be home early, I promise, Mom," she ended in a rush to forestall Jessie's objections.

"You bet you will," Jessie replied, her mind scurrying back to her plan as she picked up empty flower boxes. "It looks as if a hurricane hit your room. Be home directly after lunch, and be sure to clean under your bed. You sisters will be awake by then, so the noise won't cause an argument."

"Want to come with us, Jessie?" Mark asked hopefully. "We could take a little ride out into the country. The sunset should be fantastic tonight."

"I don't think so. I'm tired," Jessie lied. "I'll get us a bite to eat." She ignored his pique, giving him an absentminded kiss on the cheek as she headed back to the kitchen.

AN HOUR AND A HALF LATER, his good humor restored, Mark rested his shoulders against the trunk of a sheltering old oak and drew Jessie into his arms.

"How did you know this is exactly what I needed?"

Jessie turned her head from the view of hills and trees and purpling western sky. "Because I love you," she said simply, "and you've been hinting broadly enough to convince a stone you need to get out of the city."

"That bad, huh? Do you really intend to spend the entire night under this tree?" A smile quirked the corners of his mouth.

"With you, yes sir," Jessie declared emphatically. "Why else would I drag out the sleeping bag and round up enough food to ward off starvation until sunrise, not to mention sufficient bug spray to repel an army of mosquitoes, if I weren't serious? Besides, I like it out here." She settled back into the curve of his arm, munching on an apple core before tossing it down the hill heading to the old farmhouse that witnessed their early misunderstanding.

"I have to admit it beats spending the evening in front of the tube." Mark's hands found the fullness of her breast.

"No interruptions," Jessie breathed, snuggling close against his hand, twining her arms around the strong column of his neck. "Aren't you glad I planned this little outing?" Her hand strayed along the inseam of his faded brown cords. They didn't often have time to indulge in the sensual games other lovers played, but when they did she enjoyed the erotic give and take.

"This place is for sale," Mark threw out experimentally. "The whole farm. Maybe we could move out here after the girls leave home. The magazine's taking off like a rocket. I think we could afford the land. Would you like that?" He shifted his weight, taking her against him. "In a few years we can build a place of our own. You can commute to A & M with me every morning and take pictures to your heart's content."

"Sounds marvelous. The house will be so lost and empty when the girls are gone." She faltered a moment, then continued. "The loft is a lovely place...but..."

"You never thought of it as home. Funny, I haven't either. It was a hobby, a place to mark time in. I've always wanted a house away from city lights and traffic noises." How easy it was to share his dreams with her these days—all but one. Jessie shied away from the subject of children. The time was here, in the few precious hours alone together, to tear down the last barrier between them.

"A log cabin?" Jessie murmured. "With central heating and at least a bath and a half. I'd like living out here." Jessie snuggled against him in wanton invitation.

"That's settled, then. See how easy it is when you talk things out? Your house is too big for two middle-aged people." Mark leaned away from her, unrolling the double sleeping bag that Hi and Marta had sent for Christmas.

"How can you think that house will ever be empty? Have you forgotten the guppies procreating by the hundreds or the hamster the pet-store man swore was a boy or the cats...?" Jessie broke off. "Five kittens aren't so many, Mark," she pleaded, catching the gleam in his eye. "It's so hard to find good homes for new kittens."

Mark removed his shoes, pretending to ignore her plea. "Go on."

"Anyway. Speak for yourself," Jessie changed the subject abruptly, recalling his earlier remark. "I'm not middle-aged yet. I intend to live to be one hundred and four. That makes me..."

"Sixteen years from being middle-aged," he answered before she could make the mental calculations. "I thought that might get you. Start undressing, Jess." Mark twirled the ends of a villainous mustache. "You can bargain for Cecelia's offspring with your lovely body."

"Oh, stop that," Jessie gurgled. "You know as well as I do I've gained back the twelve pounds I lost last winter." Mark didn't seem to be listening. He took off his shirt and pants, hanging them over a tree branch.

"There's more of you to love. Quick, get in this sleeping bag. It may be May, but it's darn cold when the sun goes down."

Jessie didn't need a second invitation. Soon she was lying naked beside him within the comforting folds of the down bag. "On my honor, I'll have Cecelia spayed, but aren't the kittens adorable?"

"They grow into cats," Mark replied unarguably. He seemed to be studying the dark pattern of new oak leaves intercrossing above their head. Jessie didn't care about trees; she watched Mark.

"I thought you liked babies." She paused, all at once serious. It was the opening for which Mark had been waiting.

"I do love babies—in their proper place." He pulled Jessie close. She snuggled against the warmth of his lean frame. She didn't meet his gaze, tracing patterns across the hard planes of his chest. "It's been bothering you, hasn't it, Jess?" he went on in a quiet, soothing tone. "You're worrying that you aren't going to be able to give me what you think I want most. It's time to set the record straight."

"I love you more every day, Mark. You do believe that?" There was an infinitesimal note of fear in Jessie's tone. He turned slightly to kiss her once, lightly, reassuringly. Tendrils of cinnamon-colored hair brushed his cheek, beckoning his touch.

"I can't go back to formulas and two-o'clock feedings no matter how much you want us to have a family of our own," Jessie said softly. Her breath tickled his skin where she lay against his chest.

"Look at me, Jess," Mark lifted her chin with his finger. "I do know how you feel." Desire for his wife stirred and strengthened in him. She was the most precious thing in the world. How could he make her understand? Mark gathered her close. "What if I told you I've changed my mind?" He could feel more than see Jessie's tear-bright gaze searching his face in the dusk.

His intentions were the best. He wanted to settle this last hurdle between them, but the sight of her soft corral lips sent all rational arguments from his brain. He lowered his head to taste the honey of her mouth.

Jessie's lips parted; her tongue welcomed his. This was reality, Mark thought vaguely, the most secret of his dreams come true. Jessie was the loving companion, the friend he'd always wanted during the long, lonely years, the mother of his children: the daughters he'd love and nurture as though they were his own.

They didn't speak again. Jessie welcomed him joyously, glorying in the ever-renewing pleasure of joining with him. They soon found themselves reborn again, whole and complete, in the soft, damp darkness of a May night.

"JESSIE, are you awake?" Mark's voice was rough with sleep.

"No. What time is it?"

"Very late," Mark said with a chuckle at the convoluted logic of his lover's statement.

"I don't want to miss the sunrise," Jessie mumbled sleepily. "Then we have to leave. We have to be home before the girls."

"I imagine the birds will wake us in plenty of time."

Jessie rolled to her side to study Mark's profile in the light of a low-riding spring moon. She wiggled closer, breathing deeply of the mingled odors of leaves and earth and Mark. "What are you thinking?" she asked, running a finger along his jaw.

"About the conversation we never finished. Somehow I got sidetracked."

"Babies?" Jessie sounded tense. Mark caught her hand, turning his lips into the palm. Jessie lifted her face to his. The kiss was reassurance and recommitment.

"About how close I came to losing you over a misunderstanding."

"A misunderstanding? Now *I* don't understand?" Jessie threaded her fingers through his. A small corner of her brain registered the rustling of an unseen nocturnal wanderer. She slid closer to Mark's comforting bulk. She would learn to love the wilderness for his sake, but it would take some doing.

"I never made it clear to myself, though, Jess. I think I got caught up in the whole parenting thing, the joy of finding you and the girls, finding what I'd lost so long ago and thought never to have again. A baby would have been another part of us to carry on into the future. It sounds silly and macho now that I've said it out loud."

"It sounds like a loving, caring man with a well-developed nesting instinct." There was a smile in Jessie's voice.

"More like a quiet mid-life crisis," Mark snorted, hugging her close to his heart.

"Lighten up, Colonel. It happens to all good men sooner or later."

"Think so?"

"I know so, especially when you've waited so long. Have you really changed your mind about a child of our own?" Jessie leaned over him, the better to make out his features in the dim light. "I don't want to destroy your dream...your 'happily ever after.'" Jessie couldn't suppress the twinge of anxiety in her words. She wanted him to tell her it was all right between them.

"I have my dreams. They're you and the girls, a family of my own." Mark chose his words carefully. "I felt close to your girls from the very beginning. I never felt that way toward Kerry's children, although I tried. I think it's because the twins and Nell are nearly adults. Does that make any sense to you?"

"All the sense in the world." Jessie dropped a kiss on his palm, resettling his hand just below the swell of her breast. "You wanted a family. Society says you have to start with babies, not teens." The warmth of his touch stirred the embers of passion so recently banked. Small flames of wanting licked along Jessie's nerve endings, but she tried valiantly to keep her mind on the topic of discussion. Mark had told her everything she wanted to hear. Relief and passion combined to make her as giddy as champagne did.

"I wanted the companionship of your daughters. I wanted you," Mark continued, following his own line of thought, "because you are the most desirable woman I've ever known. Because you understand events and times that are only history-book memories to someone like Kerry. Damn, I said that all wrong, didn't I, Jess? I'm sorry."

"Don't be. I can be gracious in victory. I can even wish Kerry all the luck in the world if she decides to go back to David. In fact, I hope she does. California is just about far enough away for a born damsel in distress like that one."

"I deserve that," Mark admitted. "But, Jess, you make me feel so young. I thought at first that Kerry would make me feel even younger." He grunted in self-mockery. "Was I ever wrong. After you left me I felt a hundred years old. I didn't know how I'd gotten myself into such a mess."

"Love makes us do funny things. I thought I was ready to give you up to another woman for the same reasons. We deserve to have ended up with each other."

"For the rest of our lives?" Mark's lips were on her hair. Jessie shivered, pressing closer to his strength, the heat of his ardor pushing forcefully against her thigh.

"And beyond."

"I'll be the best stepfather three girls ever had, Jess."

"You already are. They love you almost as much as I do."

"You've shown me a man doesn't have to be a biological father to be good at the job."

"You're the best." Jessie had a quick glimpse of the house they'd build in this spot, small and intimate but roomy enough to stretch out to enfold a host of loved ones. "It's all in the heart." Mark pushed against her thighs, beginning the age-old rhythm that would escalate between them with each successive touch.

"I'm going to be one hell of a grandfather someday." He rolled over, his weight pushing Jessie deep into the soft warmth of the down bag. The smell of crushed oak leaves drifted upward as they moved. "By then you'll be a full partner in Abrahms and Mahoney and your pictures will be famous."

"*Meanderings* will be on newsstands all over the Northeast." She smiled up at Mark with all her love and contentment mirrored in his heated gaze. "You'll make one hell of a sexy grandfather. Know why?"

"Uh-uh," Mark grunted, his hands buried in her soft, scented hair. His lips caressed the hollow at the base of Jessie's throat where a pulse beat quickly and lightly in cadence with his heart. "Tell me."

"Because you're a natural; that's why."

Tell person she sorry
and return candy bar —